Totally Bound Publishing books by Roxanne Blackhall

Bristol Park
Abbeydon Attraction
Abbeydon Academy
Abbeydon Abandon

I0645688

Bristol Park

ABBEYDON ABANDON

ROXANNE BLACKHALL

Abbeydon Abandon
ISBN # 978-1-80250-582-5
©Copyright Roxanne Blackhall 2023
Cover Art by Erin Dameron-Hill ©Copyright November 2023
Interior text design by Claire Siemaszkiewicz
Totally Bound Publishing

ABBEYDON ABANDON

Dedication

To my family —
Somewhere between weird and wonderful, but
always amazing and supportive.

Chapter One

Stacy Barclay turned down the tree-lined drive and her eyes went wide. This was either a winter wonderland or the scene of some horror movie. She stopped the car and turned to Kylie in the passenger seat.

"When you suggested out of the way, I didn't think you meant..." She waved a hand at the snowy forest that seemed to have swallowed them up as soon as she'd pulled off the main road.

Brit leaned forward from the backseat. "I think it's kinda cool," she said. "I've been checking out their website. This place is gonna rock."

She held her iPad so it was visible from the driver's seat. Stacy rolled her eyes. She'd seen the pictures when Kylie made the reservations. Sure, the place looked amazing and supposedly had just been renovated, but she knew from experience things weren't always what they appeared. Too many places posted images that were heavily processed and taken from some magic angle to make the spaces seem bigger.

"You said you needed a break from it all," Kylie replied from the passenger seat. "We all wanted skiing, but not someplace with the usual ski crowd. Plus, this is only a few hours from the city—perfect for a long weekend. Besides, no matter how bad it is, I guarantee we've been in worse. So, drive."

Stacy blew out a breath and rolled forward. Kylie was right. They had stayed in some pretty scary places. The three of them had been best friends since childhood and traveling together since their first trip without adults when they'd all turned sixteen.

Kylie was the queen of all things tech and had a gift for finding cool places no one had ever heard of before. They always had a great time, or at least a great adventure with wild stories to share after—like their post-high-school-graduation trip to San Felipe, Mexico that had included lost luggage, a bout of food poisoning and almost getting mugged, only to be rescued by a trio of handsome young men from Guatemala.

"How the hell did you snag reservations with only a two-week notice?" No matter how much she trusted Kylie, Stacy wasn't ready to let it go. It was the last month of a busy year, and she had thought this trip would be a celebration. She'd wanted to share it with her best friends someplace quiet.

Except she'd learned this morning she hadn't gotten the promotion she'd put in for and deserved. What was worse, the guy who did had a less impressive portfolio and less experience. He was, however, a man and his father played golf with the Vice President of Operations. *Fucking old boys' network.*

"Would you relax." Brit's voice had that big-sister vibe she could sometimes get. "It's time to forget work for a while."

Stacy loosened her grip on the wheel. Brit was right. This may not be the celebratory trip she'd planned on, but it was still just the three of them enjoying some much-needed downtime.

"The directions say to follow the road around and take the right fork up to the house," Kylie said, as Stacy approached a bend in the long drive. "Park in the gravel lot to the side."

The trees opened up, and Stacy caught a glimpse of snow-covered cabins and a huge outdoor pavilion before finally focusing on the gorgeous Victorian house at the top of the hill.

"Anyone else getting summer camp vibes?" Brit said. "This has a sort of vintage feel—like *Dirty Dancing*."

Kylie laughed. "Except that was in summer. And why do we still talk about that movie? It's ancient."

She was right. The movie was more her mother's era. Yet, they'd all watched it countless times to the point where Stacy could probably still quote the entire thing.

"Is this place gonna be like totally empty or something?" Brit craned around as she gazed out the windows. "I mean, Stacy's right. You booked on Thanksgiving, and they had an open weekend two weeks later?"

Kylie still hadn't answered the question, and Stacy was starting to get nervous when she pulled up to the house and found several vehicles already parked. Kylie hopped out before their car had come to a complete stop.

"Ye of little faith." She pointed down the hill to the line of cabins. Every one of them had skis standing on their porches and cars parked along their sides.

"Hi! You must be Kylie, Stacy and Brit." The warm, rich baritone carried in the chilly air and all three women turned toward the main house. Kylie sucked in an audible breath while Brit made some squeaking noise. Stacy mentally checked that her mouth was closed.

The man was big and broad-shouldered, and everything you pictured if someone said to combine a sexy lumberjack with a splash of old-school hipster then make him hugely tall. He came down from the porch as she popped the trunk. In the blink of an eye, he had the three of them and all their bags inside the big house.

"I'm Nate Stewart," he said as they shook hands and made introductions. "I'll turn you over to my wife, Cat. She'll give you the tour and get you to your rooms. Someone'll bring your bags up."

If Nate Stewart was a giant, his wife was the opposite—a petite redhead wearing jeans and a turtleneck, but everything about her screamed class and money. Except there wasn't a trace of snobbery in her warm welcome and pleasant chatter as they went through a hall and into a large sunroom then on to the rest of the house.

"The rooms all have coffee pots, microwaves and mini fridges," Cat said. "There's a small kitchen downstairs that guests can use, and we do three meals a day. There's a handful of restaurants in town, but it's all pickup this time of year and most close early."

They climbed a flight of stairs, and Cat explained there was a small elevator, but it was out of the way. She turned down a short hall.

"You lucked out a bit," she said. "We had a cancellation, and we were able to get you into three adjacent rooms. The original design was meant to accommodate families, so the majority of the rooms have connecting doors. These days, most folks choose cabins."

Well, that answers the question about short notice reservations.

Cat stopped at the end of the hall. Everything about the place felt like you were in someone's very-well-decorated home and not a hotel or lodge. Colorful runners covered the hardwood floors and there was not a sign of ugly wallpaper anywhere. Simple holiday decorations graced the stairwell, making things feel festive, but not in your face. It was warm and welcoming and very personal and looked even better than the pictures online.

Cat handed over three keycards. "Will you be eating dinner here?"

Kylie and Brit glanced at Stacy. After a long drive, she had no desire to try to figure out food.

"Yes, please," Stacy said. "That would be terrific."

Cat pulled out her phone and tapped a few times, then pocketed it. "We do dinner in the dining room — downstairs and to the right. All the info for meals, snow tubing, skiing and everything is in the binder in your rooms, and the phone list is there as well as instructions for downloading the app for keyless entry. If you need anything or have questions, please call. Someone will be happy to help. Enjoy your stay."

She waved over her shoulder, leaving a wake of something that smelled vaguely of Christmas cookies, and Stacy turned to her friends.

"We're in some alternate dimension," she said. "First, unless I open that door and find a hell hole, girl, you outdid yourself."

Brit nodded agreement. They faced their doors in the time-honored tradition they'd observed every time they vacationed together. Stacy smiled at her friends. The first moments were always exciting. They counted to three then opened their rooms at the same time.

"Holy shit." Brit let out a low whistle.

"Fuck, I'm good." Kylie laughed with what sounded like relief.

As for Stacy, she hadn't expected much from the small Catskills resort, whose online info claimed it was still a work in progress. The once thriving family-run place had been shut down for over a decade. Then Cat had picked up her grandmother's property and decided to make a go of it.

The room in front of her belonged in a magazine. Sunlight streamed through big windows and made the room's wood floors gleam. The bed was sleek and modern—no antiquated four-poster here—dressed in crisp white linens and sitting on what had to be the plushest area rug ever.

"I don't know how you found this place. I don't care how much we're paying for this place. I don't care what body part you had to sell to get these rooms. Wow." Brit came and poked her head over first Kylie's shoulder then Stacy's.

Stacy finally noticed her bags, already sitting on the bench at the foot of the bed. Her bags. How anyone had made sense out of the jumble in the car's trunk was beyond her. She shook herself and stepped into the room, halfway expecting the illusion to shatter. It didn't.

"Let's get these adjoining doors open." She had the middle room and marched over to throw the locks on first one door, then the next. Brit opened her door and toed the doorstop into place while Kylie banged hers open, stuck her hands on her hips and looked around as if surveying her handiwork.

Each room had a bed, a comfy-looking chair with an ottoman, and a small desk and chair in addition to the promised mini fridge, coffee pot, and microwave. A spacious closet with a built-in dresser lined one wall, and a flat screen television hung opposite the bed.

"Moment of truth," Brit said as she opened Stacy's bathroom door. Then she stood there with her mouth open, pointing at the clawfoot tub. It wasn't like they'd never seen these things before. They'd stayed in everything from bug-infested hostels, and some nice ones, to five-star hotel suites. It was that none of them had expected this out of the way place to be so well done.

"Okay, it has to be said, the pics on the website don't do this place justice." Stacy flopped onto her bed. *Perfectly comfy.* The online images were clean and modern, but somehow, they'd all been thinking they were idealized pictures. Computer-generated concept images or something. She'd certainly thought mountain lodge equaled wood paneling and plaid flannel everywhere. Speaking of plaid flannel...

"Did you get an eyeful of Nate Stewart?" Leave it to Kylie to voice what Stacy was thinking.

Brit shared those thoughts, judging by the way she fanned herself and fell back on the bed. "They're both ridiculously hot."

She rolled over and eyed Stacy. "How long has it been since you've had a boy toy?"

Kylie jumped between the two of them. "Too long! I know that much."

Stacy threw a pillow at them. "How did we get from ogling our hosts to talking about my sex life? Pedro was last spring. I've been too busy aiming for that damn promotion to think about boy toys."

She'd been too busy to think about a lot of things.

"Besides," she continued, "I could pick up some rando at any number of bars in Manhattan. This isn't exactly a hopping singles destination, and this weekend is about some girl time."

She pushed herself up from the bed and grabbed her suitcase, determined to bring that conversation to a close. By the time they'd got unpacked, cleaned up, and changed, it was time to go down to dinner. Each meal had a three-hour window of service, which she supposed made sense for a place like this.

Downstairs, they found the dining room with ease and a hostess directed them to take any table, but she suggested they might like the spot by the fire. They took her up on the suggestion and settled into cozy wing chairs pulled around a small table next to the enormous fireplace.

After dinner, their server told them this was the last seating, so they were welcome to linger a bit with drinks, or every Friday there was a meet and greet in the sunroom and library down the hall.

All three immediately hopped up and headed for the library. A crowd of guests—certainly more than would fit in the rooms they'd seen in the house—filled the large space, and there was a giant decorated tree in one corner. They got drinks at the bar then settled into chairs near the fire.

"So far, I approve." Stacy sipped her drink and scanned the room. There were far more people here than she'd expected, and they weren't all couples. For once, Brit didn't have her phone out, which meant she was unplugged for the weekend. "How'd you manage to get off early on a Friday?"

"Not all of us work for hellholes that don't encourage a healthy work-life balance," Brit replied. "I went in an hour early to go over some briefs and scheduled all my clients before noon. I've got nothing to think about until Monday morning."

She knew Kylie had been up hours earlier than her usual to finalize one project before taking off, and since she was self-employed, she didn't have to worry about a boss. Stacy was the only one who had worked twelve-to-sixteen-hour days for the entire two weeks prior to ensure she was not only caught up, but ahead, and no one could complain.

Kylie's booted foot tapped her ankle, and Stacy followed her friend's subtle nod. Nate Stewart stood on the far side of the room, chatting with an older couple and a tall, good-looking blond man.

"Not in the market," Stacy replied, but her friend knew her type. Tall and lean, with shoulders that strained the seams of his shirt, he was worth a second glance. Or a third. Maybe a fourth.

The man turned their way and even from across the room, his eyes caught her attention. His gaze locked on hers and he smiled, then lifted his glass and winked. Stacy smiled, then looked quickly away. It had been too long since she'd enjoyed flirting. Work had taken too much of her time and energy.

"Bullshit," Brit said. "That little interchange was game on if I ever saw it."

Kylie palmed her half-finished drink and stood. "I am tired, and I know you do not need a wing-woman if you decide to go for that." She stepped around Stacy's chair and leaned down and whispered in her ear. "That was supposed to be encouragement, just in case you missed it."

Brit rose and gave a quick, short jerk of her head toward the blond man before she followed Kylie toward the hall. Stacy took another sip of her drink. She should go up to her room. She'd had a long week and was running on almost no sleep. Instead, she turned to where she'd seen the man and found him gone. She scanned the room, but he was nowhere to be found.

Oh well.

She finished her drink while watching the flow of people through the big room. Bristol Park was not at all what she had been expecting, but she liked it. There was an easy, relaxed vibe to the place that was different than anything she'd ever experienced.

Might as well explore.

She got a fresh drink, wandered into the sunroom and immediately caught her breath. There he was again. Stacy leaned against the wall and assessed the view. His light-blond hair was pulled into a ponytail and in this lighting, his eyes were like ice-blue water. A neatly trimmed beard covered a face that might have been chiseled into existence by a sculptor who wanted to combine masculine and beautiful into one stunning specimen. *Nothing wrong with a little flirting.*

He was standing near the big French doors, laughing with a couple. The other man had a fresh bruise on his cheekbone.

A hand on her elbow startled her, and she turned to find Cat, looking stunning in a pair of flowy black pants and a silky sleeveless top.

"Kylie mentioned skiing when she made the reservations," Cat said. "Let me introduce you to Luke Tverberg. He's our resident ski instructor. He came to us about a year ago, and we're so lucky to have him."

She linked her arm around Stacy's elbow and steered them directly toward the gorgeous man she'd been admiring. Cat let her go as they stopped facing the trio.

"Oh, Jules, what did you do?" Cat reached out and stroked the air over the man's cheek. The woman with him laughed.

"He decided we should go really off piste," the woman said. "We found the old logging camp. It's a gorgeous cross-country. We were just telling Luke you should mark that as an official trail."

The man smiled at her, then back at Cat. "I had a bit of a disagreement with a tree branch. I decided I could ski through without ducking. It begged to differ. No actual harm done. The place is coming along. Congratulations."

Cat practically blushed and bid them goodnight as they left. Then she had Stacy by the elbow again as she spoke to the blond man.

"Luke, this is Stacy Barclay. She and two friends are here for the weekend and it's their first visit with us." She turned to Stacy. "We're still expanding, so we're not a typical ski resort. Luke can get you up to speed on everything you need to know. Enjoy."

Then she was gone. Like a puff of smoke in the wind. Leaving Stacy to wonder if Cat was one of those people who could pop up at the right moment, do whatever it was she needed to do then quietly disappear, or if she'd seen Stacy drooling and was the best wing person ever.

"So, first visit, eh?" His voice was deep and soft, with a hint of some accent she couldn't quite place.

For an instant, Stacy questioned whether she'd imagined the wink before, because now he seemed like what you'd expect from anyone in a service role— polite and family-friendly. Then he leaned closer, his smile curled up on one side and there was nothing innocent about the look in his eyes.

"I thought I spotted a new face in the library earlier." His voice had dropped to a sultry whisper.

Stacy recognized interest when she saw it in a man. Lucky thing, this was one of the few times that interest was mutual. *Yep, definitely nothing wrong with some harmless flirtation with the hot ski instructor.*

"What's your usual? Alpine?"

Stacy nodded, unable to find her voice when face to face with a man who would be perfectly at home in some Viking movie.

He was saying something about the trails here being unmarked, and it was still mostly open skiing. They had great maps, though, and she didn't catch the rest because she got distracted by the complicated ink tracing up his forearm and disappearing under the rolled cuff of his shirt. He paused as if waiting for a response, and Stacy blinked, realizing she'd missed whatever he'd just said.

"I'm sorry," she said, sounding semi-like herself. She'd feared she'd come off like some breathless teenager. "I didn't catch that last part."

He smiled again, and she damn near turned into a puddle on the spot. This man was dangerous.

"I was asking about experience levels. There's one lift, and it serves a handful of easy runs. We encourage anyone who isn't a very confident skier capable of advanced blues to stick to those."

That made sense. Cat had said they weren't a traditional ski lodge, and Kylie had shown her pictures of the lift under construction during the summer.

"I've been skiing since I was a child," Stacy replied. "We all have, but I'm the only one who ever got serious about it. I've skied Telluride, Jackson Hole and Snowbird. I'm pretty confident I can manage anything the Catskills wants to throw at me."

Chapter Two

Luke, Friday, December 11

Luke Tverberg's brain came to a grinding halt at the look in Stacy's caramel-brown eyes. He'd seen her with her friends earlier and again the moment she'd walked into the sunroom. Then Cat had shown up with Stacy on her arm. He was pretty sure this night couldn't get any better.

"Well, all righty then," Luke replied. He'd heard brags like hers before, usually right before the person face-planted on an easy run. That or they casually took a double black like it was nothing. *Which is she, I wonder?*

"So, tell me how it works here," Stacy said. She leaned in a little closer, and he caught a fleeting whiff of something spicy and a little smoky.

In previous jobs, he'd have been angling to get her into bed as quickly as possible. Hell, most of the time, he didn't have to try — they came to him. He'd enjoyed that perk of the job countless times in the past. That was at big resorts, though, and after a year of keeping it in his pants at Bristol Park, he had no desire to fuck up a good thing.

"Well, it's pretty simple," Luke replied. An older couple vacated a pair of cushy chairs, and he gestured for Stacy to go ahead of him. That was a decision he both regretted and blessed. Her rich, brown hair cascaded down her back, highlighting her trim figure and drawing attention to a narrow waist, slim hips and a perfect ass. He was grateful for the opportunity to sit and hide the half hard-on that had popped up in his pants.

He tried not to stare as she arranged herself in the chair opposite him. Her long legs crossed at the ankles. He forced his mind to stay on topic.

"Back in the day, this was a typical small ski resort," he said. "Two old-school surface lifts and several runs. This time a year ago there was just the bunny slope and cross-country open. The rest was in bad shape. We've spent the last year rebuilding, and it's still a work in progress, but we've got a good half-dozen greens and three blues open so far."

Cat and Nate had drilled him on the history, and he'd honed it to perfection. Years of working at a variety of ski resorts had given him some decent people skills. Stacy leaned forward, her chin resting lightly in her hand and her caramel eyes steady on him. Yeah, it was going to take some serious willpower to keep it professional here.

"Guests like the idea of downhill," he continued. "But if you want more of a challenge, we've got a handful of marked trails, and you can go off piste. Before anyone skis beyond the groomed slopes, they have to demonstrate ability and accept that, essentially, everything else is off trail and at your own risk. That's why it's still all-inclusive — no fees for skiing."

Technically, they could charge to cover staff, and the maintenance they did on the slopes and tubing hill, but for now, they'd gone the all-inclusive route and offered day passes for folks who weren't staying at the resort. None of that mattered to Stacy and her friends, though.

"Guests have full access to everything," he finished.

She blinked, and a slow smile spread across her full lips. *Damn, she is gorgeous.*

"Everything?" The smile broadened. She'd clearly played this game before. A little light banter, some flirting, and see where things go. Some folks liked to flirt. Some flirted with a purpose. Stacy didn't strike him as the type to do anything without full, conscious intent.

"Well, my services are included," he said. "Doesn't sound like you need an instructor, though. I'm guessing you know your way around."

He leaned in, matching her posture, and was rewarded as she turned to face him more fully, giving him a terrific view of her amazing cleavage.

"True, but it's always nice to get a few pointers when you're tackling a new mountain," she replied. "Cat said you'd been here a year. Where were you before?"

Well, shit, that's a dash of cold water. Luke cleared his throat and gave her his most winning smile.

"The place before this was Vail, Colorado." Her eyebrows raised, and she gave an appreciative nod. "Last year, I'd been planning to take it easy, but my kid brother took a job at the high school here and kept telling me I needed to see this place. So…" The first part of that was a half-truth, but no one beyond his employers needed to know his reasons for leaving Vail. He shrugged.

He'd learned folks who knew Abbeydon understood that shrug. People who were visiting for the first time read it differently, but it worked equally well.

"And you've explored all the trails?" There was a teasing tone to her voice that he liked. She was certainly going to be interesting.

"Most. There's a lot of mountain out there." He chuckled and braced his elbows on his knees. "I've been on these trails nearly every day for a year and I'm still learning. But I've had outstanding teachers — both Cat and Nate can knock your socks off on skis."

Something he'd said had surprised her. She leaned closer to him and gave a quick glance around, as if she were worried about being overheard.

"Him, I can believe," she said. "But Cat? Come on. She's…" Stacy waved a hand as if she couldn't find the words.

He completely understood. He'd underestimated the tiny woman himself. "Don't let her size or prissy exterior fool you," he said. "That woman is a stick of dynamite with a purpose."

Stacy threw back her head and laughed, a rich, throaty sound that had Luke's thoughts headed straight for the gutter again. If she was that abandoned with laughter, seeing her let go in other ways would be nothing short of amazing. *Where the hell did that come from? Fuck.*

"Sounds like my friend Kylie," she said. "She's small and cute, but she's scary smart and a tech whiz."

"My turn to ask a question," he said. "What brought you to Bristol Park?"

Her face darkened, and he wondered if he'd stepped into some ugly mess like a cheating boyfriend. Then she flashed a bright smile and flipped her hair over her shoulder.

"We do regular girls' trips, and I was in the mood for something different. Quieter. Where we could just hang."

She straightened in her seat, and her gaze drifted outside, where soft lights draped in the trees and lined the way to the pavilion.

"I can get a massage any day," she continued. "I needed to unplug and not think about the city for a while."

Hell, he could understand that. Around here when someone said 'the city', they usually meant New York. There'd been a time when he was excited to be in Minneapolis rather than the suburbs. That was before he'd seen how ugly city life could get. Now he stayed as far away from them as possible. He couldn't imagine visiting New York, much less living or working there.

"And what's in the city? What do you do?" He liked getting to know people. Understanding someone's desires and drives, and who they were, made it easier to work with them and figure out what they needed from a ski instructor—because once someone got past beginner, it was never just about improving their skills on skis. There was always a deeper reason.

Stacy bit her lip, and her hands clenched briefly on the arms of the chair. She took in a slow breath and fixed him with a smile that didn't reach her eyes.

"I'm a senior analyst at a financial firm and attempting to work my way up to investment banker."

There was something flat about that statement, and her expression. Both lacked the vibrancy she'd brought to their interactions so far. Work might be a topic to avoid with her.

"Sounds challenging," he said. He nodded toward the windows. "During the full moon, it's bright enough out there to walk around at night. The moonlight reflecting off the snow is beautiful."

Stacy leaned in and rested her hand on his knee as she followed his gaze out through the glass. "Seems a little dark out there tonight."

Luke nodded. If they were anywhere else, he'd be suggesting a walk down to the pavilion. He was pretty confident she'd agree. They could step off the deck and into the privacy of the nearly moonless night. No, Bristol Park was too small a place for that behavior.

"I would like another drink. And it's a little warm in here." Stacy rose and took a few steps, then turned to him. "Care to join me?"

He didn't think twice. He stood and offered his elbow as they navigated the still heavy crowd to the bar in the library where they collected fresh drinks. Luke steered her toward the glassed-in hall that stretched along the back of the house. It tended to be cooler, and, though there were benches along the side, it was usually less crowded.

She settled on a bench halfway down the hall where the chatter from the other rooms faded, punctuated with occasional bangs from the big kitchen as the staff finished cleaning up for the night. She patted the spot next to her, and Luke wasn't about to resist that invitation.

Sitting this close, he caught a hint of something floral in with the spice and smoke.

"You won't get in trouble for being here with me like this, will you?" She tipped her head back and leaned against the wall, exposing more of her long, smooth neck and delicious cleavage peeking from her blouse.

"We're in a public space and, as far as I know, this is entirely innocent, so..." He lifted his hands in a 'who knows' gesture. "I don't think so."

Her throaty chuckle sent his thoughts headed even further south than they already were. She rested a hand on his knee and this time, her smile lit up her eyes.

"I'm never entirely innocent," she said. "And I don't believe you are, either."

She removed her hand, and Luke felt its absence. This was a complication he did not need. Until now, most visitors had been families or couples. A group of older ladies had come in last week and flirted outrageously, but he recognized harmless teasing when he saw it. There was nothing harmless in Stacy's flirtation tonight.

"Tell me about the house," she said. The rapid change of subject sent his head spinning for a second.

"Uhh..." Luke cleared his throat and tried again. "You came in the main entrance – the front hall opens to the private living spaces of the house and the stairs to the family bedrooms."

He'd never been upstairs on that side, but he'd been in the kitchen many, many times, often sharing coffee and chatting trails with the Stewarts.

"Weird to come through the family doors, isn't it?"

Luke shrugged. "When the place first opened, I think it was a bit more normal. Times were different, and there are only twelve guest rooms in the house. There is a big entrance on the side in what Cat calls the rec room, but I think it was originally a ballroom."

Stacy looked down the hall, her expression incredulous.

"There's that much back there?" She gave a low whistle. "Wow."

It had surprised him as well. From the front, you didn't see much of the big wing behind the main house. Even in winter, heavy trees blocked the view.

"This is the community's party space," he said with a laugh. "High school prom. Weddings. Whatever."

She settled back, close enough that her shoulder brushed his. "Guess we got lucky with the cancellation."

They sat for a minute, listening as the crowd down the hall thinned and the kitchen sounds faded to nothingness. The quiet as the day faded had always been one of his favorite moments at every resort he'd worked at. Early morning peace was nice, but there was a sense of anticipation or impending chaos. Nighttime quiet didn't have all of that—it was softer, almost seductive.

"So, if I plan to ski off the groomed slopes, I need to have you check out my form."

Luke snapped his head around and everything about her expression said she knew exactly what she'd done.

"That is the policy," he replied. "Come down to the bunny slopes tomorrow morning and I'll be happy to ah…" He stopped himself from saying the words. He didn't stop himself from letting his eyes slowly travel her body, from the shining dark hair to the swell of her breasts and the curve of her waist, and down over her seemingly mile-long legs.

"What if I wanted to book a lesson? Or a private tour?"

Luke nearly choked on air. Yeah, he'd been around enough to recognize the come on in those questions. As well as the plausible deniability behind them. He would love nothing more than to give Stacy a private tour that had nothing to do with skiing.

"I'm on the bunny slopes till ten and I've got a lesson before lunch, but my afternoon is free. If you and your friends want to get on the trails a bit, I can show you around."

She shifted on the bench, braced a hand on his thigh and stood. The contact felt electric, and Luke had to tell himself to stand as well. She was nearly as tall as he, though he'd noted she was in heels. Even then, there weren't too many women who almost looked him in the eye.

Stacy smiled and leaned in. For a moment, he thought she was going to kiss him, and he felt a surge of panic. No way would he have the strength to not go there if she offered. Instead, she hugged him, and even that brief, full-body contact was delicious. Too delicious.

"G'night," she whispered in his ear, then pulled back.

Watching her walk away was pure torture and judging by the sassy glance she threw over her shoulder as she turned toward the stairs leading to the guest rooms, she knew exactly what she was doing.

So did he. He was going straight to his cabin for a cold shower. *Damn.*

Chapter Three

Stacy, Saturday, December 12

Brit pushed her sunglasses up on her head and surveyed the small crowd already on the slopes. "I have not had enough coffee for this."

Stacy glanced up toward the wispy clouds and gave a theatrical sigh. "It's a gorgeous day, and we've got to get this done. Unless you wanna stick to that for skiing." She pointed at the lift behind them. She leaned over and poked Kylie. "We came here for something different, right? And you chose the place."

Both Brit and Stacy were used to being up early, but Kylie was not a morning person. She crossed her arms and harrumphed. Then her grumpy face turned to wide-eyed as Luke sauntered over.

"Morning, Stacy," he said, and a grin lit up his face. "And the rest of the girl squad."

Even all bundled up in ski gear, he was just as long and lean and even more good-looking than she'd remembered from last night. Stacy had to take a quick breath to steady herself before introducing Brit and Kylie.

"Pleasure to meet you." Luke pointed to the side of the bunny slope. "We've got a rope lift rigged over here to make it easy. Let's get you all checked out so you can go have some fun."

As much as she loved snow skiing, the only kind of fun that really interested her right now was the indoor variety with Luke. Preferably with a lot fewer clothes.

Luke told them to put on their skis, then carefully checked everyone's gear. He nodded in approval at Brit and Kylie, then took his time inspecting Stacy's setup before giving her a thumbs-up and a big smile.

"If you're going to go on any trails, you'll need to have a satellite GPS," he said, and held up a compact unit. "It's a just in case, and you check them out and get any additional gear you need at the end of the mess hall where we've set up first aid and what passes for ski patrol."

In a matter of minutes, he had them at the top of a short run not much steeper than the bunny slopes. He chatted with all three of them in a mildly flirty way, and Stacy was again reminded of folks in service roles. Maybe she'd misread him last night. Then he turned her way and dropped a wink that spoke volumes and none of them were G-rated.

"So, everybody sees this run and thinks it's boring and easy," Luke said. "And they're right. It is, but if you ski down it like it's nothing and come to some showy stop at the end, you're gonna have to do it again."

Stacy looked down the hill and chuckled. It did appear easy at first glance, but the entire slope was a field of moguls. She was scanning the patterns and trying to pick her path down and missed whatever Luke said next.

"I'm sorry, I..." Stacy stopped when he raised an eyebrow at her. What the hell? Is he seriously about to be that kind of asshole?

"Brit, you wanna go first?"

Brit gave a short nod as Luke stepped closer. She was every bit as tall as he, but Luke showed no sign of surprise.

"Don't forget," he said, with a glance at Stacy. "I want to see you pick a path, get some turns in, use your poles, and I wanna see solid edge control."

Brit dropped her glasses onto her nose. "And maybe no crashing at the end. Got it."

She pushed off and, after a couple of turns, settled into a path that had her riding the ridges. She got to the bottom and executed a perfect stop.

Luke shot her a thumbs-up, then turned to Kylie. "Any questions?"

Kylie braced her hands on her poles and shook her head. Luke nodded and leaned down close to her. "Have you picked your path?" He stood there, knees bent and head down, so he was on eye level with Kylie, the shortest of their bunch. She nodded and said something Stacy couldn't hear, but Luke let out a hearty laugh and stood. "You've got this."

She took off slowly, then found her groove and followed the same path as Brit. Kylie was a competent skier, but lacked confidence and rarely opted for anything that challenged her unless Stacy or Brit were involved. Somehow, Luke had picked up on that.

Kylie got to the bottom of the run and whipped off her hat in celebration. Her blue hair fluffed in the wind as she waved up the hill. Luke stuck both arms in the air and gave a double thumbs-up. Yeah, maybe Stacy had misread him last night. He seemed to be one of those friendly types.

He turned to her, and the genial nice-guy smile was gone. She got the lopsided smirk and the slightly narrowed eyes that made her wonder what he was thinking and exactly how non-family-friendly it might be.

"Good to see you out this morning," he said, and Stacy's heart rate picked up a beat or two. "I'm guessing Kylie does more cross-country. She's got good downhill skills, but she's not sure of herself, which means she's not as fast as Brit. Brit seems at home on the slopes and she knows her strengths and weaknesses. Where does that put you?"

Stacy had no clue how he'd gotten all that from watching her two friends go down a short run. Nor how he managed to make everything he said to her sound like some thinly veiled innuendo and yet come across as polite and charming at all times.

"Do you always flirt?" Apparently, her mouth decided it had a mind of its own and didn't need any help. Thank you very much.

Luke threw his head back in laughter, then leaned in close. "Reading people is a skill you develop, and some people respond well to a little light flirty behavior. Some don't. It's important to know the difference."

He brought his head down more and spoke close to her ear. "I don't always flirt like this, though," he said. Warm breath caressed the skin above her scarf and sent chills of pleasure down her spine. "In fact, it's a rare thing. Should I stop?"

He straightened up and, though he was smiling, there was a trace of uncertainty in his eyes. He wasn't kidding about any of that. Stacy smiled back, then winked.

"Don't you dare stop," she said and pushed onto the slope. The sun had warmed, and the snow was faster than she'd expected, but she carved into the turn and rode the outside of the first mogul. It was a tighter path and sharper turns than Brit and Kylie had taken, but faster.

She made it to the end and spun quickly to see Luke's thumbs-up a split second before he dropped over the edge himself. He came down the slope so fast she barely had time to register he had followed her path almost exactly.

He wasn't even breathing hard when he reached the bottom and pulled three green silicone wristbands from his pocket.

"I'll add your names to the list, but these are an easy way to spot who's good for the trails. If you're out there, have 'em on, please."

Kylie and Brit slipped theirs on and immediately turned to the site map, posted like a big sign, to decide what to do before lunch.

"You still have the afternoon free?" Stacy wasn't ready to leave Luke's company yet. He was good-looking and charming. She didn't normally jump into bed over a short weekend, but she might make an exception for him.

"Yep," he replied. His hand brushed hers and even that tiny contact, through thick gloves, sent a fresh round of pleasant shivers through her. He made a soft sound somewhere between a purr and a growl, and Stacy wished with all her being she could drag him to her room this instant.

Unfortunately, another group had approached and were waiting for Luke's attention. He tipped his head toward them and waved. "Be right with you, folks."

He snagged the sleeve of Stacy's jacket and pulled her to where Kylie and Brit still perused the map. Luke leaned against the frame and crossed his arms loosely.

"If you want something for this morning, stick to the groomed slopes. The greens will be fun and a nice warm-up. The blue on the far right will make you work for it, but it's not tough."

His smile broadened. "Meet me at the mess hall at two, and I'll get you geared up and show you the best part of Bristol Park. There's a great trail that combines cross-country with some downhill and has amazing views. It'll take a couple hours if we go at an easy pace."

He didn't even bother hiding the saucy wink he dropped at Stacy before he turned to the family that had come in behind them.

Kylie started fanning herself. "Well, not to say I told you so, but... I would like to point out that I did call your attention to him last night. Now we know what had you up bright and early on a weekend."

Brit elbowed her friend. "You're the sleepyhead. Is it possible for someone to get hotter overnight? Bonus, he's clearly into our Stacy."

Stacy pushed off toward the slopes and ignored her friends. Not that they were wrong. Luke was the reason she'd gotten up early — actually put on eyeliner and mascara — and donned all her gear right after breakfast.

They found the ski lift, and there was surprisingly little traffic. Stacy suspected, like Luke said, the real attraction was the abundant cross-country. The majority of the crowd on the slopes were families with young children and an elderly couple.

They got back to the main house right at lunchtime and had enough time to change into dry gear, eat and meet Luke at two. At the mess hall, he showed them around the space that served as ski shop and gear rental — or rather loans. Signs on the wall indicated next year there would be gear rental fees.

"There's a lot here still undergoing renovation as we dial in to what works. Lemme get you set up for some ski touring," Luke explained as he pulled out piles of equipment. "You're set for downhill, but most of Bristol Park is...well, slack country."

He added binding inserts to allow their heels to lift and stuck fish scale pattern friction skins on their skis. This type of skiing was more up Kylie's alley. Luke had been right. Kylie was skilled at cross-country, while Brit often got bored without the downhills.

They set off at a modest pace, Luke in the lead. Stacy did not mind following him at all — the view of his ass, even in ski pants, was nothing short of amazing. The snow-covered forests and hills weren't too bad, either.

Their first stopping point was a crest with a steep drop to a river on one side and a gentle slope leading to a wide forest path on the other. Luke stopped and pointed upriver to a swath of pine standing out in the deciduous forest.

"There's an old logging camp up there. You can still see the tree patterns and distribution are different."

Stacy scanned the surrounding hills, then back to where Luke had pointed and gasped. Everywhere else, there were bands of evergreen that ran like water through a sea of barren trees. Where he'd pointed out the camp, though, there were almost perfectly straight lines of evergreens bounding two sides of a section of forest where the trees were smaller than the surrounding area.

"Is that the camp the man at the meet and greet was talking about?" Stacy was a little winded after the climb to this peak, and she was trying not to sound breathy. Brit was bent over at the waist, stretching, and Kylie had her arms over her head like a runner who'd gotten a stitch in their side. Luke didn't even seem a little out of breath.

"That's the one," he replied. "It's a challenging trip."

Stacy recalled the bruise on the man's face. Something about a wayward branch. They rested another minute, then took the slope slow and easy before slipping into the snowy path that snaked between trees so old and gnarled Stacy half-expected elves or wood nymphs to pop out at any moment.

"The other side of the river had a lot of newer growth," Brit puffed the words out as they continued down the path. "Here it looks old."

Luke's chuckle carried on the breeze and sounded a little like rustling leaves. "This is protected land. Back in the day, it was still part of Bristol Park and never logged like that."

He paused at a fork in the trail and pointed to the right into an open field. "Go that way, and you'll find a couple easy runs, then a quick, flat trek to the bunny slopes. We're going this way."

He pushed off and veered left, where the trail hugged the edge of the forest. "So, I know Stacy is in investment banking. What about you two?"

Stacy nearly dropped her poles in surprise. He really was good at this—part ski guide, part encyclopedia of local facts, and gauging they were a group that preferred talk over silence. Or maybe he was just like that, but she suspected not.

"I'm in cybersecurity," Kylie spoke first. "Private sector."

Her short answer brought a bubble of laughter to Stacy's lips. Kylie had tried government work and found it didn't mesh with her style. The streaks of bright blue hair tended to put conservative types off before she ever opened her mouth about her left-leaning politics. Never mind that she was exceptionally good at her job.

"What about you, Brit?" Luke's tone was gentle, conversational. As if he understood Brit was often reluctant to talk about her work.

At nearly six feet two inches tall, with dark hair and striking green eyes, Brit commanded attention she didn't always want.

"I'm an attorney," Brit responded. She stopped there, like she usually did, forcing the other person to ask deeper questions if they wanted, and buying her time to sus out how much to tell them.

Luke pointed up a short rise. "We'll climb that, then we've got a series of downhills that will take us around this side of the mountain, and we'll come out at the top of the runs above Bristol Park."

Stacy stopped in her tracks. "We'll be making a big circle."

Everyone else stopped as well. Brit and Kylie looked a bit confused, but Luke smiled.

"Cat took me on this one my first week here," he said. "It's a good starting point, and I'll show you on the map later. You can make it as long or as short as you want, and it's easy to find your way home. But yes, we're making a big circle."

He started up the trail and stayed quiet until they reached the peak. "Here we'll take the left slope, then it's maybe twenty or thirty yards to the next run. What kind of law?"

He threw the question out almost casually, and Stacy watched Brit's eyes go wide. She drew herself up to her full height and smiled.

"I work primarily with gender and sexuality issues," Brit said. "The firm I'm with concentrates on marginalized people in workplaces and educational environments."

Luke nodded. "Excellent. That's important work."

Brit practically glowed under that brief praise, and Stacy felt the tiniest twinge of jealousy. The same feeling she'd struggled with throughout college as she'd watched Brit do Big Important Things That Mattered while her focus was on money making and essentially enabling the rich to get richer.

They headed down the first slope, then very quickly to the second. Luke made it all seem so effortless as his skis swished through the soft snow.

They crossed a broad, flat plain of endless white unspoiled by anything but animal tracks, and Stacy felt a thrill surge through her. Theirs were the first human tracks here since the last snowfall. Something about it felt at once pristine and profane. In the middle of the field, Luke brought them to a halt and gestured for quiet.

"Close your eyes and listen." He spoke softly, with an almost reverence. "Just breathe and enjoy the moment."

Feeling a little silly, even if he was echoing her own feelings of the experience, Stacy closed her eyes and at once, the world came alive in other ways.

The moment her world went dark, she picked up Kylie's deep breaths off to her right and Brit's lighter breathing to her left. In front of her, the nearly imperceptible sound of Luke. The air carried the crisp scent and taste of winter—a strange mixture of ozone and pine she associated with skiing.

Another breath and there was the soft drip, drip and thump of snow melting and clumps falling off trees. Then the crackling of frozen branches in the wind.

Somewhere in the distance, the distinctive sound of a woodpecker and the raucous call of a jay. The longer she stood still and silent, with her eyes closed, the more sounds she picked up. There was something so peaceful about the moment it nearly brought tears to her eyes.

She'd seen beautiful mountains in winter, and skied some famous resorts, but she'd never known this kind of simple peace of listening to the world around her. She'd asked Kylie for something different, and the reality had surpassed her wildest hopes. Bristol Park was magical. She focused again on her friends.

Kylie's breathing was slower, and Brit's so soft it was almost not there. She couldn't hear Luke at all, but she could feel him like he was standing right next to her instead of five feet away. It was as if she could reach out and touch him like he had touched her hand this morning.

She opened her eyes, and the spell was broken. Luke wasn't in arm's reach. He was in the same spot as before. With his head tipped back, face up to the sun and his eyes closed, he almost looked like a man in prayer, as if this were a sacred moment.

Maybe it was. She'd certainly felt something before while her eyes were closed. His head lowered, his eyes opened, and his gaze locked on hers. His lips curled into a smile and the lust she'd been tamping down and keeping semi-controlled raged wild and free. She wanted this man.

"Wow." Brit breathed the word, then took in a long, slow breath and rolled her shoulders before she opened her eyes. "Thank you."

Luke nodded, then shifted his attention to Kylie, who almost seemed dazed as she opened her eyes. "I don't think I've ever stood still and...well...been...like just existed before. I don't know whether or not I liked that."

Luke stretched like a lazy cat waking up from a nap in the sun. "I find my peace out here," he said. "You might not, but everyone can use an occasional moment to stop everything and listen. And this is the perfect place for it."

There was very little talk on the way back to Bristol Park. The downhills made it harder to keep up the chatter, but the quiet wasn't uncomfortable. Instead, Stacy felt like she carried a bit of that deep peace from the meadow locked inside her.

They followed Luke into the mess hall to take off their borrowed gear, and Kylie and Brit started making plans for the hot tub before they'd got everything checked in. Soaking was probably a good idea, but Stacy wanted more time with Luke.

He put away the gear and turned to her with his hand out. She almost put her hand in his, and barely stopped herself.

"Give me your phone," he said. Stacy handed it over without question, and he tapped the screen in a wild flurry, then returned it. "Added my info to your contacts. I've got a couple lessons before dinner and I've got night tubing duty, but text me any time."

She nodded, trying to find words for whatever she'd felt in the field and failing. He caught her hand as she turned away and the electric jolt promised taking this man to bed would be an experience like no other.

"I mean it," he said. "Not just ski shit, either. Text. Any time."

His next group was already filing into the space, and Stacy roused herself from whatever strange spell she was under and caught up with her friends as they expanded on their plans for the hot tub.

Chapter Four

Luke, Sunday, December 13

Luke's finger hovered over the text button. He'd tapped out two words while pouring his morning coffee then sat there alternating between hitting send and staring at the picture Stacy had sent last night.

It was just her face, but she was clearly in bed, hair in a messy bun and wearing some oversize shirt. He couldn't take his eyes off it and, dammit, he needed to not go there. No matter how tempting it was, he needed to keep his dick in his pants.

He pocketed his phone without sending the good morning text, poured a second cup of coffee into a travel mug and opened his cabin door. Another clear and beautiful day early in the season meant the snow machines were going on the main slopes. *Good.* He'd texted Cat and Nate late last night after checking on the condition of a couple of the closest runs and seeing no snow on the weather report.

Thanks to a few good storms at the start of the month, there was still enough cover on the deeper trails to allow for back-country skiing, but the closest runs had seen heavy use yesterday and were showing the wear of two sunny days in a row. The machines would have them up and going by the time breakfast was over.

"Figured you could use some help."

Luke glanced up to see his kid brother, Erik, leaning against his new Jeep. *Damn morning people.*

"Wanna throw on some gear and gimme a hand getting the bunny and tubing hills groomed?"

Erik laughed. "Kinda why I'm here," he replied. "Nate texted. The baby was up half the night. I'da been here earlier, but some of us need to eat in the mornings."

The idea of food first thing turned Luke's stomach, but Erik had to eat almost immediately after waking up. *Weird kid.*

For years, Luke had treated Erik to a week on the slopes at whatever resort he was working. He'd have done the same for his sisters if any of them had skied. Since Luke moved to Bristol Park, they'd spent time together every week. They'd hit the slopes after the first snow and even gone to the next town over for ice-skating.

"How's work?" Luke hadn't had much of a chance to talk to his kid brother since school had gotten back in session. Football season was in full swing, and Erik had his hands full as the new assistant coach at the high school. The Abbeydon Blue Devils were determined to win the championship again.

"It's different." Erik zipped his coat and gave Luke a 'hurry up' look. "Last year had its challenges, but I was insulated a bit since I wasn't regular staff. Being on as an official coach can be a bit rough at times."

Luke turned off the snow machines and did a quick check of the powder levels. *Perfection.* "What's making it so tough? I thought you liked your boss. Brandon seems pretty chill."

Erik shrugged. "Coach Waters is great, and it's nothing bad. But they created this position after the bullshit last year, and we're working harder with students who are up for athletic scholarships but whose grades aren't up to par."

Luke knew that story all too well. He'd been in that situation as a student—his performance in sports had earned him attention for scholarships, but his academics didn't match up. In the end, it didn't matter. He went to Minnesota State because that's where his girlfriend Becca was going.

This time ten years ago, he'd been making plans to propose. Then his world came apart. Ten years since he'd dropped out of college and taken up a life of being constantly on the move. A season here, a season there, never settling down. He shook himself from those thoughts.

Erik's attempt at indifference didn't fool Luke. The kid was in his first job out of college and his boss was his childhood hero. It was enough to make anyone a little stressed. He nudged Erik's arm.

"You want the bunny slopes or the tubing hill?"

Erik's face transformed as a wide grin replaced the worried expression. "Fuck, you know I can't keep that thing straight enough for the tube hill."

Luke tossed a set of keys to his brother and, for the next hour, lost himself in the simplicity of focusing on creating perfect channels for snow tubing. It seemed simple — plow a straight line down the hill — but for a great tubing experience you wanted different styles of runs. Flat, shallow ones with sharp bumper sides for the little kids, or the nervous tubers. Runs with a slight hump in the middle that ran steep and fast for the speed demons. And his favorite, the runs that were slightly cupped with banked sides that sent tubers slaloming and spinning down the hill in fits of laughter and delight.

By the time he'd finished the wedge of packed snow in the landing zone, he'd shoved his old thoughts into the hole where he kept them tightly locked away.

His phone buzzed with an incoming text as they returned the plows to the shed. He thumbed his messages open and smiled.

Good morning. I enjoyed our text chat last night.

He went to the message still sitting there and waiting to be sent. He added to it.

Good morning to you. Me too. What are your plans today?

She was probably leaving right along with everyone else. Which was a good thing. If she were to hang around for a week, or hell, even a few more days, he wasn't sure his resolve to keep it professional would hold up.

Erik leaned in and poked a finger at his screen. "Wow. Wondered if you'd ever get back to your seasonal flings."

Luke pocketed the phone and shook his head. "Just flirting," he said. "Figured my usual wasn't a good idea at a place like this."

His brother laughed long and hard and clapped him on the shoulder. "Or maybe last year was a wakeup call, or maybe you're maturing. Late bloomer and all."

Luke rolled his eyes. "Says my kid brother," he said. "But yeah, there could be some of both of those. I haven't... Well...nothing since I came here."

Erik folded his arms over his chest and leaned against the shed door. "Wow. You think you're finally ready to settle down? Mom and Dad would be thrilled. Still, I can't imagine anyone having a problem with something uh...occasional and discreet."

"You know me." Discretion was the name of the game if you were dating multiple women during a single season. Not that he ever promised monogamy to any of them, but he wasn't rude or an asshole. Fat lot of good it had done him in the end. He ignored the first half of Erik's comment.

"I know you've never kept your dick in your pants for an entire season, let alone a whole year," Erik replied. He was right, and that was another uncomfortable thought Luke would prefer to avoid.

"Bite me," he said. "We should hit the slopes later. This place is emptying out this afternoon. No one's staying the week."

Erik shook his head. "Sorry, I've got a date."

Luke raised his eyebrows. Erik was normally very private about his dating life. Rightly so. He'd caught enough hell after coming out in his senior year of high school.

"He's in Albany," Erik said, as if in reply to Luke's unvoiced questions. "I'm not fool enough to date in the same town I'm working in."

That gave Luke a chuckle. Ordinarily, he'd agree with Erik, but something about Abbeydon was different. He had a feeling folks here would roll with it. In fact...

"Didn't you tell me the head of the girls' athletic department is married to the school's office manager, or something like that? Why would who you date make any difference?"

Erik held his hands up in mock surrender. "Yeah, everybody knows Susan and Tonya, but they kept it quiet for years. And I'm still the new guy."

Something in his tone stuck a chord in Luke. "Are you worried?"

Erik shook his head. "I'm always worried—all it takes is one pissed-off parent. But no, I'm not stressed over anything specific. Just cautious. Plus, I think I'm his rebound."

Luke nodded. Erik had worked hard to get where he was, and he deserved every bit of success. Still, the caution was understandable. Luke had always imagined his kid brother winding up in some more urban situation after growing up in the suburbs. "I know you're not going to like it, but I've never asked. How much of you taking this job had to do with Brandon Waters?"

Erik had practically hero worshiped the guy. He'd seen him play during his rookie year and followed his career from that moment on. He was devastated when his favorite player had had to retire after getting injured on the ice.

"Wow! I'm halfway through my first year on staff, and you're just now getting around to that," Erik replied. "A lot of it is about him, but not the way you think. He's a good boss, and it's an excellent opportunity."

Kid has a point. Doing your first years as a new teacher in a small and relatively well-off district was a smart choice. Having his childhood hero as a boss was a bonus. Who cared if he felt like he had to drive an hour and a half to date someone. *Except no one should have to feel like that.*

"I think you're right," Luke said, finally. "If it feels good for you. Why not?"

His phone buzzed again but he ignored it until Erik tossed the keys at him and sauntered off. Then Luke pulled the phone out and tapped the screen.

We're leaving midafternoon – probably right along with everyone else.

The words sent a chill through him for no real reason. He'd just met this woman. Why should he care? The hell of it was, he did, and he wanted to see her again before she left. Though managing that would require a damn near miracle-level intervention.

Luke shifted his attention to the first visitors of the day, a boisterous family itching to get some activity time before starting the drive home.

He stayed busy right up until the very end of lunch, when the crowds started thinning out, and he debated whether to head up to the kitchen and see what they still had available or go to his cabin to heat a bowl of soup. The argument with himself came to an abrupt end when Stacy came walking up with a big lunch box in her hand.

"I had the strangest conversation with Cat a minute ago," she said as she handed over the red and white cooler. "Kylie and Brit headed up to pack after lunch, and I figured I'd come down here and..."

She stopped and glanced over at him. She looked a little confused, as if she couldn't figure out why she was telling him this.

"I wanted to say goodbye before we left and thank you for an amazing day yesterday."

She waved a hand at the cooler. "It's still warm. Eat. I was on my way out the door when Cat stopped me and asked if I was coming down here. Then she asked if I'd mind taking this down to you."

Conflicting thoughts whirled through Luke's head. If Cat was doing that, then she'd probably noticed his interest in Stacy. Cat wouldn't ask Stacy to do something like that if she didn't think that interest was mutual. Still, she was his employer, and he was trying to keep things...

Ah fuck it. He didn't have the energy to spend on that right now. Not with Stacy standing right in front of him and a cooler full of who knows what waiting. He nodded his head at the mess hall.

"Come with?"

He braced for her to say no, but she didn't. She silently followed him inside and to a table he'd pushed near a window. It was a convenient spot to get out of the weather so he could update his paperwork or grab a quick meal without traipsing all the way to his cabin or the main house.

He opened the cooler to find a Thermos of soup and a wrapped ham and Swiss on a croissant—still warm.

The soup probably came from the kitchen. The sandwich was one hundred percent Cat.

They chatted idly while he ate, then, as he was finishing the last of the soup, Stacy sat back with the confused look on her face again.

"Would you be honest with me about something?"

Luke wiped his mouth and dropped the spoon and thermos into the larger cooler. He'd take them up to the house later. He fixed his eyes on Stacy's.

"Sure."

He didn't know what he was getting into with that one, and he'd probably regret that single word.

"I'm not sure how to read you," Stacy said. "You're a flirt, but anyone in a service field uses those skills. I mean, specifically, with me, you were flirting. Then you'd kind of... I don't know. It was like you hit a pause button or something."

Luke was very glad he was done eating because he probably would have choked on something.

"Was there a question?" Maybe not the nicest thing to say, but he needed some clarity.

"Am I wrong?" She arched her eyebrows and oh, he wanted to kiss her right now. He wanted it so badly he could imagine the taste of her on his lips.

"You're not," he said. Everything in his experience said now was the time to tap dance a little. She was all set to leave, so any chance of getting together was about to end. He wanted her to have good impressions of the resort—that was the source of his paycheck, after all. This was a balancing act he used to excel at.

He took a deep breath and chose complete honesty instead.

"I was one hundred percent flirting," he said. "And I'm pretty confident you were too." He didn't need her nod to tell him he was right.

"I'm not gonna lie," he continued. "There have been times in my life when I've happily had flings with clientele." *That might be sugarcoating it a bit, or at the very least, under-representing things.*

"But that was at much bigger places than this," he said. "Places where one bad review or pissed-off client couldn't have a big impact on the bottom line. Even then, it's a risk." That was a fact he'd learned all too painfully last year, but she didn't need to hear that.

"Here? I've avoided opening that can of potential trouble."

There. That's honest, but kind. Let her think he was a total playboy — it wouldn't be that far from the truth. Or at least from his usual truth. He dared a glance over at Stacy.

Her expression had morphed from confusion to something bordering on wicked. He definitely liked this new look much more. Too much more.

"I think you're underestimating your employers," she said. "But I get it."

She stood, then leaned down, her hands pressed flat onto the table in front of him. For the second time in the weekend, he thought she was about to kiss him. His resolve to keep it professional was no stronger today than it was the night they first met. *Fuck, was that only two days ago?*

Instead, she got close enough her hair tickled his cheek and the spicy, smoky scent of her wrapped around him.

"Maybe we'll see each other again." She whispered the words in his ear, then rose and, without explaining what she'd meant, she was off with a wave of her hand.

Every bit of his attention was riveted on her retreating form. His cock had risen to full salute, as if to say it was ready for action.

He needed something physical that would allow him to shut his mind off. Maybe he'd see if he could clean up some old trails this afternoon. He reached down and adjusted himself. Or maybe he should go to his cabin and take care of this problem. *Fuck.*

Chapter Five

Stacy, Monday, December 14

A stack of files landed on her desk with a resounding thud. Stacy looked up to see Chad Higgins hanging over the partition to her cubicle. Everything in her wanted to wipe the smarmy grin from his face. Instead, she adopted her most innocent expression and forced a smile.

"Can I help you?" She pointedly did not mention the folders he'd just dumped.

"These all need digitizing." He tipped his head at the pile, as if that answered her question.

"Uh huh," she replied, then waited. And waited. When he didn't respond, she leaned forward, elbows on her desk, and propped her chin in her hands. "Isn't that what we have interns for?"

The urge to bat her eyelashes at him was almost overwhelming. Despite his recent promotion, Chad was not her boss. He wasn't even in the chain of command over her.

He rolled his eyes and leaned down as if he were talking to a child. "So, give them to the interns. They just need to be digitized, and I don't have time to deal with it. It's called delegation."

He stomped off, muttering something under his breath. Stacy took in the pile, easily six inches thick. Apparently, his climb up the ladder had made him even more insufferable than usual.

She'd applied for the same position. She'd been at the company longer, had a better portfolio, and did better work than Chad. None of that seemed to matter when stacked against his undeniable connections. *And the fact that he's a man and I'm not.*

Stacy huffed out a breath and scooped up the pile before marching down the hall to the row of desks where the interns worked. She'd spent two years at those open workstations, busting her ass to make an impression so she'd be considered for a junior analyst role as soon as she graduated. By any standards, she should have made associate by now.

She set the pile of folders down on the long table behind the intern's desks.

"Hey, Caylan." The tall redhead at the end of the row turned. On top of the flaming red hair, Caylan Stewart had fair skin, freckles, bright green eyes and a winning smile. As attractive as he was, none of those attributes could change, or make up for, the fact that he looked like he was maybe twelve. He was about as baby-faced as they came.

"I offered to take those from Higgins a few minutes ago," he replied, pointing at the folders. Stacy forced herself to remain calm. Higgins' new office was just outside the intern's space. Caylan was well known for seeing a need and stepping up to help. The fact that Chad had bypassed the intern in favor of dumping the task on Stacy added fuel to her already simmering pot of dislike for the man.

"Yeah, well." She heaved a sigh. "I'm not sure what kind of deadline he's got on those, but I'll find out. You got space for it, or should I ask one of the others?"

Caylan scooped up the pile and transferred it to his desk. "I've got it. Andy and I can get this handled pretty quickly."

Stacy nodded. "Thanks. You're a gem."

He sketched a salute but gave a bitter laugh. "We both graduate this June," he said, then leaned forward and dropped his voice. "Neither of us is applying here. I mean…" He spread his hands as if to say, 'look around'.

She couldn't blame him. Caylan was not only baby-faced, but he was also openly gay. No matter how progressive the firm claimed to be, as far as Stacy knew, there were no out staff members. Andy was a brilliant student, but his family were immigrants and the board member who championed his internship made no secret of the fact that he'd only made the request so his wife, who was one of Andy's professors, wouldn't banish him to the couch.

Not that anyone would admit those were the reasons. An internship at the company would be amazing on their resumes, but they stood about as much chance of rising up the corporate ladder as she did.

"When the time comes, I'd be happy to write a recommendation," she said. "If you think that would help."

Caylan shook his head. "It's fucked up that you didn't make associate."

"Yeah, well," she said again and mimicked his 'look at this place' gesture. Then she waved and headed to her desk.

She met Kylie for what passed for lunch—a pita filled with grilled lamb and topped with lettuce, tomato and tzatziki from a nearby food cart. Fast but delicious, even when eaten outside on a chilly day. Then she rushed to the office to finish her reporting so she'd have the morning free to prepare for client meetings.

Unfortunately, that plan was interrupted by several phone calls, an email that took an hour of her time to find the answer for, and at least half a dozen people coming by commiserating with her that she hadn't gotten the promotion.

Fuck.

It was Monday afternoon, and she already needed a break from work. She grabbed her phone and sent a quick text to the friends' group chat.

Last weekend before Christmas. What are we all doing?

She went back to her reports, knowing she wouldn't hear anything from her friends until later. Kylie would be buried in her computer, and Brit was likely in court on a Monday. She stayed at the office until she had everything done, and even got a jump start on her work for the morning—just in case there were more interruptions.

Story of my life here.

Kylie texted as Stacy stepped out of the building and into the blustery night.

I've got a wicked deadline. I'll be plugged in all weekend. We can do takeout if you need some company or something.

Stacy sent a frown face and stuffed her phone away. She wasn't ready to go home to an empty apartment, so she stopped at her favorite bar — a place that had decent drinks and good, if basic, food. She sat at the bar and ordered a soda and a chicken sandwich with fries. Maybe not the healthiest choice, but it beat going home to whatever she had in stock. Probably cereal. Or eggs and toast. She always forgot to grocery shop.

Her phone pinged as her food arrived, and Stacy stuffed a fry in her mouth before thumbing open her messages.

Sorry. Mom wants to leave early for Florida. Grams is thinking about moving down there. Sounds like there's gonna be some house-hunting going on.

Well, that settled that.

We talking about the same Grams who had kittens when we considered getting a place in the outer boroughs during college? The one who can't go a weekend without her Nathan's?

The woman loved her hotdogs. She loved to tell the story of her grandfather buying her a hotdog on a trip to Coney Island when she was a little girl. She got the same thing every time. Grams liked her dogs with mustard and onions.

The very same. Wild, right? Bunch of her friends have either moved or done the snowbird thing. Grams says moving is too much of a pain to do twice a year, and Nathan's ships now. Who knew? Surprised you don't already have boy-toy plans.

Stacy laughed, then stifled it when other patrons turned to glare at her. She stuffed another bite of sandwich in her mouth while she typed with her other hand.

Haven't had one of those since Pedro. Have fun in Florida.

Maybe Brit and Kylie were right. Stacy was firmly of the opinion that her twenties were meant for strictly casual dating as she focused on her career. Which was why she'd ended things with Pedro when he'd proposed after three months of seeing each other. She'd think about settling down later. Maybe. She thumbed open the browser on her phone and found the site for Bristol Park.

If they've got a room available this coming weekend, I'll call it fate.

She typed in the dates and hit the button, then sucked in a breath as the page popped up. She hit the reservation link and had a room booked by the time she'd finished her sandwich.

Chapter Six

Luke, Thursday, December 17

Cat shifted the baby and handed over a printed guest list. All the details were online in a brand-new guest management system that tracked everything from room or cabin numbers to dietary restrictions, but Cat had a thing for paper lists. Nate had warned Luke not to even try to dissuade her from the habit. She'd give it up if and when she was damn good and ready.

"Thanks," Luke said and slid a finger down the column of names. It was likely to be a light weekend for him. A large group of seniors had taken several cabins. The older guests tended to come in two varieties — those who would take a basic lesson or two and stick to the easier runs, and those who were cross-country enthusiasts who just wanted to get out in the woods.

His peaceful imaginings came to a halt when he saw two large families taking up the other cabins. Kids meant work. Lots of work. He switched to the house guests and hissed in a breath.

Stacy?

He opened the registry on the computer to double check. Yep. That Stacy. *No. That has to be a glitch.* Maybe the room was empty and somehow the system... His thoughts ground to a halt when he scrolled down the reservation.

Made Monday. Definitely not a glitch. *Well hell. That's interesting.*

He skimmed the rest of the rooms but didn't see her girl squad's names. *Really interesting.*

"Hey." Cat waved a hand in front of the screen. "We've got a couple high school kids coming in to handle the tubing hill. Erik said he'd take a Saturday afternoon shift on the main runs. That frees you up a bit."

She winked, then turned and left the makeshift ski office. He sat there trying to process the wink. *Was that about Stacy?*

Whatever it was, he didn't have time to think about it. During ski season when most guests were in for the weekend, Bristol Park allowed guests to select an early check-in on Fridays. The group of older folks had indicated they'd be arriving around ten in the morning. That meant he likely had to be ready for them on the slopes before lunch.

Time for some last-minute gear checking, restocking the first aid kits, making sure all the GPS units were charged and ready and maybe doing some extra grooming on the easier slopes, considering the kids.

That work kept him busy most of the day. It also kept him from dwelling too much on the fact that Stacy was coming back.

He'd had a lot of flings in his life, but he'd rarely had chemistry like he'd had with her. Maybe it was the year of celibacy talking, but he didn't think so. Still, right now, all he could think of was how good she'd smelled, her bright smile and the way her touch sent jolts through him that seemed to go straight to his cock.

Fuck.

He put everything away, locked up and headed to his car, texting his brother on the way. The drive to town didn't clear his head, and he found himself sitting in the small, but airy apartment Erik had moved into after his boss Brandon and his fiancée Gina had bought a house. The apartment used to be Gina's.

Erik slid a beer across the table at him. Luke popped the cap and took a swig.

"I'm fucked," he said.

Erik didn't bat an eye. They hadn't spent as much time together over the years as Luke would have liked. Erik hadn't even been in high school yet when Luke dropped out of college. Winter weekend ski trips and a week at whatever summer water adventure Luke was doing that year were not the stuff strong brotherly bonds were made of.

Since coming to Abbeydon, Luke had realized what he'd been missing. His kid brother had grown up and he hadn't been there for it. Still, over the past year, they'd formed a deep friendship that surpassed the years of distance.

"You wanna explain that a bit?" Erik cracked open his own beer and finished a quarter of it in one swallow. "Because I need some context here."

Luke sighed. "Stacy's visiting this weekend."

Erik threw his head back and laughed. "Yeah. I know. That's a big reason I'm helping out."

Luke opened his mouth to say something, then shut it with a shake of his head. *What the hell?*

"Excuse me?"

Erik shrugged and took a slow pull on his beer. "Cat said you seemed to really click with a particular guest last weekend. And since you just said, 'Stacy's visiting', I kinda assumed it's the same person."

Luke nodded.

"Cat texted and asked if I might be able to cover some time Saturday afternoon. She said it wasn't likely to be a busy weekend, and she had a feeling you might be wanting a little free time."

Aw shit. Well, he'd figured Cat had noticed his interest. *And Stacy's, too, it seemed.* He wasn't sure what that meant, and he didn't like uncertainty. There was too much water under that bridge for him to be happy about it.

"So why, exactly, does this mean you're fucked?"

Luke scowled at his brother, then shoved his hands through his hair. "I don't know."

That was the best he could come up with. Anything else went deeper than he was willing to go in his own thoughts. He sure as shit wasn't going there with someone else — not even his brother.

"This isn't a big resort," he said. "A fling isn't gonna go unnoticed. Hell, Cat winked at me when she told me you'd cover Saturday afternoon."

Erik looked like he was about to burst with laughter. "Why are you so torn up about this? I'm serious. You think I was blind all those years? That I didn't see the women — different women — coming and going at all hours? Come on. I was a teenage kid still trying to convince myself I was straight."

Luke traced a finger through the condensation on his beer bottle. "Why are you staying in Abbeydon?"

His brother blinked as if the question confused him. Then he chuffed a short laugh. "This place grows on you."

That was all he said, but his eyes said there was more to it. Maybe it was some residual hero worship for Brandon Waters. More likely, it was something like what Luke was feeling himself.

Abbeydon accepted him as he was but challenged him to be better.

The question was, where did Stacy fit into that? Was flirting with her falling into his old behaviors? Or was this something different?

"You want a second?" Erik clinked his beer bottle, and Luke rose and chucked the empty bottle into the recycling bin.

"Nah," he replied. "I need to check the snow machines yet, and tomorrow's gonna be an early morning. Let's grab a burger."

Chapter Seven

Stacy, Friday, December 18

"You're leaving early?" Chad Higgins stopped on his way in the front door, effectively preventing Stacy from doing just that.

She smiled sweetly and gestured for him to move. He didn't.

"I've completed all my work and also gotten a jump start on the projects for next week. We're set to be able to close early on the twenty-fourth." She hated justifying herself to him, but fighting back meant causing a scene and that wouldn't go over well. Still, he wasn't her boss. "Last I checked, I don't report to you, so I don't need to explain myself."

Chad rolled his eyes and blew out a breath. "You'll never get anywhere in this company taking Fridays off."

More like I'll never get anywhere in this company unless my daddy paves the way. Not that she'd say that.

"Considering I've been pulling sixty-to-eighty-hour weeks since well before you came here, I'm not sure it matters."

She wouldn't be petty and remind him that her work was better. He wouldn't agree, and even if he did, he wouldn't care.

"You're leaving early to interview!" His eyes went wide, then he looked around as if afraid of being seen talking to her or something. Then he stepped closer and leaned in. "You putting in at Godmann?"

Stacy took advantage of him moving away from the door and skirted around him, flashing a bright smile as she went. "Again, I don't need to explain myself. Ta!"

She waved and pushed through the doors, thankful to be leaving her annoying coworker behind. Let him think she was applying elsewhere. She wasn't, but maybe she should. The last week had made it abundantly clear that she was going nowhere fast in this place.

She had five more years to reach her goal of complete financial independence by her thirtieth birthday. At the rate she was going here, she wouldn't make it.

Maybe she should have taken her stepfather's advice and gone to law school instead of pursuing her dream of investment banking. When it had come time for an internship, she'd had plenty of options, but chose this firm for its reputation of supporting its analysts on a career track.

Sadly, that had turned out to be utter bullshit — a complete show with nothing real behind it. It was the same old story — it didn't matter how hard you worked. It was all about who you knew. *And worse for women.* She swapped her shoes out in the elevator and pulled on her coat. Mid-December in Manhattan could be miserable. It might only be a five-minute walk to her place—an apartment her grandfather had kept for when he worked long days on Wall Street—but it was a windy walk.

The apartment was top on her list of things to ditch as soon as she was making enough money to afford a decent place on her own. She was renting at well below market, which she supposed put her in a better place than Chad. At least in one way. It was common knowledge he'd lived in Brooklyn when he first started and now had a shoebox of a studio just to have a prestigious address.

Let Chad think whatever he wanted. If he spread a rumor she was job hunting, it might hurt her chances of getting any good projects, but it wouldn't get her fired. Stacy needed downtime. She'd made that decision on Monday night, then worked till nearly midnight the rest of the week getting everything ready so she could take off.

She'd gone above and beyond, but all that would be seen was her leaving early. In college, she'd scoffed at people touting some mythical 'work-life balance' and now she was justifying taking personal time. *Oh, the irony.*

Inside her building, she rushed into her small apartment, changed clothes and grabbed the bag she'd already packed. When she'd decided to take the weekend off, just for herself, fate must've been on her side, and she landed the last room at Bristol Park.

Getting a car meant stopping by her parents, but her stepfather was out of town for work, and her mother at a museum event. She'd had the conversation via text. Story of her life.

She was pulling down the long drive by six. The sky was already dark, and her headlights carved sharp shadows into the trees. Her tires crunched over the gravel and some of the tension around Stacey's chest lessened.

By the time she was on the porch, her shoulders felt like a ton of weight had been lifted from them, and by the time she was in her room, she was practically humming.

Kylie and Brit had both sent smiley devils and eggplant emojis when she'd told them where she was going. Not surprising. Her friends knew her, and Stacy had every intention of getting to know the hot ski instructor.

She couldn't decide if he was the laid-back ski bum he made himself out to be, or if he was some bored, rich frat boy who'd never grown up. Either one was fine with her, though if she was being honest, right now, the ski bum had more appeal. She'd had it up to her eyebrows with rich frat boys—her office was full of them.

She tried to convince herself it was the place—Bristol Park felt comfortable and welcoming, like going to your grandparents' house where you knew there would be your favorite snacks and unconditional love. At least, that's how Kylie and Brit's grandparents seemed to her.

Stacy's grandmother's house was more like stepping into some combination of museum and library where you had to be on your best behavior at all times. As a teen, she'd joked you even had to be polite in the bathroom.

She cleaned up, changed clothes, and even put on a bit of makeup then made her way down to dinner.

There were no other solos in the big dining room, and Stacy chose a table near a corner so she could people watch. Sitting alone was always a different experience than with a group. You saw a place through a different lens.

It was a diverse crowd — families with young children, a handful of people about her age, and a large group of older folks. It was even more crowded than it had been the week prior.

After dinner, she headed for the library and the bar. Drink in hand, she caught sight of a certain man sitting on a barstool at a small high-top table in the sunroom and made her way over to him. When she tapped him on the shoulder and he turned, she found herself face to face with a man who looked like a slightly younger Luke.

"Oh, hey there." The voice was almost the same. A little brighter and not quite as deep. "I uh, think you want my brother." He whisked off his beanie and stuck out his hand. "Hi, I'm Erik Tverberg."

Stacy blinked. Under the beanie, he had the same blond hair, only his was close cropped while Luke wore his longer and usually contained in a ponytail. Erik had the same cool-blue eyes. Same smile, even, though he sported more stubble than beard. They were practically twins. She remembered her manners, cleared her throat and shook the man's hand.

"Stacy Barclay." She had to bite her tongue to keep from asking where Luke was.

Erik's eyes flicked to her left a split second before a warm hand landed on her shoulder.

"Back again so soon?" There was the rich voice she'd imagined in her dreams. Not that she'd admit that to anyone.

"I see you've met the bratty kid brother," Luke said. Erik flipped him off and scooped his drink from the table.

"Stay," Luke said and tapped his brother's arm. "I think…" He nodded his head toward the door. Cat stood talking to a devastatingly good-looking man with dark hair and a close-trimmed beard. She pointed in their direction and the man nodded, then wove his way through the crowd.

"That the guy from Albany?"

Erik's cheeks pinked. "Andre? No. This is someone Cat wanted me to meet."

Luke smiled and shook his head then grabbed Stacy's hand.

"That's our cue to leave," Luke whispered in her ear as he pulled her toward the quieter hallway and the same bench they'd settled on before.

"In case you haven't figured it out, Cat is very good at connecting people," Luke said. "Sometimes, romantically." He nodded his head toward the sunroom. "Erik works at the high school. He did his student teaching year here and somehow charmed his way into a permanent job."

Stacy leaned against the wall. She could listen to him talk all day. There was something soothing about his voice — low and rich with the slightest hint of an accent. It was stronger in Erik. Maybe because Luke was older and had been away from home longer.

"No girl squad this trip?" Luke nudged her gently and Stacy chuckled.

"Nope," she replied. "This trip is all for me."

He sat back, his shoulders brushing hers. He folded his arms over his chest, and she had a hard time not reaching over and tracing a finger along the cuffs of his shirt. They were rolled just high enough to show off the bulge of his forearm and a complicated tattoo with roses and what looked like a dragon tail.

"That's beautiful work," she said. Luke shifted his arms, rotating so she could see more of the design that snaked around his forearm. "How far up does it go?"

The smile that crossed his face was so slow and delicious, it was filled with promises of slow, deep kisses, mussed hair and rumpled sheets. He licked his lips and cleared his throat.

"Full sleeve," he replied. "Up to my shoulder. You got any ink?"

Stacy shook her head. Her grandparents thought tattoos were vulgar. A perspective her stepfather shared. Her mother, however, had a tiny butterfly on her hip—a remnant of her rebellious years.

"I admire them on others," she said. "When they're well done, of course. It's not something I ever thought of for myself."

Luke tipped his head toward the sunroom. "Erik is the good boy. We've got four kid sisters, and they're all more like him than me."

Stacy arched an eyebrow at him. "Oh? How so?"

She couldn't imagine growing up with six kids in the house. She was an only child. Kylie and Brit both had siblings and their homes seemed at once delightful and chaotic in their activity and noise.

"Erik and the girls are all a bit bookish," Luke said. "They're more likely to be in the library than playing sports, and yet, he's an assistant coach."

She turned to him, reached out and plucked at his sleeve, sliding it up his forearm to see more of the design. Well, she tried to slide it up his forearm. The cuff wouldn't budge more than half an inch.

"Any other time in my life, I'd be offering to show you all of them," he said. He leaned closer and placed his mouth near her ear.

"I think you'd really enjoy my newest one."

Oh, two could play this game of tease.

"You keep saying you would have in the past, and want to now, but can't." She rested her hand on his knee and got close enough to smell some subtle cologne she couldn't identify. "Then you go and say things like that. Mixed messages. Should I back off?"

Luke didn't flinch from her words. He didn't even blink or tell her she was behaving like a man. She'd heard that a time or two in her life. As if women should be passive rather than actively pursuing something that interested them.

"We both know the answer to that question." His hand covered hers and slid it up his leg. He stopped shy of what she'd been hoping to get a feel of, and he smiled. "I'm trying to be a good boy, but I don't have a great track record there. Let's go for a little walk."

Luke stood, and she didn't miss the very obvious bulge in his pants. He offered a hand and led her down the hall. For a moment, she dared hope he would turn up the stairs and suggest they go to her room, but he walked past them. He stopped at the end of the hall, turned into a narrow alcove and pushed her against the wall.

Luke's body pressed against hers, rock hard from top to toe and Stacy gasped at the sudden contact.

"What do you want here?" His voice was lower than usual, gruff and sexy. "I'd like to think I'm pretty good at picking up signals, and all signs here point to yes. Am I right? Or should I back off?"

Stacy sucked in air. Luke made her feel like no one else ever had — she was used to guys who fell over themselves if she expressed interest. Luke's confidence was something different, and as sexy as fuck.

"You said it yourself last week," she replied. "You've had flings with clients before. I'm pretty sure you recognize when a woman is trying to get into your pants."

He let out a low growl and pushed a knee between her legs. If there had been any doubt in her mind that he was aroused, it was completely wiped out by the hard bulge against her hip.

He tipped his head down to her and she lifted her face, expecting a kiss. Instead, he cupped her chin in his hand, turned her head and pressed his lips to the spot under her ear. Stacy's skin prickled in delicious shivers she felt all the way down to her toes.

"I think we need to play a little game," he said, and the words whispered across her skin. "I like the way your skin flushes when you think of something naughty. Right here." He traced a finger along her neckline and dipped down to caress the tops of her breasts.

"What game is that?" She managed to keep her voice steady, despite the fact that she wanted to rip his clothes off right here in the hallway.

"Something you seem to excel at," he said. "Teasing."

His lips brushed her ear, ever so gently, then he withdrew.

"We keep it discreet," he said. "And we see how much we each can handle."

She cocked her head to the side and gazed into his icy blue eyes. "And why would I want to do that? What's to stop me from giving in?"

His tongue snaked out over his lips, and Stacy nearly melted. A week ago, if someone had said she'd be turning to puddles over that gesture she'd have laughed.

"Your competitive streak," he replied. Then he slowly pulled away as if he were peeling himself off her. The last point of contact was his hips, still firmly against hers, then that, too, was gone and he grinned.

"I've got a busy morning, but I'm free after one if you want to explore some more trails." He winked and pointed down the hall. "Your room is that way. See you tomorrow."

He slipped through a side door she hadn't even noticed, and Stacy stood there wondering what in the hell had just happened and thanking all the powers that could ever possibly be that she had thought to pack her vibrator. She was going to need it if she wanted to sleep tonight.

Chapter Eight

Luke, Saturday, December 19

The last giggling child set off down the bunny slope as the snow started getting heavier. The kid took the shallow hill in a perma-snowplow position, and Luke forced himself to not appear disapproving. *Whatever.* He'd spent all morning working with the entire group, despite begging the parents to have the kids do a thirty-minute session on their own—he had a great intro to ski class geared specifically to children under ten. As expected, the youngest ones had tuned out and run around squealing.

Just because he was used to a large, noisy family didn't mean he wanted that for himself. He'd been booked all morning with the combined family group. That meant four parents and ten kids, none of whom would be ready to tackle any of the regular runs, let alone the trails in Bristol Park this weekend.

Not that it seemed to bother them. They were here for the hiking, the nearby ice-skating, and the overall scenery. The free ski lessons were a bonus. He followed the family down the slope, helped them all out of their gear and sent them on their way to lunch, then checked the weather on his phone.

This morning, there had been some light flurries. He'd seen Stacy from a distance, looking like she was on her way out, so he had texted a warning to check the weather, then promptly gotten distracted from checking it himself.

Shit. The flurries had turned to a light snow by the time he'd finished with his lessons, and things were getting heavier. He texted Cat. If this kept up, they'd have to call everyone in.

Stacy had mentioned she might do the loop trail he'd shown her and the girl squad last week. Which meant she should be back by now. That thought sent at least some of his thoughts rushing to points south.

He was pretty sure he'd regret his suggestion of their little game. It damn near took everything he had to walk away from her last night. He wanted nothing more than to get her into bed. The sooner, the better. The game was as much for him as it was for her.

She awakened desires he'd buried for the past year, and his ability to deny himself pleasure wasn't exactly the best, but put in the context of a competition — who would hold out the longest? Oh, he'd win. Hands down.

He didn't want to tell her no. Everything in him wanted to say yes. He figured she had a bit of a competitive streak of her own and would rise to the challenge he offered. It was going to be torture, that was for sure, but it would also be fun as hell.

He'd have to find her and suggest lunch. He stopped at the ski check-in, set up at the end of the mess hall. The closest thing they had to a ski patrol—a staff member checking GPS units in and out and periodically checking status.

"Stacy come in yet?"

The young woman on duty frowned and ran a finger down her notes. They didn't have lift tickets or anything complicated, but they did keep track of who went out, where they were going, and when they returned. Plus, anyone going out in the back country had their satellite tracker.

The attendant shook her head and a trickle of something cold began in Luke's stomach. He scanned the log. She'd gone out hours ago.

He checked his phone. She'd sent a thumbs-up to his text about the weather and nothing since. Not surprising. Cell service was spotty on the trails. That was one of the reasons behind the satellite trackers. It wasn't time to panic yet. Maybe she forgot to check in.

"Can you get the location of her tracker?"

A few taps on the keyboard and the attendant pointed to the screen. The trickle became a bucket of ice dumped into Luke's veins.

Stacy was near the river. How the fuck did she get there?

Luke tried calling her phone. Nothing.

He called Cat.

"I don't want to be alarmist, but…" He explained the situation and less than a minute later, Cat stood next to him, glaring at the screen. He booted the attendant out of her seat and took over.

"Has she moved?" Cat asked. They'd had cases where someone had lost the tracker. Luke nodded.

"Yeah." He pulled up another screen that showed the tracker's pings. Something must have happened because she'd gone along the same set of trails as before, but suddenly veered off.

"She's got the maps," Cat said. "She's an experienced skier, so what's going on?"

The pings showed Stacy spent some time going in circles.

"I don't know for sure, but best guess?" Luke toggled the screen to show the route and timestamps. "Unless I'm very wrong, and I doubt it, something fouled the trail, and she can't get past it. All of this," he drew his fingers along the screen, "is her searching for an alternate route."

Luke pulled up the radar.

"I do know that I don't like the look of this." He pointed to the screen. They were about to get hammered. The original predictions for a couple of inches of snow over the next twenty-four hours had been updated to nearly a foot on the ground before midnight.

"Fuck, we can't even run a drone out to check with that coming in." Cat picked up her phone and called Nate. "I'm pulling everyone off the trails."

She nodded at Luke. The trackers were set up on a messaging system. With one click, he could ping every active tracker with a message to return home due to impending weather.

The policy required an acknowledgment, and they started pouring in. Nothing from Stacy's unit. Luke pinged her tracker again and this time a response came within a minute.

Trail blocked. Downed trees. Bit of a mini avalanche. Unstable AF. Tried to route around but there was more. Visibility sucks. Figuring on following river in.

Forget the bucket of ice, Luke's entire body had just been dumped into arctic waters. Cat looked at him wide eyed.

He swallowed hard and typed out a message to Stacy.

Find someplace stable, in the trees or near large rocks if you can. Not out in the open. Weather is getting worse. Don't risk getting lost or losing footing. You need better equipment. Will come to you.

He waited the agonizing minutes for her response.

Fuck. Yeah. OK.

That brought a chuckle at least. He glanced up at Cat to find she was already pulling gear down.

"Oh, hell no," he said. "You are not going out in this. Nate would kill me. Like seriously kill me. Get him down here. We can't risk a snowmobile if there's been avalanche activity, plus the visibility is too low for that. Nate, Erik and I can move faster, better and safer than anyone else here."

He sent one more message to Stacy telling her they were on the way and to conserve battery. Nate was already suiting up when Erik rushed in. Luke updated him on the situation, then started packing supplies.

It took nearly two hours of rough going in blinding snow for them to reach the fork in the river where Stacy had stopped. All three men stood at the edge of the field and tried to take in the chaos. Or as much of it as they could see. A churn of snow must have come down the hillside and barreled through.

Luke pinged Stacy's tracker again and it said she was right there. He gulped. If she'd been caught unaware. The broad, gentle slope was a practical invitation for roiling snow coming from higher up. *Shit.* He didn't want to think about it.

"Hey." Nate held up a small box. Stacy's tracker. His face looked grim as he followed the track toward the river. "The ice around the shore is all broken up, but that could be anything."

Erik whistled from further into the field. "Skis!" He pointed to a stand of trees near a rocky outcropping where a pair of skis stood in an x-pattern. Luke was halfway there when someone stood up on the rock and waved their arms above their head.

"Here!" Stacy's voice was almost lost in the wind and snow. The three men made their way to her and clambered up the rock. Luke took one look at her and something in him soared.

Aside from a small cut on her cheek, she seemed fine and swore there was nothing hurt. Luke ran a gloved thumb over the scrape.

"There was this quiet moment," she said. "Then a weird rumble like the earth was shuddering or something. I was rushing and missed a half-downed tree. Me and most of the tree both went flying. That's when I lost the tracker, and I wasn't gonna take time to find it." She was practically yelling to be heard over the wind.

Nate tapped his watch and Erik held up a screen. More snow.

"You good to ski out?" Luke yelled, near Stacy's ear. She nodded, and he clipped her tracker onto the loop on her front pocket. They all clambered down and gathered around her to give her a little break from the wind as she refastened her skis. Luke checked her fittings, and she didn't even complain.

Nate navigated around the area where the tracks were the worst. Luke gave a low whistle as he scanned the debris field. There would be a lot of work after the storm passed. They'd have to get out here and figure out which trails were safe and clean up any mess.

"We need to stick as close to the trees as we can," Luke said. "Avoid open space."

Halfway back, Nate came to an abrupt stop. An eerie hush filled the air and the wind died down as if something were holding its breath. A low whomp echoed down the hill, followed by sharp, crackling sounds.

"Shit." Luke had felt this before. That sense of calm before the storm and an almost vibration that tickled the hairs on the back of your head. "Move!" He barked the word out and headed toward a large rock cleft.

Stacy moved ahead of him and kicked out of her skis to clamber up onto the rock. She thrust a hand down to help Luke up and he hauled their gear up after himself.

He glanced around, frantically searching for Erik and Nate. They had made it to a stand of trees against a huge boulder on the other side of the trail. Luke heaved a sigh of relief as Nate helped Erik to the relative safety wedged between the trees and rock.

The crackling gave way to a rushing sound as a slide of snow, broken tree limbs and debris barreled past them.

Stacy covered her ears. When the roiling mass finally passed, Luke looked across what seemed like a mile of churned snow and earth dotted with tree limbs. Erik stared at him with eyes wide and mouth open.

"We're not making it over this." Luke waved a hand at the mess between them. The snow would be too unstable. There'd be no way to guarantee sure footing.

Stacy pulled up her GPS and handed it to Luke. "We're not making it to Bristol Park from this side, either. I marked the areas that were impassable."

Luke glanced at her map and flinched at the sea of red x-marks. She was right. Nate and Erik had a clear path back, but he and Stacy had only one route that wasn't fouled, and it wasn't in the right direction.

"There's an old hunting cabin about a half mile from here," Nate called out, his voice carrying in the crisp, still air. "A lot of hikers still use it. It's on the map. You have cold-weather gear. Weather's about to pick up again."

Shit. Fuck.

Luke checked his weather app and sure enough, another band of snow and wind and ice was headed their way. The hundred yards between them and Nate and Erik might as well be miles. Crossing a fresh avalanche path was an invitation to disaster. He didn't like their odds of finding a way around either.

He shot a thumbs-up at Nate and cringed at Erik's worried expression.

"Let's go." He stuck his hand out to help Stacy up. They refastened their gear and mapped out a trail. Stacy grabbed his elbow as they headed in the opposite direction from the other two.

"What are we doing?" Her words echoed the confused expression on her face.

They didn't have time to stop for a discussion, but Luke paused and focused on her eyes.

"We can't cross unstable snow," he said and was relieved when she nodded. "You already know we're blocked in. We don't have time to go around."

Stacy squinted at the radar map he held up and cringed. "What about...?"

She mercifully stopped when he glanced up at her sharply. "Erik grew up in Minnesota. He knows what he's doing. Nate can handle himself. They'll make it to Bristol Park. We're headed to the hunting cabin Nate mentioned."

Stacy's eyes went wide and horrified. "Overnight?"

She'd put everything together. Not only was snow about to come their way, but they were rapidly losing daylight.

"Yeah." He didn't like it either. He didn't like any of this, but it beat the alternatives. "Tomorrow, they can come with snowmobiles."

He didn't add the part he was thinking—assuming the weather cleared and there were clear and stable paths. Otherwise, he and Stacy would be in for a grueling all-day cross-country navigation to Bristol Park. Or hunkering down for another day or so. He had emergency rations for maybe two days. It was possible the cabin might have some supplies as well—a lot of hikers would leave shelf-stable goods in shelter spaces.

He needed to focus on the right now. Luke set his poles and gestured for Stacy to follow. He wouldn't think about whatever came next. All he had to think about was getting them safely to the cabin. One problem at a time.

The wind picked up as they made their way down the slope, but thankfully it was at their backs. Stacy didn't complain and managed to keep up, despite the fact that Luke was pushing them hard. He had a shelter, but he had no desire to cram the two of them in that tiny space overnight out in the open. That and there was no way he'd trust any of the ground out here right now.

"That it?" Stacy's voice rose above the wind, and Luke followed her pointing finger to see the edge of a roof. Relief flooded him. He was cold, despite layers upon layers. He was also hungry, and he knew damn good and well Stacy had to be.

They finally made it to the cabin and while it wasn't great, it was at least solid and out of the wind and snow. Stacy looked about ready to drop, and it wasn't like they had a whole lot of choices.

He popped on his flashlight as he shut the door behind them and pulled down his mask. "Well, it's not The Ritz, but under the circumstances, it'll do."

Chapter Nine

Stacy, Saturday, December 19

Stacy propped their skis in the corner and scanned the space. There wasn't much to see. Luke's flashlight illuminated the small, empty wood cabin with shuttered windows. A large fireplace dominated the wall opposite the door, flanked by a raised platform she assumed was where you'd put an air mattress or something and a built-in bench. A couple of cabinets and a sturdy table made up the rest of the place. That was it. There wasn't even the trash or mess you'd expect of an abandoned building.

"Why is this place so clean?" The question came out before she could think, and Luke started laughing.

"I think we crossed into Bristol Park property," he said. "Anyone coming from forestry land behind would likely be an experienced hiker or skier — those folks tend to take care of potential shelters."

He lifted the top off the bench and there were canned goods covered in a layer of dust. The idea of eating cold baked beans straight out of a can turned her stomach, but she'd manage.

Then Luke pulled his pack and jacket off and motioned for her to do the same.

"Get out of as many layers as you can stand," he said. "Here. Wrap this around you. It'll keep you warmer while I get everything set up."

He handed her a tiny packet that resembled aluminum foil, but when she opened it, turned into a thin blanket of some shiny and very crinkly material. She peeled off her top layer, wrapped the blanket around herself and sat on the bed-platform thing.

Luke pulled several small bags and boxes from his pack. After some fiddling with one of the boxes, the room lit with pale blueish light. "Battery lantern," he said, then tossed three bundles onto the platform next to her before he went searching around the cabin.

"Aha!" Luke turned from digging in one of the cabinets with an armload of wood. Then he dug out a battered pot and a few other things he laid near the fireplace. In minutes, he had a fire going, then he went outside and brought pots full of snow and stuck one on what looked like a miniature lunar lander he'd unearthed from his pack and sat on the stone hearth.

"What are you doing?"

He shrugged out of another layer and laid his clothes along the bench.

"Getting some heat going," he replied as he picked up her discarded ski jacket and laid it next to his. "The snow will melt, then boil, and once it cools, we'll have drinking water. And I can make us dinner. Take off your outer pants and at least one more top layer, open up the blanket and stand by the fire for a minute so you warm up more."

Stacy did as he said, relishing the feel of warm, dry heat. She'd felt like the cold and damp had seeped all the way into her bones. Luke lifted the top on the bench again and came up with a few cans.

"So, ah…our menu is very limited tonight," he said with a laugh. "We've got baked beans, some clam chowder and apple pie filling." He held the cans up as if they were gourmet treats then nodded at one of the bundles he'd laid near the fire.

"Plus, I've got some freeze-dried meals — chana masala with rice, beef stew and a nuts and quinoa mix. I've also got some dried venison sausages and beef jerky."

Stacy's stomach gave an involuntary grumble even as her brain rebelled at every one of those options.

"I highly recommend we save the apple pie filling for tomorrow," he said. "We can have that with some jerky and the quinoa. It'll make a good breakfast."

She should be back at Bristol Park right now, all freshly showered and headed down to a delicious dinner. Instead, she was chilled to the bone, sitting in some bare cabin who knew where and thinking freeze-dried food sounded pretty good.

It was definitely better than the alternative — stuck on a rock with nothing but some dying warming packs and a bottle of no-calorie sports drink. And she had Luke to thank for that. Maybe if she focused on how good he looked in the firelight, things wouldn't seem so bad.

He squatted by the camp stove and poured water from the pot into metal cups that he set into a tray of packed snow. Then he poured more boiling water into the pouches of freeze-dried food he'd pulled out. Finally, he dropped the pack of sausages into the last bit of water in the pot.

"Five minutes till dinner," he said. He smiled at her as if they were on a date and he was cooking at home. In that brief flash, it was easy to forget their situation and imagine the possibilities of hours alone with Luke. The crackling fire did little to drown out the sound of the wind whistling outside, or the fact that she was wrapped in a foil blanket that crinkled with every move.

Stacy pulled in a breath, trying to steady herself, but it turned into a sob. Luke was on his feet in an instant. His arms wrapped around her, and he pulled her tight against him.

"I shouldn't have gone on that trail today," she murmured into his shoulder. A rumble started deep in his chest and finally burst forth in a laugh.

"Nah," he said, his voice a soothing hum near her ear. "You didn't do anything wrong. The weather shifted. You can't be blamed. From what I saw on the tracker history, you did the right things."

She knew the risks of skiing solo, but in all her life, Stacy had never had to be rescued. She'd never taken more than a minor spill. Never gotten really lost. Sure, she'd been the friend marking a downed skier and waiting for the ski patrol. She'd even been through an avalanche before and managed to ski out.

"Hey," Luke whispered. He tucked his finger under her chin, and Stacy turned her head to look at him. Those amazing blue eyes crinkled at the corners and his lips hovered inches from her own.

His hands clenched, crinkling the blanket at her back.

"You have no idea how much I'd like to kiss you right now."

Music to her ears. Stacy tipped her head and smiled. "What's stopping you?"

The words were no sooner out than his lips were on hers. Everything in her exploded in a warmth that spread from their kiss. She let go of the silly blanket and wrapped her arms behind his neck.

Luke made a sound low in his throat, then his tongue joined the kiss, boldly sliding between her lips. His shoulders felt like slabs of marble beneath her hands, and she clenched her fingers into the thin material of his base layer.

Luke's hand slid under the hem of her shirt, and Stacy arched into his touch. She was wearing far too much clothing for her tastes.

A loud pinging echoed in the tiny cabin, and Luke lifted his head with a look of amusement. "That would be Cat or Nate," he said. "Maybe Erik."

He tugged the blanket up around her and grabbed the tracker from the table.

"Nate and Erik made it to Bristol Park," he said. Stacy nodded and kept her eyes on the fire. She didn't want to be thinking about any of that. She wanted to get back to what she and Luke had just been doing, because that man was an amazing kisser.

He tapped out a response then set the tracker down. The flickering, golden firelight skimmed his torso, highlighting every bulge and dip of muscle the tight undershirt revealed. If she'd thought he looked like a Viking before, it was even more true now. His hair had tumbled from the short ponytail she'd always seen, and his normally tidy beard was mussed.

She pouted as he turned away from her, but it turned to a smile when he started laying food out. He pulled the table near the bed platform, and they sat. Stacy hadn't realized how hungry she was until he opened the pack of sausages and she nearly drooled at the smell.

Neither of them spoke, as they tore into the food. She was sure it was mediocre at best, and under other circumstances, she'd find it all gross. In that moment, however, it was the most delicious thing she'd tasted. Well, second most—the most delicious was definitely Luke's kisses.

After they'd eaten, he packed all the trash into the smallest bundle ever and handed her one of the now cooled cups of water.

"Drink up," he told her. "You're bound to be dehydrated after today."

The boiled snow water wasn't the worst thing she'd ever drank, but it wasn't great either. She downed half the cup before the realization hit.

"What if I have to...?" She shuddered and didn't finish the question. The cabin had no bathroom that she'd seen and the only idea more horrifying than going outside was trying to pee with him in the room.

"I'll step outside," he replied. "You can have privacy."

That was all well and good, but there would still be a container to be dealt with.

"I know this isn't ideal." He covered her hand with his and some of her fears eased. "We're here and we'll deal with it. I'm gonna drop one last message to Bristol Park then shut down the trackers to save batteries."

Stacy nodded and thanked her lucky stars for Luke. She didn't want to think about what would have happened otherwise. Still...

"What can I do to help? I feel like I'm being kinda useless. I don't like the whole damsel in distress vibe."

The smile that crossed Luke's face was sex personified, then he bit his lip and cleared his throat. "You can grab the three bags on the platform and unpack them." He pointed at the bundles. "Open the gray one first. It's a flexible shelter. Grab the shelter itself and stretch it out on the platform. Leave the other stuff in the bag."

His face turned serious. "The others are ultralight sleeping bags. Unroll them and lay them out on the table so they can fluff and warm up a bit. We're gonna be sleeping close tonight."

His fingers squeezed her hand and Stacy swallowed hard. Sure, she'd thought about getting him to bed more than once, but not like this.

"I'll get water boiling again and dig out more wood," he said. "Luckily, there's a well-stocked wood bin with indoor access."

He rose and fiddled with the trackers. Stacy snagged the two bright green and yellow packs and tossed them on the table, then turned her attention to the shelter.

She pulled out what looked like a deflated pyramid of gray tarp and stretched it out on the platform. This wasn't like any tent she'd ever seen. Not that she'd seen that many tents. Her only camping experiences had been in cabins.

The rumpled mass made no sense, and she couldn't imagine how that could possibly help and why they would need a shelter indoors. The sleeping bags were at least more familiar. Sort of. These weren't the cute rectangular bags of sleep overs. These were narrow at one end and wider at the open end.

She was shaking the second one out when Luke stacked a huge pile of wood next to the fireplace, then knelt and fed a few small sticks into the growing flames. He rose, nodded at the platform, then the bags and pointed to her water cup.

"I'm serious," he said. "You do not want to get dehydrated."

She dutifully drank the rest of the damn snow water, hoping her body wouldn't betray her and need to pee before this was all over. Then she got distracted by the sight of Luke stripping another layer of pants. As if she needed any further evidence that he may be lean, but he was built. His shoulders strained the seams, and his shirt skimmed over a flat stomach. Stripped down to his base layer, every single muscle in his thighs and ass was lovingly sculpted by the light-blue fabric.

He turned toward her, and Stacy hissed in a breath as her brain went completely into the gutter. She hoped like hell he was a shower and not a grower, because damn.

"How much are you planning on taking off?" It was warmer in here than before, yes, but she hadn't peeled all of her mid-layer off yet.

"I'm moving around, I'm gonna get warm," he replied. "When it's time for bed, I'll put clothes on."

She wasn't sure if she was disappointed or relieved. She was sure she was fascinated by watching him as he pulled straps and clips from the bag and arranged the weird not-tent thing into a sort of cave on the platform then lined it with the shiny, crinkly blanket.

"We'll tuck the sleeping bags in here," he said, pointing at the opening that arched up on an angle to face the fire. "The back sides will help trap any body heat that escapes the sleeping bags, and the open front will let heat in from the fire."

He tossed both bags into the space and shuffled them around a bit. Stacy glanced around at the cabin. He'd had a big pack on — he'd skied out while carrying everything.

"How do you know all of this?" The words blurted out without thought. He was a ski instructor. Maybe they all knew this stuff.

Luke shrugged. "I've uh… been doing this for nearly ten years." His voice broke and he paused and looked away. He turned and flashed a smile. "Different resorts. Different jobs. I've done ski patrol. Had to have rescue training to work Vail."

He stepped closer to her but stopped short of touching, almost as if he were afraid.

"I hope I wasn't out of line earlier," he said. "The kiss, I mean."

"My only complaint is that you stopped." Stacy moved into his reach, and Luke let out a low growl before curling one arm around her waist and hauling her against his body.

His lips found her ear, her neck and jaw, then finally her mouth. Stacy wasn't about to be passive at this point. She curled her fingers into his gorgeous hair and kissed him back, eliciting another growl from him.

She backed them up to the table and leaned against it. Luke gripped under her ass and lifted until she was sitting on the edge, her legs straddling his hips. The heat of him baked into her, and she longed to peel off the last layers of clothing and feel skin against skin.

The cabin shook with a gust of wind and tree branches scraped along the closed shutters. Reality slammed into Stacy's brain with brute force. She was stranded in this cabin until at least morning. True, Luke was possibly the best person to be stuck in this situation with. Bonus that he was hot, but she was unshowered and there wasn't even a toilet, never mind a way to clean up. It was a safe bet neither of them had condoms handy, either.

Luke's hands loosened, then slid off her and he stepped back. She missed his touch, instantly.

"You okay?" Gone was the sexy cockiness. His eyebrows arched up in the middle and his eyes were wide with concern. He took in a deep breath, as if he were about to say something, but Stacy stepped into him and wrapped her arms around his waist.

The sexual tension that was threatening to erupt moments before now sat at a simmer. Luke's arms wrapped her shoulders, and he held her.

"Let's get ready for bed," he said, his voice soft and low. He dropped a kiss on her forehead then let her go slowly.

Stacy eyed the makeshift bed. There was no way she could sleep without going to the bathroom. *Dammit.* She tugged on her outer layers and sat to pull on her boots.

"You wear your shoes to bed?" Luke waved a hand at her feet.

"I've uh… I mean, I need to…" Anywhere else, she'd say she needed to pee. Unfortunately, here, that meant either peeing in a bucket or whatever container they could find indoors or braving the outside and peeing in the snow.

She'd take the snow, thanks.

"And you're gonna insist on going outside." He shook his head, then rummaged in his pack and handed her a silvery envelope.

Stacy turned it over in her hand. The package crinkled like the blanket and the packaging caught the light, but she had no idea what the thing was.

"It's an emergency urinal and it includes a little sleeve, so you don't need a penis to pee standing up," he said. "I'll step out..."

"No." Stacy cut him off. She'd take freezing her butt off, literally, over trying to pee into this thing. "What the hell do you do with a bag full of...of...liquid?"

Luke tugged on his pants then shrugged into his jacket. "It has gel in it. Like a diaper. It'll sorta solidify. Also, use this."

He handed her a small packet that looked like the kind of wet wipe you'd get with barbecue.

"It's PH balanced so it's safe for use on your bits," he said. "When you're done and cleaned up, put the trash into the bag the urinal came in, seal it up and put both of them on the bench. Then get into your sleeping bag and start adding some body heat in that space. I'm gonna need it."

He grabbed a second silvery thing and headed for the door. He was seriously going to traipse out into the cold to give her privacy.

"Wait," she said as his hand fell on the latch. "Just... I dunno... Turn your back, I guess."

Chapter Ten

Luke, Sunday, December 20

Luke powered up the trackers and checked for messages. Sure enough, Cat had already sent a note.

Weather is holding. Nate and Erik are packing snowmobiles. They'll get as close as they can, but we had a drone out earlier and some of the passes might be rough. Stay put till they figure out how they're coming in.

He sent a quick acknowledgment and glanced down at Stacy. A lock of hair had slipped from her braid and lay curled across her cheek. The urge to brush it behind her ear and kiss her awake was nearly overwhelming. His body ached, not from sleeping on the hard platform, but from desire. What had started as a game to keep from taking her to bed had turned into a torture he'd never imagined.

He stirred the fire to life and lit the stove. By the time he had breakfast done, Stacy was up and grumbling about the need for a toothbrush.

"Can't help you there," he said. "I can offer food and instant coffee."

Something he'd learned years ago — being stuck in snow in less-than-ideal conditions was no fun. It was made even less fun by lack of food. So, he always had emergency rations on hand. Always.

Stacy mumbled something and accepted the cup of steaming black liquid. She made a face, but swallowed half of it at a gulp.

The tracker pinged as they were cleaning up. Stacy's eyes went wide and hopeful.

"Nate thinks they can get all the way here on snowmobiles," Luke said and her body visibly relaxed. "Um…about last night…"

A pink flush crept up Stacy's cheeks, then she smiled as if recalling a fond memory. "Don't you dare apologize."

Well, that took him back. He'd been about to do just that. "Uh…okay. I won't. But I will ask if you're okay. A switch kinda flipped there at one point."

Her smile turned to a chuckle, and she looked away for a moment before turning to him and answering.

"Everything sort of hit me all at once," she said. "I was tired. I felt gross. And I'm not sure why I'm telling you that."

Luke covered her hand with his and squeezed. She squeezed back and smiled.

"I tend to bring that out in people," he replied. "I wanted to make sure I hadn't stepped on any boundaries."

Her head snapped to his and those caramel-brown eyes went wide, then narrowed in laughter.

"You are some sort of unicorn," she said, the giggles making her words hard to understand. "No boundaries crossed. It's all good."

Luke stood and offered his hand. When she took it, he pulled her to stand. He held his other hand out, and she stepped into him. He wasn't sure if she was still interested in their little game, and now wasn't the time to ask.

Stacy tipped her head and grimaced. "I really want to kiss you, but…"

"No toothbrush," Luke said. "Let's get packed up and do what we can to leave this place better than we found it."

Luke found more firewood stacked at the side of the cabin and refilled what they'd used. He made a mental note to check with Cat and Nate about maintaining the place. He couldn't replace canned goods—those had to be from folks who came in on ATVs or something. No hiker or skier would carry cans. He could restock the first aid kit and add a couple of the emergency urinals.

Stacy had finished stuffing the sleeping bags into their packs when the hum of engines buzzed the air. It took another fifteen minutes before the snowmobiles crested the hill and made their way down to the cabin.

Nate pulled off his helmet and a large purple bruise covered half of his jaw. Luke hurriedly turned to Erik, but he looked unscathed.

"What the hell?" Luke pointed at Nate's face.

Nate shook his head and ran a hand over the mark. "Yeah, you oughta see my ribs."

That didn't answer the question, but Nate hefted Luke's bag and stowed it in one of the snow mobiles. Erik leaned in and pointed his thumb at Nate.

"We hit some nastiness on the way home yesterday navigating over a fresh track. There wasn't any other way around it. Buried tree shifted and slammed right into him."

Fuck. Shifting snow after an avalanche was always dicey. There was no guarantee what could be under the surface, and triggering a new cascade was always a risk that could knock someone down, or even sweep them away. Nate had gotten lucky.

After they'd got the gear stowed and the skis tied down, Nate beckoned Luke onto the porch while Erik and Stacy gave the cabin one last pass to make sure everything was tidy and locked down.

"How are you physically?" Nate asked. "I'm not gonna lie, getting here took more outta me than I expected."

"I can handle driving. You wanna double up with Erik? He's lighter than I am."

Nate handed over the keys with a wince.

"Break anything?" Luke wouldn't be surprised if the man had a few broken ribs.

"Don't think so," Nate replied. "One of the guests is a doctor, and she gave me a once over. Poked good and hard, too." He gave a chuckle, then winced again. "She thinks it's just bruising."

Erik closed and latched the cabin door then pulled up a map and showed Luke.

"We didn't have too much trouble coming down. Using the drone ahead really helped." He pointed at a path outlined in green — it took them a little out of the way, but along easier terrain.

"Cat said they've been running the drone along the way we came, and it all appears good." He pocketed the tracker and fastened his helmet. "Let's go."

Stacy slid on behind Luke and her arms around his waist felt so good, he had to resist the urge to reach back and pat her knee.

They made good time on the return trip. Under any other circumstances, it would have been a beautiful trip — sunny skies and almost no wind meant sparkling white snow and gorgeous mountains and forests. If you ignored the occasional evidence of the series of rolling avalanches that had torn their way through the valley the day before.

Back at Bristol Park, Stacy was almost immediately swept up by a fussing Cat, leaving Luke standing with his brother and a bemused looking Nate.

"I suggest you get cleaned up and plan on company for dinner," Nate said as they stowed the snowmobiles and hung the keys.

"Also, thank you." Nate offered his hand to Luke and shook. "That was above and beyond the call." He clapped Luke on the shoulder, then turned for the main house and headed up the hill.

Erik hung the last of the gear and sketched a salute. "I'm out of here. Canceled a date last night because we got back so late. Calling in the raincheck."

Luke should have been exhausted. He should have been heading straight for a shower and maybe a real meal. Instead, he scanned the bunny slope and tubing run, both still bustling with activity. Someone had groomed them this morning.

On the board, the ski report indicated everything else was closed — there would be no back-country skiing until they could get out and check trails for downed trees or other dangers. With nothing left to do, he headed to his cabin.

The hot shower was a welcome sensation, and he stayed under the cascading water longer than usual. Having Stacy in his arms had been like nothing he'd ever experienced before. He was pretty sure that was a year of celibacy talking.

Luke had pulled on fresh clothes when there was a knock at his door. He'd bet Cat had sent someone with food. That is if she was done with Stacy.

He tugged open the door to find the tall brunette standing there with her hands shoved in her jacket pockets.

He held the door wide, and Stacy breezed into the room, trailing the scent of soap and shampoo and something intoxicating and floral. In an instant, he forgot the fact that his stomach was reminding him it had been hours since breakfast and all he'd had since then was trail mix.

Stacy stood in the middle of the small cabin, her hands twisting in front of her. Maybe he hadn't been the only one with questions this morning.

"I got the feeling you were a little uncomfortable earlier," she said, her hands tugging on the hem of her sweater. The nervousness seemed out of character for her.

Luke took in a slow breath and blew it out. "We've been flirting, and we started this little game, but last night, there was a distinct moment when you went from yes please to putting on the brakes," he said. Before she could jump in, he continued, "You explained that this morning, and it made sense, but…"

He held his hands out in a shrug. "Stuck alone together in a remote cabin didn't seem the time to get into a conversation about that. I take consent very seriously, and your comfort even more so."

Instantly, her demeanor shifted. She dropped her hands, and a smile lit her face. Holy hell, he'd been played. She knew exactly how to get honesty out of him, and the expression on her face had his cock springing to attention.

He glanced at his watch, then to her. "When are you headed back?"

"I really should be going in the next hour or so," she replied.

"Not much time left, is there?"

Stacy arched an eyebrow at him in a move so perfect it had to be practiced. "Well, I never took you for the quickie type, but…"

He had her in his arms in half a breath and up against the wall before the next. She hiked one leg around his waist, and he lifted the other until she wrapped around him.

He didn't know who kissed who first, but her hands tangled in his hair while he gripped her ass and their tongues danced. Somehow, her jacket came off and got tossed to the couch.

She was liquid fire around him, and he wanted, no he needed more. She pulled back slowly, and her smile said everything he was thinking.

"Maybe just this once," she said. Her lips were swollen from their kisses and her hair had tumbled from its usual tidy ponytail. "Like an appetizer. I mean, I'm not coming up next week. Family holiday stuff."

That thought cut into Luke like shards of ice. Not his favorite time of year. Far from it. He'd been managing to keep from dwelling too much, though. Stacy's forehead creased into a frown.

"You okay?"

Luke forced a smile. He held her in his arms and kissed her gently.

"Are you forfeiting?" *Fuck. What the hell is wrong with me?* An amazing, intelligent, beautiful woman wanted into his bed, and he wasn't jumping at the chance. *That's a new one.*

Stacy raised her eyebrows. "I said appetizer, not main course. But you didn't answer my question."

He hauled in a slow breath. This wasn't one of his casual season-long flings. He didn't know what this was, but it wasn't that. He swallowed hard.

"I don't have a great relationship with the holidays," he said. Understatement of the century. He seemed to specialize in those with her. He cupped her face in his hand. "You've kept me from thinking about it too much."

Her eyes went wide, and her mouth opened, then snapped shut. "I'm sorry. Shit... I mean..."

Luke shook his head. "It's okay. I do a good job of keeping anyone else from seeing my mess." He chuckled and pressed his forehead against hers. "So, how long does this family holiday stuff take?"

He must've hit the right notes because she smiled. "Just Christmas with the family," she said. "Then Kylie, Brit and I are doing a charity thing on New Year's Eve, but I can come up that weekend. If you're open."

New Year's Eve. He'd be a mess. He could pull himself together by the weekend. It wouldn't be the first time. Working on the holidays was the norm at resorts. This was different.

"I like the sound of that," he replied. He wasn't even sure who the fuck he was any more. None of this was his normal. "For now, do you have time for dinner before you go?"

Stacy tipped her head up and kissed him lightly. "Yeah, I can swing that."

Chapter Eleven

Stacy, Tuesday, December 22

Stacy waited until the door closed behind her clients before she danced a little jig. *Yes!* The Abbots were high profile and high dollar, and they were happy. To the point they expressed their desire to continue working with Stacy rather than be handed off to a more senior staff member.

This was the way she always imagined work going. Stacy practically floated to her desk and drafted an email to Sam Smith, the mentor she'd been assigned during her first year as an intern. A fact that baffled her. She'd expected to be paired with a woman based on the company's public assertions of promoting women in finance. Now she knew it was all lip service.

Still, her record of work was solid, and this latest achievement should be more than enough to put her at the head of the line for any future promotions. This was a good time to ask for a meeting. She'd play nice – ask for help identifying areas where she needed improvement and highlight her strengths. That's what mentors were for. Rather, what they should be for.

She made sure she stayed later than the people above her — she still had a full week of work to do even though they were closing early on Thursday and wouldn't be open on Christmas Day. Plus, she'd left early last Friday and taken half a day off the Friday before. If she wanted to get ahead, she needed to be seen as a hard worker.

Luke might be tempting, but she needed to keep that in perspective. He was a distraction. A very sexy and fun distraction, yes, but that was beside the point. He was a boy toy. Nothing more.

A few coworkers passed her desk on their way out and each congratulated her on today's win. Stacy left the office feeling hopeful for the first time in a long time. A feeling that was soon squashed by a text from her mother as she headed up the street.

Grand-mère wants formal dinner dress for Christmas. And keep it tasteful. She's still on about the year you wore bright green.

Stacy stuffed her phone in her pocket. Leave it to her grandmother to remember something she wore ten years ago. She'd been fifteen and chafing at her grandmother's outdated rules. When the mandate had come down from on high that dinner wear for the holiday should be 'festive colors', Stacy had picked out a bright emerald-green sheath dress.

It was a fabulous color on her, and very flattering, but when her grandmother said 'festive', she meant muted silver or gold. Dark red or dark green, were acceptable of course. Winter white was fine, black would be boring, unless accented with a proper red plaid, in small doses. Stacy's bright dress stood out, and not in a good way.

She waved at the doorman and made her way to the bank of elevators. Still, she couldn't be too resentful of her grandmother. She was the reason Stacy had this amazing apartment a short walk from work. She never understood why Grand-mère had kept the place after her husband passed, but she wasn't complaining. And if having this benefit meant meeting her grandmother's often over-the-top expectations, so be it. That was one of the reasons for her drive to climb the corporate ladder.

She unlocked her door, got out of her coat and took her phone to the kitchen to brew coffee. Another text popped up, this one from Luke. That brought a smile to her face. She'd tackle that after the one from her mother. Palate cleanser.

Are there any other guidelines? I don't want to show up in silver only to find all of her decor is cream and gold. I'd clash.

A bit snarky perhaps, but oh well. She could get away with that with her mother. To an extent anyway. Her stepfather would roll his eyes and call her childish. She never understood why her mother married the man. She vaguely remembered her father—a vibrant, smiling man who always seemed to be laughing.

Stacy was barely three when they divorced. He'd hung around for a couple years, then he'd trekked off to who knows where. The last she knew, he'd been working with some disaster relief organization. She'd kept in touch with her paternal grandparents for a while, but even that had faded over the years. Her phone pinged again as her coffee finished brewing.

Light blue, silver and white this year. I'll be wearing dark blue.

Of course she would. Chloe Astor-Barclay had survived her mother's home by not rocking the boat. Most of the time. She'd had a rebellious moment or two, when the tiny tattoo happened, and when she'd gotten married during college—to a nurse who was completing his education to become a physician's assistant. Other than those two things, and getting pregnant, most of her life, she'd played it safe.

I promise I'll behave.

She was tired of the near constant fight anyway. Always scrambling for her grandmother's approval. Whether it was grades, or how you dressed, or your choice of major or career—that had caused some serious discussions. Grand-mère did not believe women belonged in finance. *Ugh!*

Stacy stopped that train of thought before it went down a negative spiral. Everything with her grandmother was a mixed blessing. She clicked on the message from Luke and immediately gasped.

He stood in a bathroom, naked but for a towel draped dangerously low on his hips. Every chiseled line of his body highlighted to near perfection by droplets of water still clinging to him. The ink on his arm traced up to his shoulder, another design coursed along his ribs, and there was a hint of something at his hip.

Memories of his kisses rushed in, and she could smell the spicy scent of him as if he were in the room with her. She tapped out a message on her phone.

Is this part of teasing? If so, two can play at that game.

She poured her coffee and waited for his response. She wasn't disappointed.

Bring it.

Another picture followed. He'd dropped the towel, but his hand and body angle hid everything. Still, the man looked like he could be sculpted from marble. She wanted to run her fingers over every single inch of him.

On impulse, she stripped down to her panties, then hopped up on her kitchen counter. Naughty selfies were nothing new to her. She set her phone to video and propped it up. A little creative use of her coffee cup and she was able to screenshot a pic that showed off her legs and gave a flash of cleavage.

She sent the picture to Luke and went to shower. Maybe they could exchange even naughtier pics. Or have a sexy chat or call. She rummaged in her nightstand and plugged in her vibrator. *Make sure that sucker is charged.*

She stepped into the shower humming.

Chapter Twelve

Luke, Wednesday, December 23

The smell of fresh coffee wafted out from the kitchen, and Luke pushed through the door to find Cat and Nate seated at the long counter. A twinge of nerves hit his gut even though he'd known this meeting was coming—his agreement with the Stewarts was he'd work for a year, then re-evaluate. Usually, you signed on for a season and hoped no one was an asshole.

"Pour yourself a cup," Cat said as she pushed a stool out across from her. "Well, we got through a potential disaster, thanks to you."

Luke got his coffee and sat. He wasn't sure what to expect. Nothing about working at Bristol Park was anything like anywhere he'd ever worked before, and while he kind of liked that fact, he wasn't exactly in a clear headspace today.

He could have, should have said something. They'd postpone the meeting, he was sure. But he did what he always did — swallowed everything and sucked it up.

"You've been here a year. What do you think?" Nate laid his elbows on the table and smiled.

Luke breathed a little easier. He was still kicking himself for what had happened over the weekend — nearly losing a guest like that. That it was Stacy made the whole thing worse. He didn't even want to consider how the Stewarts might react to him fooling around with one of their guests.

"Bristol Park is amazing," Luke replied, and he was being one hundred percent honest. "I mean, yeah, there's a long way to go yet, but everything is top-notch. I think the only question is where you go from here."

Nate tipped his head at Cat and his smile turned to a grin. She leaned forward and bright green eyes bored into Luke. Erik had warned him it was virtually impossible to say no to her, and he'd found that to be true.

"We have some big decisions to make about how to further develop the property," she said. "We have plans for an assessment, but it's nice to have someone on staff who knows their stuff."

It didn't take much to read between the lines. They'd had talks about adding another lift and doing more to develop the ski side of the property. That would take a lot of work and a lot of money, and it made sense to call in experts to evaluate what they could and couldn't support.

"Bristol Park is a four-season resort," Nate continued. "And you have experience with all of the amenities we offer. We'd like to offer you an expanded role here if you're interested."

Luke nearly choked on a swallow of coffee. Cat had made some passing remarks about him settling in. Hell, he'd even joked about the place growing on him. He hadn't taken it seriously, though.

"I'm flattered," he replied. He'd never considered staying anywhere. Getting tied down wasn't his style. Still, he couldn't deny the appeal. There was something about the place that said home.

"We said we'd re-evaluate after a year," Cat said. "And I know this is sudden, so we figured we'd throw the idea out there and let you consider it."

She thumbed open her tablet and spun it so he could see the screen with two job descriptions.

"Realistically, even with snow machines, we'll only be able to run skiing through sometime in March. We could maybe push into April, but we'd rather shut it down earlier and get to work on evaluation and maintenance."

She tapped the screen, highlighting the first job. Same as he'd been doing—with a decent raise. A year-by-year contract for Memorial Day through Labor Day tubing, then start prep for skiing in mid-November and wrap it up mid-April. The time in between was his.

Then she hit the next one.

"The other option is moving into an operations role," Cat said and fixed him with a bright smile that nearly had him agreeing to anything she suggested. "The big things wouldn't change—skiing and tubing. Plus being the resident expert on all things trail related—maps, maintenance, safety, you name it. Including managing seasonal staff as needed and coordinating and overseeing future improvements."

That one came with a significant raise, and benefits. It also meant settling down. Staying in one place year after year.

"I can definitely agree to the first, right now," he replied. He usually bounced around resorts, but it was at least his normal seasonal pattern. Once the slopes closed in spring, put in a couple weeks marking trails for rerouting or maintenance, then it was a six-week vacation before the summer season started.

"We expected you'd have to consider a position with increased responsibilities," Nate said. "All we ask is notice by the end of March, so we have time to find and train the right person before next summer."

Wow. Holy shit. This was a lot to think about. His entire life had been nomadic since losing Becca in their sophomore year of college. He'd walked away from the path everyone expected him to take and had never looked back.

He had no desire to play corporate whatever. This was something different. This was...it was wild and free. He knew the history—how Cat and Nate had fought corporate developers and basically saved Abbeydon.

He swallowed hard and nodded. "I can do that," he whispered. "By the end of March. You got it."

They all shook, then Cat produced a new contract that he signed without batting an eye. It felt good. It felt right. Something he'd never experienced when agreeing to a job. They'd just been places to pass the time. Money in his pocket for doing what he loved. This felt different.

"Two more things," Cat said. "What are your plans for Christmas? Going home? You're always welcome here."

Luke hissed in a breath at another reminder of the time of year.

"Thank you, but um… I don't do Christmas," he said. "Or New Year's. I work because it's a busy time of year, but otherwise, I stick to myself."

A cloud passed over Cat's face as if some dark memory intruded on her usually sunny disposition, then it was gone so quickly Luke wasn't sure if it was real or imagined.

"I hope someday you'll trust us enough to share more, but I won't push." She leaned forward and stuck her elbows on the counter. Her smile went from sweet to sly. "There's no rule about fraternizing with guests. Within reason."

Shit. He braced himself for whatever was coming next, but Cat chuckled.

"Don't be indiscriminate or cause drama. Don't be creepy or predatory. Don't make messes. In short, don't be a dick."

Soft cries came from the baby monitor next to her. She rose from the table and deposited her coffee cup in the sink. "Excuse me but seems like Brody woke up early today."

She headed out the door, leaving Luke staring across the counter at Nate. The big man's expression was hard to read, but Luke wasn't getting any negative vibes from him.

Nate rolled his eyes after his wife then scratched his jaw where the bruise was turning mixed purple and green.

"Stacy is a beautiful woman," Nate said. "And one who clearly knows what she wants in life. Or at least, what she thinks she wants. Like Cat said, don't be a dick."

He gave a salute with his coffee cup before finishing the last swallow and dumping it in the sink. Luke took that as his cue to leave. He thanked Nate for his time and tried not to rush as he went for the door.

He didn't let his mind dwell on anything until he was in his cabin, where he could pace to his heart's content. That didn't calm him. His fingers itched to open his phone and the series of pictures he and Stacy had exchanged last night. Nothing too racy — neither of them had shared an actual nude. It was all sensual and suggestive. In keeping with their teasing game. Definitely a path his brain didn't need right now.

The airy cabin felt too confining and stuffy. He dropped a text to Cat and Nate letting them know he was heading out to check trails, then pinged with his tracker and suited up for off piste work.

Luke made it to the field where he'd told Stacy and her friends to stop and listen. The air was crisp and clean and here there was little sign of the devastation from the avalanches. He stopped, closed his eyes and listened as the wind whispered through the trees.

He loved nothing more than skiing perfect powder and tackling runs that had most people doubling back the way they had come. That was pure adrenaline and it made him feel alive and invigorated.

He liked living every day as if it were his last. And yeah, sure, if someone wanted to analyze that, it was probably in response to Becca's death. Whatever. It worked for him.

Sometimes, though, he found something different. A moment of pure peace. This spot was tranquility and calm. Here, where if he silenced himself enough, he could hear the tiny sounds that lived in the eerie quiet of snow. The sounds most people missed. Animals scurrying in the underbrush. The tick and drip of snow melting in the warming sun.

He opened his eyes and recalled the meadow when he'd come up on it last spring — wildflowers blooming and birds everywhere. Summer would bring deeper greens and the smell of the forest, rich with life before the heat and sun faded into fall. The leaves would turn, and the scent would change to something earthy with the hint of death, then back to the crisp, clean scent of winter.

He pushed off again, heading for the trails Stacy had taken over the weekend. He'd already marked the major paths with red flags — off limits. Time to see if they could be made safe for next weekend.

He paused for lunch near the river where they'd found Stacy, and the landscape looked very different today. The heavy snows that night had blanketed all signs of them being there. The river had refrozen where the tree she'd tripped over had gone into the water.

She could have died out here.

Luke sank against the big rock outcropping and his stomach roiled. Ice and fire burned through his gut and forced their way up to a sob.

Over the years, he'd dealt with injuries and lost skiers, and even had a guy have a heart attack on the slopes. None of that had dug at him the way Stacy going missing had. He'd never had the gut-wrenching fear he'd experienced when he thought she'd gone into the river.

He'd been numb since winter break his sophomore year. *Ten years today.*

The whole family had been at his grandmother's house two days before Christmas when the call came in. He'd listened to the voice on the other end of the line telling him his girlfriend had been shot in a carjacking as she was leaving work. The two-and-a-half-hour drive from Duluth to Minneapolis had passed in a fog.

The nurses led him to her bedside, then a doctor came along and told him Becca would never wake up. She was somehow physically hanging on, but she had no brain activity. They'd stopped the bleeding and were keeping her alive until next of kin could be notified and decide what to do.

Except she had no family. Just him. She'd stayed for work. "I'm in retail and it's that time of year," she'd said. Then she'd kissed him and promised to drive up in time for Christmas Day. "I love your family, and I wouldn't miss it for the world!"

He sat by her bedside and held her hand. He pulled the ring from his pocket—a simple emerald he'd saved up for. Emerald because it was her birthstone, and she thought diamonds were ridiculous. They let him stay the night in her room and the flurry of activity in the morning gave him some hope. False hope.

His parents had shown up after he'd downed coffee in lieu of leaving Becca's side to get breakfast. By noon, he'd had the awful news and faced a decision no one should ever have to face.

She had an advanced directive on file naming him as power of attorney and her appointed health care agent. A thing they had done the year before when she'd had to undergo surgery after she broke her arm ice-skating, and he'd entirely forgotten about it since.

He sat at her bedside and cried bitter tears. It took him days to make the decision, then another few days while the hospital got everything ready. She was an organ donor, so there was a lot of planning.

In the end, he'd slipped the emerald on her finger and kissed her one last time, then held her hand as the medical staff disconnected all the beeping and hissing machines.

He'd been nineteen, and this New Year's Eve would mark ten years since she'd passed.

An involuntary shudder passed through him. *Shit.* He hadn't thought of that night in years. Not like that. Not in detail. He tried not to. He forced himself not to.

Luke told himself it was because he and Stacy had been flirting. He'd had a lot of flings over the years, but had never dealt with any of them missing, or even injured. Not so much as a broken nail.

That's all it had to be. Seeing Stacy in danger was one step too close to things he tried to keep locked away in a deep and dark place where they couldn't bother him.

He pushed his way up and wiped his face. He was done out here for the day. Even if he wanted to do more, his brain was not in the right space for it. It was late afternoon by the time he made it to his cabin. His phone buzzed with a text from Erik.

Hey, wanna come ice-skating?

Luke could definitely use the break from his own company.

Yeah. Sounds like a plan. You're not still on about starting a hockey team at the school?

It was an ongoing joke. Erik had somehow convinced Brandon to help with a youth club at the local rink. It had spawned renewed speculation that with a former pro-player coaching at the high school, maybe they'd get a team together, despite Brandon insisting the club was as far as he was willing to go in the world of hockey.

You never know. It could happen. Abbeydon is…special.

A shrug emoji followed the text. Luke knew exactly what his brother meant. Something about this place made you feel at home, but that comfort seemed to come at the price of hauling out your darkest secrets and seeking answers to questions you didn't want to ask.

Chapter Thirteen

Stacy, Friday, December 25

A manicured hand closed over Stacy's phone and tugged. She looked up into her mother's disapproving face.

"I've lost count of how many times you've checked that thing." Her mother's whisper managed to be soft enough to not be heard by others, but still carried the weight of parental threat. "This is family time. Put it away."

Stacy stifled a snarky response and slipped her phone under her thigh. *I am so not doing this next year.* Christmas Eve was spent with her stepfather's family — that meant an entire dinner listening to a bunch of lawyers discuss cases and politics. *No thank you.*

Christmas Day started with breakfast at her mother and stepfather's home. When she was a child, that had been followed by lunch with her biological father's parents and her perpetually single aunt. Boring, but at least not excruciating. That practice had faded away after several years of her father not making an appearance, not even for holidays.

Dinner with her maternal grandmother, on the other hand, was excruciating.

"Stacy, dear. Why do you insist on taking your coffee like a man?"

Case in point.

The Astor family matriarch reigned supreme at the head of the table — her son and daughter, their spouses, her three grandchildren, and one grandson-in-law, were arranged down the table by how in favor they were.

This year, that meant Stacy's very pregnant cousin Amanda sat at their grandmother's right. Her father, Stacy's uncle, sat to the left. Stacy landed in one of the farthest seats, across from her other cousin Matt who'd had the poor taste to get caught having an affair with a married woman. No one was allowed at the foot of the table. Not since Grandfather had died and Grand-mère had abandoned her normal place and taken his at the head of the table.

"Ladies take their coffee with cream," her grandmother continued. Stacy hadn't bothered to answer the question. There was no acceptable response. It was best to sit in silence and let Grand-mère speak her piece. "Though I am glad you chose an appropriate color this year."

Stacy managed a polite 'thank you' in response. The simple pewter dress had seemed a safe choice. After dinner, Stacy slipped away to the downstairs powder room. As soon as she had the door latched behind her, she pulled out her phone and thumbed open text messages. She opened the group chat with Brit and Kylie first.

So, what did you do to get banished to the end of the table?

Same family drama, different day. Job – it's time to move on. Hot Ski Dude – it's time to move on him.

A series of high five emojis, an eggplant and a drooly face followed. She sent an eyeroll emoji and tapped on the message thread with Luke. She'd wished him a happy holiday first thing this morning and gotten nothing in return.

When she'd heard nothing by lunch, she'd tried again. Then again before dinner. It wasn't like her to pursue a man like this. Sure, Luke was hot, but there was something more about him.

He'd finally replied during dinner. She'd been trying to read the message when her mother chastised her.

Sorry for the late response. How is the family dinner?

That was it. No reason. Just a terse apology and polite question. She stared at the screen as if focusing on it could make more words appear. *What the hell do I care? He's just some hot ski bum.*

Except she did care. She sighed, leaned against the door and let her fingers fly on the phone.

NP and it's classic Astor family all the way – Grand-mère doling out her approval as if it's some prize to be won. Scary thing – it is. I'm apparently not in her good graces this year, though I'm not even sure why and I can't muster the energy to care.

She scanned the text and nearly deleted it all. It was too much. Too raw. Only Kylie and Brit saw this side of her. She hit send then nearly dropped the phone as the door behind her rattled.

"It's time for the envelopes." Matt's voice was an urgent whisper that still carried through the thick wood.

Stacy stuck her phone into the pockets some genius had thought to put in the dress's full skirt and opened the door. One did not miss this annual tradition. Their grandmother did not give presents. She gave envelopes. If you were lucky, yours included a generous check. You did not want to see a letter.

They made their way to the family room where everyone gathered. At least here, Grand-mère's strict seating order crumbled. Stacy sat on a couch with her parents, while Matt took a chair on his own. His parents were already clustered around his pregnant sister and their son-in-law.

Grand-mère sat in the same high-backed antique chair she sat in every year, and Stacy had the same thought as always—that it was her throne, and like a petty monarch, she reigned her money over the Astor family.

Well, Stacy was determined to break that cycle herself. It was why she pursued investment banking—there was good money to be had. She'd been slowly weaning herself off her grandmother's support. Or trying to, anyway. In this family, if you owned a house, it was a safe bet that Grand-mère had gifted you the down payment. Every gift came with strings.

The family matriarch picked up a stack of red envelopes and called them up one by one. Stacy waited her turn, second to last, no surprise. She went to her grandmother, kissed her cheek, thanked her, took her envelope, returned to her seat and waited. Just like everyone else.

The recipients would open their envelopes in the same order they were given out. They would exclaim over the generosity, and Grand-mère would proclaim how they were to use this gift. Stacy listened as six others received their checks and the strings attached to them.

She opened her envelope and slid out a thick page of monogramed stationery. The already quiet room turned so silent the ticking clock sounded like a bomb about to go off.

She unfolded the page and forced her eyes to focus on her grandmother's still elegant handwriting. Stacy cleared her throat and read aloud, as expected.

"'Dearest Stacy,
It has come to my attention that you are not excelling as you expected in the world of finance. I told you time and again that was a world for men, but you were stubborn and wouldn't listen. Now you are finding the cost of your pride.

Should you decide to come to your senses and wish to pursue an education more befitting you, I will cover your tuition at an acceptable university.

All my love,
Grand-mère'"

Stacy swallowed hard. This was her gift. The year she'd declared her major, she'd been banished to the farthest seat at the table, and her check was for twenty dollars. This year, she hadn't even merited that. She didn't want to imagine what Matt's envelope would contain.

She was supposed to say thank you. She was supposed to be grateful. She was supposed to show humility and respect and turn from her own path and put her feet on the path her grandmother approved.

She was supposed to be like her mother who did as Grand-mère instructed. Mother had changed her major from political science to museum studies. Then Stacy came along, and three years later, she had divorced her first husband and moved herself and her daughter back into her parents' home. A year later, Chloe had married Pierce Barclay, a successful attorney from a good family. They'd even changed Stacy's last name, so everyone matched. *Whatever.*

Everyone stared at Stacy, waiting for her to express her thanks.

Stacy rose to her feet, crumpled the letter into a ball and dropped it in the middle of the floor.

"I don't want to change my career," she said through gritted teeth. "And if I do go back to school, it will be one of my choosing."

Stacy didn't wait to see the reactions. She marched to the hall, grabbed her coat and purse, and was out the door. She caught a fleeting glimpse of her mother rushing toward her before the door slammed shut.

Great. Christmas night, and I'm standing on the fucking sidewalk. At least it's not snowing.

The door of the townhouse opened, but Stacy didn't look back to see who had come out to check on her. She'd lay odds on it being Matt. He was already in trouble, so wouldn't mind a little more. While her mother would fear being shamed for Stacy's behavior and wouldn't dare risk disapproval by going after her wayward daughter.

Stacy took off up the street, cursing herself for wearing heels. She had no one to call. Kylie would be in Connecticut with her family and Brit was in Florida, a family tradition Stacy had joined in on once or twice.

Well, she wasn't walking the five miles from East 76th Street to home. She could damn well make it to the subway station on 77th, though. This was New York, trains ran on Christmas. Or she could call a cab, though that splurge might not be a bright idea after she'd pissed off her landlord.

She turned onto Lexington and braced herself against the wind as she hurried the short block to the stairs into the subway. She fumbled her card out and mercifully made it to the platform in time to catch the next train.

Bare legs and high heels were not the ideal attire for the train on Christmas night, but Stacy had arrived with her parents. She hadn't expected to be out walking after dinner. Her coat was warm, but the thin dress underneath did nothing to protect her from the late December chill.

She sank into a seat without paying attention to the handful of other passengers. Normally, she'd take the six straight down and make the third-mile walk to her apartment, but tonight, she'd transfer. The four got her closer, and she was cold.

Plan in place, Stacy pulled out her phone and tapped Luke's response.

Family is always challenging but sounds like yours take it to new levels. Sorry.

She'd answer him later. Once she was home. For now, she sent quick notes to Kylie and Brit, then pocketed her phone and looked around. A man with two kids, all bundled up in holiday gear and carrying bags with new toys sticking out sat near the end of the car. The only other passengers were an older couple huddled over a cell phone. By the way they were smiling and swiping, Stacy imagined they'd spent the day with their grandkids and were scrolling through pictures of the happy family.

Not something she was terribly familiar with.

Chapter Fourteen

Luke, Thursday, December 31

The glow of the bonfire cast flickering golden light over the snow. The sounds of laughter and music filtered down the hill. He'd hoped his staff cabin was far enough away from the festivities at Bristol Park that he wouldn't have to hear it. No such luck.

Still, he forced himself to stand on his porch and listen. After ten years, the pain of saying goodbye had faded a bit. The guilt had not. He should have stayed. He could have picked her up from work. He should have insisted she take the time off. So many thoughts, many of them conflicting. Most of the time, he kept them locked away and buried, but at this time of year, they burst out and consumed him.

"Not up for celebrating?" Brandon Waters held up a thermos and two cups. "Hot spiced cider. Rum or whiskey optional."

It was tempting to say no thank you — he'd rather be alone. Except he wasn't sure that was true anymore. Luke nodded and moved to one of the rocking chairs. Brandon took the other and silently poured two ciders. He held up two small bottles, but Luke shook his head.

"Drinking when I'm in this state is not a great idea," Luke said. Brandon pocketed the booze and sat back in his chair.

A loud pop echoed down the hill, and Brandon flinched, then closed his eyes for a long breath. He opened them and shrugged. "We've all got our demons. I'm still figuring out how to deal with crowds and sudden noises. Not a great combination for a high school coach." He laughed and a big grin crossed his face, but the smile didn't reach his eyes. His eyes reflected pain — maybe dulled by time, but pain nonetheless. "What brought you to Abbeydon? Aside from your kid brother's invite?"

Luke had gotten that question before, and he'd always answered with some form of the same thing — I needed a break. I wanted to take some time off the grind. Or — the thing that seemed to work well around here — I came for a visit and...then a shrug. People understood.

He didn't think that would work with Brandon right now.

"I made a mistake at my last resort," Luke replied. "I got personal with the wrong guest. Despite me having made it clear it was casual, she got hurt and it got ugly. Not a good thing when you're the replaceable employee and they're the daughter of the company CEO."

This time, the smile started in Brandon's eyes and spread until he was laughing. "Okay, that was the easy one." Brandon shifted in his chair. He leaned forward with his mug of cider cupped in his hands, elbows on his knees.

"Why are the holidays so rough on you?"

The question slammed into Luke as if it were a physical thing, knocking the breath from his lungs and leaving him wide eyed and gaping like a fish.

Anywhere else, he'd tell the man to mind his own fucking business. Even here, if it were anyone else asking, he'd say the same thing, but this was Brandon Waters. His kid brother's childhood hero. Hell, Luke admired him as well, and envied him a little. Brandon was only three years older, and Luke wanted to skate like him and play hockey like him. The man had been through his own shit show, and he knew trauma.

Luke took a deep shuddering breath. "I lost someone I cared very deeply for." Even saying that much was like digging a knife into a wound. He clenched his fingers around the mug and forced himself to continue.

"We were in college. I was about to propose. Y'know, the tacky, in front of the whole family, 'Merry Christmas will you marry me' thing."

Okay, made it through that part. Brandon didn't need details. Luke wasn't sure he could give them, even if his life depended on it. The memories that sometimes played in his dreams like movie trailers were bad enough, he didn't want to put words to his torment.

"She died in a carjacking before that could happen."

That didn't encompass even a fraction of the whole story as far as he was concerned, but it was the best he could do.

"And since then, you've isolated yourself," Brandon said. His voice was soft and kind, but his words still tore into old hurts. "I won't tell you how to heal, or even that you need to," Brandon continued. "I will say that I think you're in the right place to do it. Abbeydon is a place for fresh starts. Maybe there's some magic to it, I don't know, but healing happens here if you let it."

Luke didn't doubt that. He'd gotten that sense from his first day, and maybe that was what had kept him here. It wasn't just that Cat and Nate were so welcoming. It was like when he found that meadow where he'd taken Stacy and her girl squad. There was a sense of peace here.

"You of all people know it's not always easy," Luke replied, and instantly regretted his words as Brandon's face creased into a frown. "Shit, man, I'm sorry…"

Brandon waved off the apology. "Don't be. You don't have to apologize to me for saying hard things. You're right, it's not easy. Ever. It does get *easier*. Especially if you've got help."

He rose and picked up their empty cups. "Come to the fire if you're up to it. Sit at the edges if you need to. Find me, or Gina, we'll run interference for you if you need a crowd buffer. Well, she'll run interference on people. But maybe consider not being alone this time — out with the old and in with the new and all."

Brandon headed up the hill toward the bonfire and the celebrating group. Luke sat back in his chair. Had someone sent Brandon down here to talk to him? The thermos of cider suggested Cat.

He pulled out his phone and opened the last message from Stacy. A picture of the three women, all with glittery happy new year hats on, standing on a rooftop somewhere in New York City. The view included the Statue of Liberty.

She'd said they were doing a charity thing, and Luke had imagined the kinds of things his folks did — serving dinner at a local soup kitchen, delivering backpacks filled with warm mittens and hats and coats, or bags of groceries. He should have known better.

Stacy and crew were all wearing sparkly, fancy dresses. Their hair and makeup looked professionally done. The men in the background wore tuxedos. That was her life. She was radiant and beautiful. He couldn't recall the last time he'd worn a tie, let alone a tuxedo.

Luke tapped the screen and typed out a message.

You all look amazing. Happy New Year! Hope to see you this weekend.

He hit send. He wasn't sure what kind of headspace he'd be in this weekend, but he was sure he wanted to see Stacy. No, he needed to see her.

He pushed up from his rocker, tugged his hat firmly on his head, and marched up the hill. He found Brandon sitting in a folding chair at the very edge of the firelight. It didn't take long for him to spot Gina — she was a few feet away, dancing in place with baby Brody in her arms. Cat and Nate were in the middle of the crowd by the fire.

Luke found the table with hot cider and got another cup then settled in a chair near Brandon. Maybe there was magic here, because for the first time in years, Luke faced New Year's Eve with a tiny sliver of hope.

Chapter Fifteen

Stacy, Saturday, January 2

The week from hell faded the moment Stacy turned down the drive. By the time she'd reached the house, it felt like work was a distant memory. She climbed out of the car to the sound of squeals and laughter echoing up from the bunny slopes. She'd spent all week putting in extra work and preparing for the upcoming meeting with her mentor. Her New Year's Eve had been spent playing socialite at a charity event. Fun, but draining.

She needed a break, and Brit and Kylie both had plans.

Well, so did she and they involved getting one Luke Tverberg into bed.

She'd tried to get a room at Bristol Park, but they were all booked, then Cat had offered one of the staff rooms at the day-use rate. Stacy had snatched it up. She'd hoped to come up on Friday, but work took so long it was too late to make the drive. She'd texted Cat to say she'd come up first thing Saturday morning.

The crisp mountain air helped drive thoughts of the city from her head. Nate came out onto the big porch, and Stacy waved then shouldered her bag.

"I got it," she said before he could come down to help. "It's just overnight."

Last month, if someone had told her she'd drive hours from the city to spend the night in some rural Catskills resort that didn't even have a spa, she'd have laughed. Now, she could think of no place she'd rather be.

"Luke's on till lunch, then I think Erik is giving him the afternoon off." Nate held the door for her then led the way to the floor above the guest rooms. He handed her an old-fashioned key with a number tag attached.

"I really appreciate this," Stacy said and palmed the key. "This place is more restful than a ninety-minute massage."

Nate threw his head back and laughed. "I'll take your word on that," he said. "All of our staff are locals, so we only use about half the staff rooms right now. They're not quite as nice as the guest rooms, and not all of 'em have keyless entry yet — so don't lose that."

He paused halfway out the door. "If you're hungry, you can still grab something from the kitchen staff. They've always got some breakfast basics hidden away and they know you might pop in."

Once he'd gone, Stacy tossed her bag onto the queen size bed and looked around. Nate had said the staff rooms weren't as nice, but though the space was a little smaller, it was clean and modern, and the bathroom had a big shower stall.

She dropped into the chair and pulled out her phone to text Luke.

Hey. Finally here.

She hit send and set her phone on the table. She and Luke texted at least a few times a week. It was always casual and mildly flirty and nothing of real consequence. All of that was just fine as far as she was concerned. Her phone buzzed, and she snatched it off the table.

Good. Meet you in front of the house at noon. Lunch and ice-skating sound good?

Stacy sent a thumbs-up. Lunch in his cabin or her room sounded even better, but maybe that wasn't on the table. He clearly had some issue around the holidays. Maybe he'd gotten in trouble over flirting with a guest. Though that made no sense considering Cat went out of her way to make space for Stacy, and Nate's comments today.

She shrugged and headed to the kitchen. All she'd had this morning was coffee and a granola bar. Maybe she'd luck into something with protein, then she could spend a couple of hours skiing. She didn't want to be cooped up indoors.

Two hours later and in a much better mood, Stacy rushed into the mess hall to return her borrowed skis and found Erik on duty.

"Cutting it tight?" Erik smiled as he checked in Stacy's skis and GPS unit. She glanced at the big clock on the wall. *Shit.* Erik was right, it was already noon. She waved at him then hurried out the door and up the hill. She got to the house as Luke walked up from the trail to the cabins.

One look at him and any lingering tension disappeared. All she wanted was his arms around her and his lips on hers. She wanted to lose herself in the bliss of great sex—and she was certain sex with Luke would be nothing short of spectacular.

"I need to change," she said. "Wanna come up?"

If she hadn't been watching, she'd have missed the flash of undisguised lust on his face. A sheepish grin quickly took over, and he shook his head.

"I uhh…" His face flushed, and the sheepish grin turned into shy boy.

It hit her. This was his work. Despite all their flirting and what had happened two weeks ago, she needed to respect the fact that he was at work.

"Scratch that," she said. "I'll be back in ten."

She made record time changing clothes and pounding down the stairs to where Luke waited in the sunroom.

"You said ice-skating?"

He nodded and beckoned her to follow. He led her down the same hall they'd walked before, bypassing the busy dining room and bustling kitchen. They wound up in the same alcove where they'd almost kissed when he'd suggested they play their little game.

Luke had her up against a wall in seconds. Stacy didn't wait for him to make the next move. She tipped her head and kissed him. His fingers clenched on her hips as he gave passion for passion. She arched against him, wishing she could get closer.

She pouted as he broke the kiss, but he didn't move away. He dropped his forehead to hers and let out a soft chuckle.

"I didn't want you to think me saying no to going up to your room meant I'd lost interest," he said.

It was her turn to laugh. "I realized after that I was being unfair at best," she replied. "This is your work, and you did say discretion is important."

He reached up and cupped her face and his thumb traced circles over her lips. "Sounds like it's still game on then. How much teasing can you take?"

His words had her wanting to suck his fingers into her mouth, then beg him to come upstairs, or go to his cabin, or hell, find an even more secluded corner. She'd made up her mind on the way here—she'd play the game, because it was fun, but at some point, she planned on getting this man out of his pants and into a bed.

She smiled and licked the tip of his thumb before pushing off from the wall and heading down the hall. "We taking my car or yours?"

Luke caught her hand and tugged her the opposite direction. "Mine, and I'm parked behind the house."

He pushed out a side door and into a small lot with half a dozen cars, then led her to an older Subaru. She arched an eyebrow at him as he opened the passenger door. The car might be old, but at least the interior was spotlessly clean.

"I saw that look," Luke said as he slid into the driver's seat. "I know, it's not flashy or cool, but it's great on winter roads and can hold all my gear."

He had a point. And who was she to judge.

"You've got me there," she replied. "Besides, I live in the city and don't even own a car. I either rent or borrow from my parents if I need to drive somewhere."

He pulled around the house and pointed the car down the long drive.

"You never talk about your work," Luke said.

That was not where she expected this conversation to go at all. "I come here to get away from work," she replied. "No one here cares where I went to school, or who I know, or where I work."

All those things were true, and the break was nice, but she wasn't about to tell Luke the real reason she came back was him. She'd been playing this game of theirs all wrong. She suspected he was very used to being pursued. Well, so was she. Maybe it was time to see where he'd take things if she let him.

"And you don't talk much about anything beyond where you've worked," she continued. "And a little bit about your siblings. You and Erik could pass for twins."

Luke laughed. He took his hand from the wheel and rested it on her knee. "Oh yeah. Poor kid has heard it all his life. We're six years apart," he said. "What do you want to know?"

There was something guarded in his tone, as if he were asking the question while at the same time closing doors and windows inside his head. *Tell me why you suddenly switched off at the mention of the holidays.*

"You said you've been doing this for ten years." She mentally cataloged their conversations, trying to recall details, but all that came up was how good he looked and the feel of his lips on hers.

"What got you started?" She shifted a bit to have a better view of his face. Tiny lines etched near the corners of his eyes, suggesting he smiled a lot, but the beginning of a frown line between his eyebrows said otherwise.

"I was always athletic," he replied. "Not good enough to go pro, but good enough to leverage those skills into work."

His non-answer shouldn't have surprised her. Not really. It wasn't like he was evasive, but he never gave many details about himself.

"What about college?" She'd initially wondered if he were some bored frat boy — grown up and missing his partying days so he took occasional work as a ski instructor.

"I dropped out," Luke said, his tone flat. The hand on her leg retreated. "That a problem?"

His defensiveness surprised her. She reached over and laced her fingers in his. "It isn't unless you make it one."

It wasn't like she was planning to get married here, or like she'd care even if she was. Judging by his expression and body language, whatever happened, it was deeply unpleasant.

"So, I don't want to talk work, and you don't want to talk about the past," she said and squeezed his hand. "How about you tell me why we're going ice-skating."

He took in a deep breath, and it was as if everything relaxed all at once. He signaled, got off the highway, and cracked a wide grin.

"I supposed I should have asked if you can skate." Luke lifted her hand to his lips and planted a kiss on her knuckles.

"I had childhood dreams of being a figure skater," she replied. "My mother was in love with the sport — she wanted to skate, but her mother wouldn't let her. Mom had me in classes by the time I was three."

Luke raised his eyebrows. "Wow. How'd that go?"

Stacy snorted. "It was great till I hit puberty and suddenly turned into a gangly giraffe. I was reminded on a near constant basis that there are not that many tall figure skaters. You planning to answer the why?"

He pulled into a strip mall and parked.

"We're ice-skating because it's fun and I'd like to spend time with you away from work," he said. "Let's grab lunch first. There's a decent burger place."

Stacy cocked an eyebrow at him. "Sounds good."

Eating was a good plan. If all went well, she'd be having him for dinner.

Chapter Sixteen

Luke, Saturday, January 2

Luke tucked in the laces on his old skates and waited for Stacy to finish lacing up the rentals. There were only a few other people skating, which seemed odd for a Saturday afternoon, but the manager said they tended to be busier on Saturday nights and Sunday afternoons.

Stacy stood with a shaky smile, but she was steady on her feet.

"How long has it been?" He took her hand as they walked to the ice.

"The girl squad and I skate at Rockefeller every year, so not that long."

He gestured for her to go ahead of him onto the ice. "Show me what ya got."

She shot him a smirk, then pushed away from the edge. In seconds, she was sailing smoothly down the ice. She made the first turn fast, cut tight across the middle of the rink and executed a perfect jump that brought her within feet of where he stood.

He clapped his hands in slow applause. "Not bad."

She rolled her eyes. "Damn near missed that landing. Your turn to show off."

They set off down the rink at a slow pace. "I'm more a hockey guy," he said. "Nothing fancy. There's no one else on the ice right now. How's your speed? Down and back?"

Stacy came to an abrupt stop and shimmied backward until she was nearly against the wall.

"You're on. Count of three?"

Luke counted it down, and they took off. He pulled ahead to start, but she was only a foot or so behind him at the far side. She executed some fast turn and was headed for their starting point before he could blink. It took effort for him to catch up, and they reached the wall at the same time.

"Wow!" Luke pulled in air. He hadn't pushed like that in a long time. "I was right about you having a competitive streak."

She blew on her knuckles and polished them on her shirt. The rise and fall of her breasts gave away that she was as winded as he was. He'd already accepted the fact that he might lose in this battle of who could hold out the longest but he was not ready to give in yet. The more he got to know her, the more fascinated he was — and there was more to whatever this was between them than the physical.

He took her hands and skated backward, bringing her along with him. Her caramel eyes focused on him, and his world narrowed to just the two of them on the ice. After ten years of rolling wherever the world took him, he'd landed at Bristol Park. His conversation with

Brandon on New Year's Eve had made him start questioning, maybe it was time to figure himself out. Maybe Stacy was a part of that.

"I'm glad you were able to come up," he said as he pulled them into a shaky half-spin so she was the one moving backward. Not as smooth as he'd have liked, but it's not like he spent a lot of time on the ice these days. "I'm excited at the opportunity to continue our little game."

The look on her face said she was more than ready to end the competition. The trouble was, Luke still had too many conflicting feelings swirling around to make sense of any of it.

"Here I was thinking you were ready to give in," she replied. "I can't really come up until late Friday nights. More likely Saturday mornings. Work is…well, it's a lot right now."

He noted that she didn't suggest he come to her. Good thing, since there were a couple of reasons that wasn't happening. On top of his absolute hatred of cities, he had to be here on weekends during the ski season.

She talked about her New Year's Eve but didn't bring up Christmas. Then she mentioned a new restaurant she'd tried. Their conversation stayed light as they zoomed around the ice, alternately holding hands or switching places facing each other.

It was easy and ridiculous fun and entirely surface. Just the way Luke liked it. Except this time, there was something tugging at him. Something saying, 'is this it? Is this all there is?'

He shook himself from those thoughts, pulled Stacy close and whispered in her ear.

"I think we need someplace more private."

It took them no time to get off the ice, return Stacy's skates and get to his car. The drive to Bristol Park passed in a blur, and before he knew it, they were in his cabin.

He had Stacy pressed up against the door, his hands on her ass, holding her to him as he sank into her kisses. She tugged at his shirt until he released her to step back and strip it off.

Stacy's gaze roamed his body, admiration and desire clearly painted on her face. She stepped closer, and her hand slid up his thigh, then in. Her fingers closed over his hard cock, and Luke hissed in a breath.

"Oh," she breathed the word out slowly. "Big boy."

Luke grasped her hips and turned her around, holding her tight against his body. He guided her hands to rest against the door then leaned in to nibble on her neck. He wanted to devour her, to use his fingers and tongue on every inch of her body.

He grasped the hem of her shirt and pressed his lips close to her ear. "You okay with this?"

She nodded and held her arms up for him to whisk the shirt over her head. A pink lacy bra suggested she knew something like this might happen.

"The game is how much teasing can you handle," he said against her neck as he grazed his hands down her flat stomach. His fingers plucked at the button on her jeans. "I don't have to stick my cock in you to make you feel good."

She let out a sigh. "Oh good, you're not one of those guys who thinks he has a magic peen."

Luke chuckled. He knew better. He was more than average and that meant doing a lot of warm-up before a woman was comfortable taking him. But he didn't plan on going that far yet.

Instead, he hooked his fingers into her waistband. "May I?"

He didn't have to ask twice. Stacy unbuttoned her jeans for him. She started to slide them down, but he placed his hands over hers, then guided her fingers to the door.

"Don't move," he whispered.

She whimpered when he stepped back but sighed in pleasure when he stroked his fingers down her sides.

"I don't even have to take my pants off," Luke purred in her ear as he inched his fingers under her jeans. "How many times can I make you orgasm before you want more than that?"

Another inch, and he slid beneath the band of her panties. Lace, by the feel, and he'd be willing to bet they matched the bra.

"Should I stop?" He kissed the nape of her neck and gently stroked his fingers a little lower.

"No," she said. "Don't stop."

He slid his other hand up to cup one breast, then kissed her neck again before he stopped and placed both hands on her hips. Stacy shot him a pout that almost had him laughing.

"Stay right there." Luke knelt and removed her boots, then pushed her jeans down her legs. He reveled in her smooth skin and placed kisses along her thighs.

He was right. A lacy pink thong greeted him, but instead of burying his face between her thighs, he moved to the couch and beckoned her over to straddle his lap.

Having Stacy sitting facing him, in nothing but a lacy thong and matching bra, was the most intoxicating thing he could imagine. He wrapped a hand in her hair and pulled her down for a kiss. She rewarded him by rocking against the raging hard-on in his jeans.

Luke cradled her perfect breasts and let his thumbs graze her nipples, and Stacy gasped. He slid the lace down and drew one perfect bud between his lips, then stroked gently with his tongue until she arched against him. He kept up the gentle touch as he moved to the other nipple.

He didn't know how much of this he could take, but her reaction was more than worth any torture. Her fingers dug into the back of his neck as if she were trying to pull him closer. He trailed his hands down her sides, curving over her waist and around her hips until he wrapped his fingers against the firm globes of her ass.

Stacy rolled her hips so she was grinding against his hard cock. Her fingers curled into his hair and tugged. Little gasps and moans escaped her lips as she rode him.

"Harder." The word came out on an exhale as Stacy arched her back, giving him even better access to her magnificent nipples.

Luke was happy to oblige that demand. He moved a hand to her breast and gently pinched the nipple between his fingers.

"Yes!"

Luke sucked her other nipple more firmly into his mouth and got an even louder moan of pleasure from her. He lifted his head to admire the look of abandon on her face.

"Don't stop," she said. "Please, don't stop."

Screw their game. He was right there on the same page with her. Luke brought both hands to her breasts and teased her nipples, brushing, then pinching, and back to brushing. She threw her head back, and he had the most glorious sight in front him — Stacy lost in ecstasy at his touch.

He slid a hand down and let his thumb rest below her pubic bone. She responded by pulling his mouth to her breasts. Her panties were soaked. Then she reached down and pulled them aside, so his thumb grazed bare skin.

She guided his hand until the pad of his thumb rested on her swollen clit. He loved when a woman showed him what she liked. Stacy clearly reveled in her sexuality, and it was a huge turn-on.

"More, please."

He timed his strokes with her rocking hips. He would need no lube to enter her in this state.

Her legs quivered and her muscles tensed as she sped up again. Luke matched her pace, changing only the pressure he applied until Stacy gasped and cried out.

"Oh, just like that!"

He'd learned long ago what those words meant. *Don't change a thing.* He wasn't about to complain. He had a beautiful and wonderful woman mostly naked in his lap, and if her trembling muscles were any indicator, she was on the verge of an orgasm. The world could end right now, and he would not care.

"Oh, yes!" Stacy's entire body tensed. Her legs shook and her back arched. The hands clenched in his hair released and landed on his shoulders. Then she exploded. A rush of warm wetness spread against him, and Stacy collapsed forward, breathing hard.

He slid his hand from between them and cradled her against his chest. *Fuck.* If she was like this from foreplay, sex with her was going to be mind-blowing.

He didn't even want to consider how he'd gotten from 'it's gonna stop at teasing' to knowing he would have her in his bed.

"Well, you were not bragging," she said, her words muffled against his chest. "You absolutely can make me feel good without even taking your pants off."

The laughter came unbidden, but fortunately, she laughed along with him. Luke tipped her head up and kissed her, long and slow.

"Wait till you find out how good I am with my tongue," he said.

She shifted off his lap and onto the couch next to him, then arched a brow. "Guess this changes the tone of our game. Hmmm…"

She slid to her knees in front of him and slowly unbuttoned his jeans. He had a moment to curse the fact that he'd put on underwear, then her fingers slipped into his boxer briefs and circled the head of his cock. Stacy hissed in a breath.

"Oh goodness," she whispered. She leaned down and planted a kiss on the head then rose. Luke slid forward, cupped her ass and pulled her to him until his face buried between her legs.

She tasted sweet and salty and smelled like heaven. He wanted her laid back in his bed where he could lick and kiss every inch of her body and take his time wringing as much pleasure from her as he could.

Instead, he kissed her gently, letting his lips graze the edge of her thong until her hands cradled his head and pulled him tighter.

She wanted more. *Perfect.* Luke slid his tongue along the crease of her thigh, and she shuddered. Oh yeah, she wanted more. He could happily spend the evening making her orgasm over and over again. As much as he wanted more, it would have to stop there tonight since he didn't have condoms.

His phone jangled. The emergency ring that meant work. *Fuck.*

He pulled back and straightened Stacy's panties. It was the hardest thing ever to not slide his fingers inside her as they brushed along her entrance.

"Gotta take that," he said and reached for his phone. His gut churned at the text from Nate.

Sorry to interrupt. We've got a downed skier on the logging trail.

He turned to Stacy with real regret. "Duty calls."

He showed her the text, and her eyes went wide. Then she leaned in and kissed him. When she pulled away, her wide-eyed look had turned to a sly smile.

"You might want to clean up," she said. "You smell and taste like me. I like it."

She rose and started pulling on her clothes. "Text when you're done. Maybe I'll find out how you taste."

Luke sent a quick acknowledgment to Nate, then wrapped Stacy in his arms. Everything in him was twisting into knots. His body had responded to her when his brain had been saying it wasn't going to happen. She felt so good, so right.

He kissed her again, not the smoldering passion of before, but soft and gentle.

"I'll see you later," he said.

His blood turned to ice when he met Nate at the mess hall. Erik was suiting up and his face looked stricken. Cat was at the computer rattling off trail information.

"I'll get the drone up ahead of you," she said. "You're gonna have to go fast because we're losing light, and the sheriff says they won't fly in after dark."

Luke was ready by the time Nate and Erik had the snowmobiles rigged for a rescue. Luke turned to his brother and saw the tension.

"Who is it?"

Erik tugged his helmet on. "Andre. And don't even think of telling me I'm not going."

Fuck. That was the guy in Albany. He laid his hand on his brother's arm.

"You can come. But keep your head on straight. We'll get him off the mountain."

He turned to Nate and raised his eyebrows. Nate leaned in as soon as Erik pulled forward on his snowmobile.

"It's Andre and his sister. He broke his leg and from what she said it's bad. He's in and out of consciousness. We called for a mediflight, but their time was too long, plus there's no landing space near where he went down. The sheriff's helicopter dispatched and will meet us back here. Best we can do."

Luke nodded. They weren't going to be done any time soon. He picked up his phone to text Stacy and was surprised when it pinged with an incoming message.

I need to go. Parents just called. Grand-mère is in the hospital. I may think she's an awful person, but she's family. Let's try this again next week.

He sent a quick response and pocketed his phone. *Guess the universe thought I wasn't ready for this either.* Next week was going to be interesting.

Chapter Seventeen

Stacy, Monday, January 4

The long hallway leading to the conference room seemed to stretch for a mile. Stacy pulled her shoulders back and started walking. It wasn't that far. It was all perspective. She'd requested a meeting with her mentor before Christmas. He'd put it off till after the new year and he'd invited his supervisor. Which had her a little nervous.

Show no fear. Her stepfather's motto that he'd drilled into her every time she complained about being in a space that was hostile to women. He didn't believe it was actually hostile, only that she was responding in fear to an unfamiliar environment and wanted coddling.

She pushed through the doors and greeted James Babcock, the Vice President of Operations, and her mentor, Sam Smith.

The two men rose, shook her hand, and Mr. Babcock gestured for her to take a seat. Stacy forced her breathing to remain slow and tried to contain her nerves to letting her toes twitch. No one could see her toes.

"Mr. Smith asked me to join in this meeting because he said you had expressed some concern over your career trajectory." Mr. Babcock didn't raise his head to look at her. His eyes scanned a thin folder on the table. Her employee record, she assumed.

"Yes, sir," Stacy replied. Might as well get right to it. "As you may know, I put in for the position that went to Chad Higgins. While I would never question the choice, I would be remiss if it didn't make me question what, if anything, I should be working to improve."

She took a deep breath and pressed her fingers into her thighs to stay calm. "I believe my academic record, my tenure here and my portfolio of work all speak for themselves. So, I have to ask myself—what am I missing or doing wrong? Where am I lacking? Which is why I turned to my mentor. I appreciate you taking the time to be here as well."

There. That seemed like a semi-politically correct way of saying 'why him and not me'.

Mr. Babcock flipped a page and made a noncommittal grunt. Mr. Smith gave a slow sigh and folded his hands on top of the table. Stacy braced herself for whatever shit show she was about to hear.

"No one is denying your work is stellar," Mr. Smith replied, and his tone dashed any hope she had of this conversation going in a positive direction. "You've got some high-profile projects in your portfolio, but when it comes down to it, we feel you still need a bit more under your belt before you can move on to associate."

Her fingers dug into her thighs, but she kept her face calm and serene. She had a far better, and more high-profile portfolio than Chad, as well as more experience. On paper, in every single way, she outperformed him.

"I see," Stacy said. "I appreciate that candid assessment. I feel that my recent projects are very strong, but I recognize I may be viewing things from a different perspective. What do you suggest as a next step? What should I be doing differently?"

Mr. Smith looked uncomfortable and shook his head. Mr. Babcock stood and patted Stacy on the shoulder as he headed to the door.

"Keep doing what you're doing," he said. "Keep fighting the good fight. You do good work. It takes time to work your way up the ladder."

The door swung closed behind him, and Stacy turned to Mr. Smith, expecting to see some sympathy. She didn't and her ability to maintain calm was stretched to its breaking point.

"What exactly did that mean?" She managed to keep her tone even, despite wanting to scream. "You tell me I need more under my belt, but I clearly have more experience, and a better portfolio than Chad Higgins."

Shit. She needed to get control of herself. Losing her cool would not help her case. "I'm sorry," she said and placed her hands flat on the table. She kept her eyes focused on the wood between her fingers.

"Respectfully, I do not believe the vice president answered my questions. What he said amounts to 'keep your nose to the grindstone, don't complain, and hope to get lucky someday'."

She hauled in a breath and forced herself to look at her mentor. Mr. Smith sat rigid, his lips in a thin line, but his expression otherwise neutral. This man was not in her corner. He probably never had been. Stacy felt defeated. Still, she had to try.

"This business is not built on luck," she replied. "You said those words to me when I first interviewed for an intern position, and I told you I felt lucky to be here. I took them to heart. I've worked hard, and I believe my portfolio reflects that. All I would like to know is what do I need to do in order to take the next steps?"

She didn't want to plead or beg, or sound as if she lacked confidence. She knew, deep down, that no one would ever admit the truth—Chad was promoted because he was a man, and because of his family connections. Her stepfather, on the other hand, was a high-powered corporate attorney who had probably made some enemies on the way up. Hell, it was the late eighties when he headed to college. Reagan had still been in office—corporate greed was practically a religion.

Mr. Smith rose slowly. He kept his eyes on the table, as if he were struggling with some monumental decision. Finally, he set his mouth, nodded and glanced up.

"You came here because you saw us as progressive," he said and shook his head. "Nothing in this industry is truly progressive. I have no suggestions for how to help you speed up your trajectory. I'm sorry."

He turned and left the room. Stacy sank into her chair and winced as the door clicked shut, leaving her alone.

Instead of focusing on what she could and should be doing—like spending every free hour searching for opportunities elsewhere—her traitorous brain flashed to Luke and the way he smiled at her. The way his voice dropped into a low, sexy tone that sent shivers down her spine. And how he seemed to know how she liked to be touched.

She slapped her hands onto the table, relishing the little sting. Luke was not where she needed her thoughts going right now. She'd lost count of the times she'd masturbated to the memory of their last encounter and the feel of him between her legs.

No, she needed to get to her desk, finish the report she was working on, and figure out her options. She stood, swiped a hand over her face and schooled her features into pleasant neutrality before she went back into the fucking vipers' nest she worked in.

By the time she'd finished for the day, she was the last one there. The cleaning crew arrived as she was switching off her light, and she greeted them by name. Every night, it was the same faces. It had been the same team for over a year now. A couple of the crew had been around since Stacy had started and she'd spent enough late nights that she'd gotten to know them.

"You shouldn't be walking this late at this time of year. It's too dark." Andrea was the head of the group. An older woman with salt-and-pepper hair in a tidy bun. She always fussed over the weather, if Stacy had eaten, if she was working too hard.

Stacy smiled and shook her head. "I'm grabbing a cab and going out for a late dinner with a friend. Should I get coffees?"

Long ago, when she'd first started, she'd befriended the crew by picking up coffees and sodas. They could get them any time, but Stacy always figured it saved them taking the trip two floors down.

Andrea nodded. "Always appreciated. Thank you. You take care of yourself and don't drink too much."

Stacy waved and headed down to the cafeteria where the coffee machines sat always ready. She popped pods in and waited for everything to brew. The team did the cafeteria last, so they could eat their meal in here, then clean and be out the door to their next client. Still, Stacy made sure to toss all the trash and wipe the counter after carefully putting the coffees in two carriers and heading upstairs. She left them on her desk, waved to Andrea and headed for the elevator.

She didn't bother going home. She met Brit at a small bar she'd found that was far enough off the beaten path to not be too busy. Quintessential New York—a tiny neighborhood place you could overlook if you didn't know it was there.

Brit gave her a hug that felt like being wrapped in warm blankets and teddy bears with a side of hot cocoa. That was the power of Brit. Somehow, she could channel everything warm and cozy and soothing. She could also be as scary as fuck, but Stacy had never been on the receiving end of that. She'd witnessed Kylie get it a time or two, though.

"So, are you venting about the job, or mooning about the man?" Brit curled her long fingers around a glass of red wine and settled into the deep corner booth she'd somehow commandeered. Probably because, on a Wednesday night, the place wasn't too crowded.

Stacy ordered a Paloma—it was definitely a tequila night—and settled into the booth next to Brit. She dropped her head onto her friend's shoulder and groaned.

"Both, I guess?" She hadn't told her friends much about her weekend adventure at Bristol Park. They knew she'd gotten stuck in the storm, of course, because she'd been incommunicado most of that

Saturday and Sunday. They'd assumed she was getting laid.

"Before you start on the job, know that I will listen with a sympathetic ear, but..." Brit poked her finger into Stacy's arm. "I will also say I told you so."

The server appeared with Stacy's drink. She took a long sip before tipping her head back against the booth.

"Yeah, I know." And Brit had warned her. She'd warned her before she even formally declared her major. At every decision point, Brit had been there pointing out how hard it was for women in finance. She'd also been standing behind Stacy every step of the way, cheering her on. It was a mixed bag.

"How's your grandmother, by the way?" Leave it to Brit to bring that up.

Stacy rolled her eyes. "By the time I got back to the city, she was home. She was sure she was having a stroke. Doctors said migraine."

She took another sip of her drink. "Most of us agree — it was because Amanda won't come stay with her after the baby is born. They're going to his parents. In Massachusetts."

Brit nearly spat out her drink. "So, the whole emergency room trip was a ploy for attention?"

Stacy nodded. "When I showed up, she was propped up in bed and making plans for Aunt Vivian to stay with her. Which, as far as she was concerned, meant Amanda and the baby should as well."

"Why did you go?" Brit reached across the table and squeezed Stacy's arm. "After the shit show of Christmas."

She didn't have a good answer for that. She'd answered the phone and known something was wrong the instant she heard her mother's voice. No matter what she thought of her grandmother, she was a big part of the reason Stacy had been able to make the choices she had made in life. She might not show it in ways her grandmother understood or accepted, but she loved her family. And that was reason enough.

"Family," she said and shrugged. "Change of subject. I don't want to vent about work. You're right. I knew the shitshow I was getting into. I believed I could be different if I worked hard enough. I was wrong. I need to think through options."

Brainstorming they called it. Anytime one of them had a difficult decision to make, they'd outline all options—even the bad ones. Especially the bad ones. Somewhere along the way, the right solution appeared. Usually something they hadn't thought of first, but that spun off one of the bad ideas.

It had served them all well so far.

"I could go to my stepfather," Stacy continued. "He'll be an ass. Like he always is. He'll make me feel small. Like he always does. But he will help. He's got connections, and I know he has at least a couple of clients in finance."

She toyed with the straw in her drink. She didn't want to do that. In her mind, that was only one step better than continuing with the status quo, which was not an option. There was always her grandmother's offer—which would make her feel even smaller, and less in control of her own life.

"I could just suck it up and deal," she said.

"I hear an automatic *fuck that*. Don't think I didn't notice what you left out. Fuck that as well," Brit chimed in, and Stacy nodded.

"Smart thing to do is start looking elsewhere." There might be other options. She could probably go to

Human Resources and file some kind of grievance. She could talk to Brit and get a referral to another attorney who specialized in gender equity. Neither would likely go anywhere, and even if they did, would she want to be working at a firm where that was what it took for her to move ahead.

No. She would forever be the woman who couldn't hack it so got her lawyers involved.

Not an option.

"That was a quick brainstorm," Brit said with a laugh. "But I think that's because you already know what you want there. So, the man? How is the hot ski instructor?"

Talking about work had been easy. Thoughts of Luke, however, sent her stomach soaring and her body shivering at the memory of his touch.

"That good, huh?" Brit sat back and cradled her wine glass. "Tell me all about it."

Chapter Eighteen

Luke, Tuesday, January 5

Bright, early-January sun glinted off the runs. If the predicted cold snap and snow didn't hit this week, there might be some trouble come the weekend. For now, Luke ran the snow machines at night and made sure the runs were groomed first thing in the morning. Things were holding.

Weekdays were slow, with few guests on the property. It gave him time to follow up on any reports of fouled trails. They'd still had quite a few guests on Monday, so he hadn't gotten a chance to get out. He packed his lunch, suited up and checked the logs.

As expected, a few tree branches the skiers couldn't shift themselves. Those would be easy. A family reported a large, downed tree near his favorite meadow. He planned out a route that let him finish with that.

He cleared the first few reports quickly — he didn't even need to break out tools. The next one made him work for it and it was noon by the time he made it to the meadow. He'd find the offending tree then break for lunch before doing whatever he needed to do. A whole tree over the trail would eat up the rest of his afternoon.

He skirted the meadow, scanning the trail and tree line but seeing nothing out of the ordinary. Finally, on the far side of the clearing, he spotted it. It wasn't a downed tree, just a very large branch off an eastern cottonwood.

The branch hung at an odd angle, still partially attached to the tree, but obscuring a good part of the path. He could see why it had got reported the way it had, but it would be a quick fix. He unshouldered his pack, sat it on a rock and pulled out his lunch. Might as well enjoy the sunshine.

Once he'd eaten, getting the branch free took only a few minutes of work with his folding saw, but Luke was sweating in his layers. He peeled off the outer jacket and looked around. The forest was loose here, a scattering of deciduous trees with wide spaces around them. He could haul the branch off the trail without having to cut it up.

A loud screech pierced the air, and he ducked instinctively. January. About time for owls.

This was the perfect spot for owls to nest and it was the right time of year. He spotted it sitting in the cottonwood maybe ten feet away.

"Oh, hello, you beauty," he whispered. "If you're here, there's another somewhere."

It might be a little early for owls to start their annual mating routines, but not by much. He pulled out his tracker and set a pin at the location, then made a note about the owl. He dragged the downed branch away from the tree where the owl still roosted, watching him the whole time.

The bird made a series of soft hoots and chittering calls. Luke paused and listened. Another owl hooted in response. He couldn't find it, no matter how hard he searched, but there were definitely two.

Work done, he pulled out his phone and zoomed in on his feathered friend and snapped a picture, then on impulse, switched to video. The bird hooted at him, long and low, then let out a series of short hoots that were answered by the other owl. After nearly a minute, Luke stopped filming and watched.

The owl alternated between turning its head and hooting as if in search of something and fixing its big yellow eyes on Luke and letting out a louder, sharper sounding call. He'd never felt like an animal was trying to talk to him before, but that was exactly what this felt like.

He shook his head, pocketed his phone and retrieved his pack then made his way to the mess hall. As soon as he got out of his gear, he went in search of one of his bosses.

He found Nate replacing bulbs at the pavilion.

"You look like you've got something on your mind," Nate said by way of greeting.

Luke perched on the railing and thumbed his phone on to pull up the picture.

"Great horned owl," Nate said. "You got that close?"

Luke chuckled. "Not intentionally." He relayed what had happened in the meadow, then played the short video. "Sounds like we've got a pair thinking about finding a nesting site."

Nate tapped the screen to play the video again, then nodded. "Yeah. You'll have to keep an eye on that area. If they nest too close to the trail, we might wanna close it off."

Luke pulled up the map on the tracker and showed Nate the pin. "Already on it," He replied. "I'll get this into the system and make that part of my weekly checks. Beautiful bird. A little scary, though."

Nate regarded him with narrowed eyes that would have made Luke uncomfortable if he didn't know the man so well.

"The ancient Greeks saw the owl as a symbol of wisdom," Nate said. "Not too different from many indigenous tribes who believed they represent vision and insight."

Luke chuckled. "I always thought they were bad omens and harbingers of death." He'd meant it to be funny, but somehow it came out gloomy.

"Aren't those tied together?" Cat's voice carried in the chilly air as she stepped onto the pavilion. She had three mugs in one hand and a thermos in the other. "Coffee," she said as she sat the cups down and started to pour. "Wisdom, vision, insight, transformation, all of those things could be linked to the afterlife or to messages from well…beyond." She handed Luke a steamy mug and smiled. "Why are we discussing the symbolism of owls?"

Nate filled her in, and Luke showed her the video. Cat exclaimed over the beautiful bird, then she turned to Luke.

"Maybe seeing an owl is meaningful here," she said. "You said it yourself, you've never stayed in one spot for more than a season, and yet, here you are. And planning to stick around at least another year. Maybe you're on a path of discovery."

They all chuckled, but Luke couldn't help but wonder if she might be right. Owl symbolism aside, of course. He still had the offer on the table for a bigger role here. All he had to do was stick around.

Then there was Stacy. The first woman in years who had made him think with anything other than his dick. *What could we ever be?* He'd never given it thought before. Never cared with anyone else.

Stacy would never leave Manhattan and even if he wanted to venture into the city, he had to live where the work was. Which meant places like this.

Ten years ago, his entire life was derailed by a single bullet. All of his hopes and dreams were shattered. He'd had no plans that didn't involve Becca, and so he'd walked away from everything.

Now, he'd landed somewhere that felt like home, and he'd met someone that made him want more than a fling. *Forget path of discovery, this is a whole life upheaval.*

Luke shook himself.

"I'll stick to focusing on the tangible," Luke said. "Like needing to keep an eye on that trail to make sure no one disturbs nesting owls."

Chapter Nineteen

Stacy, Thursday, January 7

"How is it you haven't gotten laid yet?" Kylie slid into their favorite booth at the quiet bar and waved at the server.

Stacy waited until the woman left to place Kylie's order. "We kinda got interrupted last time."

Brit sputtered and coughed, then held a hand up to cover her mouth. "Please, warn a girl. His work emergency was one thing. Your grandmother's emergency did not require you to run all the way back to the city."

Kylie nodded agreement. "And you're going up this weekend."

"Yep," Stacy replied. "Tomorrow after work."

That was a decision she'd made as soon as she'd gotten back to her apartment from the last visit. It had been cemented after her conversation with her mentor and Mr. Babcock on Monday, and again this morning.

"The weekend plans had better involve lots of dick," Brit proclaimed. "Because, girl, you need some stress relief, and that man looks like he knows how to provide it."

On that, Stacy could agree. Everything she knew about Luke so far pointed to him being a very good time. Sure, he was a boy toy, like every other guy in her life had been, and usually they were a dime a dozen, but Luke seemed different. And she was determined to have him.

"Believe me," she replied, "he is on my to-do list. Right now, I'm more focused on what to do about work."

Kylie's drink arrived along with refills for Brit and Stacy. Brit smiled at their server and slid her fresh drink closer.

"I'm out of the loop," she said. "I know about Monday, has more shit happened?"

Both her friends leaned forward, as if this were big news. It wasn't. None of it should have surprised her, but she appreciated their support.

"Mr. Smith asked me directly if I was applying elsewhere," she said. "Apparently he heard a rumor. And that could only have come from Chad. The prick."

She took a sip of her fresh drink. The gentle fizz of the French Seventy-Five was just the thing she needed after this week.

"He pulled me off the Abbot's project, even though they said they preferred working with me." She had struggled to keep her cool when he'd delivered that news earlier today. "Instead, I got handed an audit on long-term accounts—these are people who sit on their investments and don't change anything. I was doing these in my first year as a junior analyst. It's a step backward."

She pulled the straw from her drink and dropped it onto her napkin before taking another sip.

"That bites," Kylie replied. "I mean, really."

Stacy snagged a chip from the bowl in the middle of the table, suddenly realizing she was starving. She'd skipped lunch today. She signaled the server, then placed an order for wings.

"Part of me thinks I need to knuckle down and do what I can to clean up this mess," she said. "I'm already working sixty hours a week on the regular, eighty when I have to. I always work extra hours before I take time off."

She'd had her plan all laid out. She'd chosen this company because they tended to produce rock stars and she'd been naive enough to not notice none of them were women. When Brit had pointed it out, Stacy had been foolish enough to believe she could be the first because the company made a lot of noise about diversity and equity.

Brit's hand landed on hers and squeezed. "The rumor is out there, and you're already paying the price for it. Time to start shopping yourself elsewhere."

Stacy nodded. Her friend was right. Maybe her years at the company would land her a position at a better company—assuming she got a good reference. What was more likely, however, was that she'd have to take a position at a less prestigious institution.

None of which would help her goal of reaching financial independence. Nor would it allow her to break free of her grandmother. She was already skating on thin ice after Christmas. Her grandmother hadn't kicked her out of the apartment...yet.

"Two years interning," Stacy said. "Three as an analyst. First person to spend only one year as a junior analyst." She threw her hands up in the air. She was good at what she did, and she knew it. She'd been good in college, even better once she got into the real world. Every single thing she'd done at work had been top-notch.

The server slid a plate of wings onto the table and serious conversation halted as the friends dove in. Once hunger was sated, they could resume, until then, it was joking, neighborhood gossip and current events.

"You have choices," Brit said as she leaned back and wiped her hands. "I imagine you don't want to pursue a complaint because you don't want to be 'that girl', and I understand that. I disagree with it, but I understand it."

She tossed the wet wipe onto the pile of bones and sighed. "Absent complaining, you start job hunting, or you stick it out. My advice? If you decide to stay? Don't make it easy. If you keep your head down and stay quiet, they'll continue to treat you this way.

"Be in your mentor's office every week. Apply for every promotion you're eligible for. Do not let them shuffle you into a corner and forget you."

Kylie leaned an elbow on the table. "All great advice, but personally, why stay? You've seen they don't value you. They're willing to have you do all the hard work but offer none of the rewards. What's in it for you?"

They were right. They were both right. The trouble was this was Stacy's dream job. This was the company she'd wanted to get in with from the moment she declared her major. Walking away wasn't an option.

"I can't quit," she said softly. "Not yet. But I won't go hide in a corner, either."

Chapter Twenty

Luke, Friday, January 8

Cat shifted the sleeping Brody to Nate's arms then turned to Luke. She was only two years older than he was but somehow exuded mom vibes. No, that wasn't right. Maybe big-sister vibes fit better. Luke had plenty of kid sisters, but he didn't know what to do with a fussing mother hen like Cat.

"Thank you for going out of your way like this," Luke whispered, so as not to wake the baby. Nate winked and headed for the stairs. Cat laid a hand over Luke's and smiled.

"If we'd had openings, I would have put Stacy in a cabin where she could get herself settled. I mean, she could check herself into the house at this point."

She tapped the piece of paper on the long kitchen table. "All the info is here—she is in one of the updated staff rooms, so it's keyless. That's her door code. She knows the routine."

She slid off the stool and stretched. "Don't give me any noise complaints. Good night."

Luke waved. "Night. And thank you again."

Cat flapped her hand and rolled her eyes, then disappeared through the door, leaving Luke alone in the kitchen for the first time. The house was quiet and only a handful of soft lights glowed. Out of the window was a stunning view down the hill to the cabins and pavilion. He'd guess in daylight you could see the river.

He also had a great view of the end of the tree-lined lane. Stacy had texted to say she was leaving work a little after eight. She still had to get home, get her bag and go pick up a car. Then make it out of Manhattan on a Friday night.

Last weekend, he'd almost taken Stacy to bed. Despite his own reservations, the only things that had stopped him had been a lack of condoms and the emergency call. He'd had all week to consider his own change of heart. He'd never thought this much about any of his flings before. Then again, he'd never wanted to spend much time with any of them outside of skiing or the bedroom.

Stacy was different. He'd felt it the moment they met, and every interaction they'd had since. Luke didn't do emotions. He'd shut that shit off when Becca died. Even if he did, it was way too soon to be feeling this way.

A pair of headlights turned at the tree line, and Luke grabbed his jacket, ready to open the door for Stacy. He rushed onto the porch as soon as her car pulled to a stop. She shouldered a bag and was halfway across the lot before he made it down the steps.

She came into his arms and Luke knew — too soon or not, he was falling head over heels for her. He tipped her chin up and kissed her lightly.

"It's cold out here, let's get you inside." He snagged the backpack from her. "This it?"

She popped the trunk, and Luke pulled out a small suitcase, then led the way up the stairs. He grabbed the paper with her room details on the way by the kitchen. They kept their hands to themselves all the way down the long hallway and to the third floor.

In front of her door, Stacy logged into the app and the lock opened with a quiet whir. Luke put her bags just inside the door and stood at the threshold. He didn't want to assume.

Stacy bit her lip and bounced from one foot to the other. The look she gave him was somehow shy and naughty at the same time.

"Do you wanna come in?" She stepped back to give him space. Luke didn't think twice. He walked into the room then closed and locked the door behind him.

Every fiber of his being wanted to pick her up and see how quickly they could get clothes off, but there was something to discuss first. A conversation he'd never failed to have.

"I hope I'm not being presumptuous, but my last testing was negative. It's old, but I've not been with anyone since. And condoms are a must."

Stacy peeled off her jacket and hung it up, then kicked her shoes into the closet. She looked for all the world like he'd asked her the weather.

"My annual physical was in November," she said. "Also negative. Also no one since. Agreed on the condoms, and I'm on the pill."

She came to him and slipped his jacket down his arms then hung it next to hers. He'd imagined when they finally did decide to have sex, it was going to be a frenzied rush to the bed. Instead, it felt like they'd done this a thousand times before.

There was anticipation, but also a sense of calm as he took off his boots and put them in the closet as well.

"I need to um..." She waved a hand at the bathroom. "Will you stay?"

Luke nodded. Wild horses couldn't drag him away from her right now. He pulled his sweater off so he was in his undershirt and jeans. The longer she was in the bathroom, the more the anticipation built until his fingers twitched with the need to hold her.

After what seemed like an eternity, Stacy emerged in nothing but a bright red silky thong. Any sense of restraint went right out the window as he scooped her up and pinned her against the wall.

She wrapped her legs around him, and her kisses were fire. Her hands tugged at his undershirt, but it was wedged between them. He carried her to the bed and laid her down with her ass right on the edge.

"Don't move," he whispered. He peeled his shirt off then leaned down to kiss her, filling his hands with those magnificent breasts. She guided his hand down her belly. He slid his fingers into her thong and stroked gently. She was already getting wet, and she spread her legs for him.

He trailed kisses down her body, then pushed the thong aside and finally got to truly taste her. Luke curled his arms around Stacy's hips and held her to him. He loved going down—it gave him a sense of power like nothing else. He could take his time, prolong the pleasure and tease until she was begging for more. Or he could find how she loved to be touched and see how quickly he could have her calling out his name.

Too many women shied away from letting him spend as much time as he'd like. Lessons learned from bad or impatient lovers. Not Stacy. She curled her fingers into his hair and stretched herself out, arching into his touch.

She came with an explosion of wetness and a cry she muffled with a pillow. Then she was pulling at him, urging him up. Luke stood, and Stacy slid back on the bed, openly admiring him.

He fished a condom from his pocket and tossed it on the nightstand then ditched his jeans as slowly as his thinning patience would allow. Stacy's eyes went wide when he sprang free from his boxers. He wrapped a hand around his cock and stroked.

"Tell me," he said. She licked her lips and reached for him, but he shook his head. "What do you want?"

Stacy rose to her knees and came to the edge of the bed. Her hand joined his in a slow stroke that had him wanting more.

"Fuck me, Luke," she whispered.

"That's what I wanted to hear," he replied. "Get on your back. It's gonna kill me, but we're gonna take it slow and easy to start."

She fixed him with a saucy grin as she shifted to make room for him. "I've got a better idea. You lie down." She took his shoulders and guided him to the bed. In a blink, she'd straddled him, and her mouth was on his, then on his neck, his chest, and down his belly.

Her hand wrapped around the base of him a breath before her lips grazed the head of his cock. She took him into her mouth, and Luke's eyes rolled back. She gagged a bit but didn't lose a stroke. He didn't know how much more of this he could take. As if reading his mind, she knelt next to him and rolled the condom down his length.

Stacy straddled him and ground against him like she had on his couch. She rocked and slid until she was gasping and sighing again. She shifted position and he slipped into her warmth. *Fuck she is too tight.*

Luke grasped her hips to lift her off, but she shook her head. "Just give me a minute to get used to you." She guided his hands to her breasts, then trailed her own hand to her clit and stroked. Her hips rolled as she slowly moved down. It was an exquisite sensation — and an even better view.

She was panting and moaning softly, and her fingers sped up on her clit as she took the last of him. A slow smile crossed her face, and she started a smooth, even rhythm. Her body trembled and her muscles tensed, squeezing him even tighter.

She grabbed one of his hands and pulled down, guiding him between her legs. "Make me come."

Luke had no problem complying with that command. He stroked his thumb over her swollen clit, moving in time to the rhythm of her hips. It didn't take long before her trembles turned to shaking. She clamped her mouth shut, and her fingers dug into his chest. The muscle spasms around his cock nearly sent him over the edge.

She collapsed against his chest, but she didn't stop. She nipped his ear with her teeth. "Roll me over and fuck me," her words came out breathy and sexy as hell. "And don't you dare take it slow and easy."

Luke's entire body gave an involuntary twitch at that. His muscles moved before his brain could process her words and he had her on her back in a heartbeat.

"Careful what you ask for," he said and levered himself up on his arms. She pulled her legs up and around his waist and tangled her fingers in his hair.

"I'm counting on getting it," she said.

Chapter Twenty-One

Stacy, Friday and Saturday, January 8 & 9

His first stroke was tentative, short, and Stacy tugged his hair until his gaze locked with hers. Luke's fingers caressed her face. He pushed deeper, and she gasped at the feel of him.

"Don't stop," she whispered. Luke shifted his hips and this time when he moved, it was a long, deep grind that sent delicious waves of friction over her clit. She'd expected he'd be *good*, and he did not disappoint.

"You like that, baby?" Luke repeated the move to Stacy's absolute delight. Then he sped up, as if he'd memorized her rhythm from earlier. Every stroke sent her higher and higher. He lowered his head and claimed her mouth. His tongue slid between her lips, and she felt consumed and filled at the same time.

She wanted, no, she needed more. Before she could find the words, Luke's next stroke was harder. She clutched onto him and begged for more. Sex had never been like this—they moved as if they were one body, their breaths mingling, both of them gasping at the intensity.

Luke spread his knees wider than gripped her hips and somehow slid her up his thighs. With her legs draped wide, she felt like she was on display.

"You're beautiful," he whispered. He pressed her legs outward and his next thrust hit that magic spot inside. Stacy moaned as he did it again. Then he trailed one hand up her leg until his fingers rested on her clit where he stroked in time with his movements.

Stacy's entire body tensed. Every muscle quivered until she was shaking all over. Fuck good, this man took sex to whole new levels.

Her fingers clenched into the sheets and her back arched. Luke leaned forward, wrapped an arm around her waist and lifted her to him without missing a stroke. She braced her feet on the bed and held onto his shoulders.

They pushed and pulled at each other — their skin slicked with sweat. His kisses got more demanding — teeth nipped at her neck, her shoulders and breasts. She gave back in kind and her fingernails dug into his skin as another orgasm shuddered through her.

Luke threaded his fingers into her hair and held her tight. She couldn't tell which of them was panting, or maybe it was both. She was pretty sure the tiny gasps and moans were coming from her.

Every muscle on his chest and shoulders stood out in sharp relief. His fingers clenched in her hair, pulling her body even tighter against him. Every time he moved another spasm of pleasure rushed through her. She wrapped her arms and legs around him, and Luke buried his face in her neck.

"Ah fuck, that is so good." His voice was thick and rough, and his beard tickled against her neck. He let out a soft moan, and her name escaped on a whisper as his body tightened. He tipped her into the bed and his last few strokes were hard and deep. His gorgeous blue eyes locked on hers as he pushed deeper and held himself there until his body stopped twitching.

Luke kissed her gently. "Gimme a sec."

He pushed up and padded to the bathroom. The view of his backside was just as spectacular as the view of his front. Water ran for a minute, then he came in with a washcloth in one hand and a towel in the other.

His touch was gentle as he cleaned her up, then patted everything dry. Stacy had never known a man to do that before, and she wasn't sure how to take it. Usually, she was jumping up to go pee and clean up. Then again, usually she was confident her legs would still support her.

He climbed into bed with her and wrapped his arms around her from behind. He nuzzled her neck, then planted a kiss below her ear.

"You smell amazing," he said. "And that was mind-blowing."

Stacy couldn't agree more, but her brain didn't want to make words. Her eyelids felt heavy. She was warm and happy. Luke's strong arms cradled her body and a pleasant ache had settled between her legs. She'd be sore tomorrow. A wonderful reminder of the evening's activities.

She should get up, go to the bathroom and wash her face. But that meant leaving Luke's arms, and she was pretty sure that was something she never wanted to do.

The stress of the past couple of weeks slipped away as she snuggled in closer to Luke.

The next thing she knew, light crept from under the bathroom door and the smell of shampoo and soap hung in the air. The door opened amid a cloud of steam and Luke stepped out in nothing but a towel.

"Go back to sleep, baby." Luke grabbed his pants and pulled them on with nothing underneath. "It's early, but I've got to get clean clothes, then check the snow machines and make sure we're set to open."

Stacy rolled over and watched as he found the rest of yesterday's clothes.

"Busy day?" She couldn't help but admire his ass as he bent to pull on his boots.

Luke straightened, then leaned in and kissed her. "Busy morning, but I got coverage this afternoon so we can spend time together."

He kissed her again. "Seriously. It's six in the morning. Sleep."

She closed her eyes, determined to do just that, but no matter how quiet he was, it was still someone moving in her space. Then her door opened and closed. She curled on her side, but the pillow smelled like Luke. She gave up and threw the covers off.

Might as well shower. She could get breakfast when the dining room first opened and still have time for skiing before lunch. She stretched and stood, parts of her body protesting.

She thumbed open her phone to find a series of texts in her group chat.

You'd better be getting laid.
Seriously. WTF. No arrival text.
PS – the D better be worth it.
???

Stacy ran a hand through the tangled mess of her hair. She hadn't even taken time to comb it out last night. She tapped her phone and typed.

You're right. I'm sorry. I fucked up on that. I owe you drinks and dinner. But yeah, the D was worth it. More than worth it. And I mean MORE.

She hit send, knowing she'd be bombarded with questions. These were her best friends, and they talked about everything, but she wasn't sure how much detail she wanted to share about Luke.

Like the fact that he was very much not just a 'shower'. The persistent and gentle ache between her legs was enough evidence of that. Or that he seemed to be hardwired to understanding her needs. And was very skilled at meeting them.

She cranked the shower to as hot as she could stand and stepped in. This thing with Luke could definitely become a regular thing. *Too bad he's not closer.* Still, the distance might be a good thing. The perfect friends with benefits arrangement. She had no desire to settle down. From everything she'd seen in her life, the keyword when it came to relationships was 'settle'. *Not happening.*

She took her time getting cleaned up and dressed. She made the bed, not sure if housekeeping did the staff rooms or not. Besides, if she played her cards right, they'd be in his cabin tonight, where maybe she wouldn't have to worry about being overheard by staff members on either side of them.

As predicted, she fielded a barrage of texts from Kylie and Brit over breakfast. She told them some, but not all, of what had happened. Kylie responded with a gif of a woman fanning herself. Brit replied in text.

Yeah, okay. Forgiven. Totally worth worrying your best friends over;-)

I'm serious on the forgiven part. I wouldn't have been thinking of anything else either.

With the friends' crisis averted, Stacy finished her breakfast as the dining room slowly filled up. Every time she'd been up here, it had been fairly crowded, and this was no exception. The property was so large it never felt that full when she was out and about, and with only twelve rooms in the house, it didn't feel busy.

Then she'd come to a meal and realize how many other people were here. She needed to find some appropriate way to thank Cat for giving her a staff room instead of just saying they were full.

After breakfast, she suited up for skiing and decided to do an easy cross-country trail. She wasn't sure her legs could handle downhill during the day and Luke at night.

She caught sight of him as she headed to the mess hall to get a tracker. He stood on the bunny slopes with a group of older women. *Oh, I bet they love him.* He looked up and sketched a wave, a smile cracked on his face. Stacy waved back.

Once on the trail, she lost herself in the beautiful snowscape that surrounded her. Tall pines flanked the wide path while farther up the hill winter bare branches swayed in the breeze. She checked the map and turned at the next trail juncture. A short uphill brought her to the edge of the clearing where Luke had asked them all to pause and listen.

Stacy skirted around the snow-covered meadow until she found a large rocky outcropping. She kicked off her skis and sat, then she closed her eyes and slowed her breathing.

As before, the world came alive in new ways the moment her eyes closed. There was quiet like she'd never known. This wasn't the hush of a library or the silence of an empty church. This was something else entirely. It was a living, breathing thing—she could understand why Kylie found it disconcerting.

Without anything else to distract her, she was faced with her own thoughts and feelings. About work. About family. About Luke. None of which she wanted to deal with. Stacy snapped her eyes open. She came here to escape stress, not to dig into her life's direction.

She shoved her feet into the bindings on her skis. Still, the whisper in the trees echoed in her mind—what was she doing in her life? Was this the path she really wanted? Why was she fighting so hard?

She started across the meadow, intent on returning to the main property by a different trail. Halfway across, in the wide-open space, she stopped again. There was peace here, but it was peace that came at the cost of self-examination.

She shook her head and kept moving toward the trail. She'd be back by lunch, then she could shower and have some time with Luke.

Something whizzed past her head, and Stacy nearly lost her footing. Whatever it was landed in a nearby tree. A giant owl perched on the branch, fluttering its wings and staring directly at her.

What the hell?

The thing hooted at her and ruffled its feathers. It seemed like it was demanding something. She was no bird expert, but she was pretty sure owls were nocturnal. Tufts of feathers on its head looked like ears and it was much larger than Stacy ever imagined an owl could be. The thing hooted again, a deep sound that reverberated in the snowy field. Then it screeched, never taking its eyes off Stacy.

She moved away. Maybe she'd disturbed its nest or something. *Do birds nest in January?* The owl flapped again, spreading its wings wide. *Holy hell that thing is huge.*

Afraid to turn and go back the way she'd come, Stacy cut wide around the bird. It watched the whole time, yellow eyes following her every move. Finally, she made her way to the trail well beneath where the damn demon bird perched in the tree.

It hooted, only this time the sound was plaintive rather than demanding. The bird rustled and chittered. She kept her eyes on it for the first few feet of the trail. She'd never heard of anyone being attacked by a giant owl, but she didn't want to be the first.

The owl let out a series of low hoots that sounded almost like it was laughing at her, then it spread its massive wings and took off. Stacy ducked instinctively, but the bird sailed harmlessly overhead and disappeared.

She wasn't about to wait around to see if it came back. She pushed off with her poles and set a rapid pace to Bristol Park. Yep, definitely a shower and an afternoon with Luke. That would do wonders to take her mind off the weird wildlife. *Another reason to love the city. No giant demon birds. Just pigeons.*

Chapter Twenty-Two

Luke, Sunday, January 10

The alarm buzzed and Luke rolled over. Or tried to. His arm was pinned under Stacy's head. He fumbled for his phone and managed to hit the snooze. Stacy sprawled on one side of the bed, her head firmly in the crook of his arm. There was definitely more room in the queen size bed in her room than in the full size in his cabin, but the added privacy had been nice.

Waking up to her was even better. Stacy turned and snuggled in closer, and Luke's cock twitched. It would be great to wake her up with kisses. Maybe see where that led. The blankets had slipped down from her shoulders, revealing smooth skin that he ached to touch and kiss.

The alarm buzzed again, and he slid his arm free, gently guiding her head to the pillow. He silenced his phone and headed to the shower. It was still dark, and tempting though it was to stay curled up in bed with

Stacy, he had work to do. This wasn't a big resort where he could come in late.

After getting dressed, he poured his coffee and sent a text to Stacy, suggesting she sleep in, shower, grab herself coffee, whatever. He wanted her to make herself at home.

Well, that's a first.

He insisted his past flings either not stay the night or leave before he did — discretion was key. Yeah, he'd have to think about that some other time. He had ski slopes to open. Guests liked to get skiing in before they checked out, and he knew they had a new group coming in the afternoon. Folks staying during the week. It was going to be a busy day.

A few hours later, his phone pinged with a text. An image of Stacy, still in his bed, popped up. Her hair was disheveled, and she still looked sleepy, but a soft smile curled her lips and Luke wanted to drop what he was doing, rush to his cabin and see what kind of trouble they could get into. Instead, he sent a heart and a smiley demon face emoji.

He went nonstop until lunchtime when he pulled out his phone. Stacy had sent a text with a picture of brown bags in the seat of a car.

I wanted something different, and Cat suggested Dolly's. I got for both of us. Should I bring it to the mess hall?

Luke sent a thumbs-up and closed out the report he'd just finished. He dragged an extra chair over to the makeshift dining table and cranked the heat a little more. Stacy came in with the bags in one hand and two bottles of pop in the other.

God, she's beautiful.

She dropped the bags on the table and handed him a bottle. The look on her face was pure mischief as she leaned in close.

"Am I supposed to keep it polite in public?" she whispered into his ear, then sat in one of the chairs and started unwrapping a feast.

Luke shook himself and sat. "I uh... Well, I guess family friendly would be good. But I don't think that means entirely hands off."

What the fuck am I saying? I've always maintained hands off in public.

He cleared his throat and eyed the wrapped sandwiches. It smelled like...

"I didn't know what you liked, but according to the diner staff, your usual is the brisket pastrami or one you apparently introduced them to."

Oh yes. He unwrapped a sandwich and there it was. A perfect soft hoagie bun piled with lettuce, tomatoes he knew Dolly grew in a greenhouse behind the diner, homemade tartar sauce and the best part, a crispy fried walleye filet.

It was a little taste of home. Everywhere he went, he'd tried getting folks to make this sandwich, and all of them had tweaked it somehow. Sure, they'd been good, but it hadn't been the little bit of nostalgic heaven he wanted.

Dolly had nailed it.

Stacy unwrapped another fish sandwich. "Figured it was worth a try." She shrugged and picked up the roll. Luke watched, his own food forgotten, as Stacy sank her teeth in. Her eyes went wide, and she made a humming sound in the back of her throat.

"Oh damn, that's good." She mumbled the words before she'd even finished chewing, and Luke picked up his own food. At some point, he paid attention to the sides — coleslaw and tater tots.

Between bites, they talked about their mornings.

"So, I've got to get out of here fairly early, I'm afraid," Stacy said. "What's the rest of your day like?"

Luke scowled. He'd hoped she could leave late, so they could find a little more time. "The afternoon is packed. It's a busy week. And I need to find time to go check the meadow before we have another crowd."

Stacy's head popped up and her eyes narrowed. "What's wrong with the meadow?"

Something in her tone set off little warning bells in Luke. "I think we have an owl pair considering nesting there. If they settle too close to the path, I'll need to mark it off."

Her eyebrows tried to meet her hairline and her hand flew to her mouth. "I forgot to tell you!"

Before he could ask what, she explained she'd seen a 'giant demon bird' there yesterday and it had acted pretty aggressively.

"Supposedly, owls are symbols of wisdom and transformation, or something like that," he said. "Or at least, according to Cat and Nate. I saw a great horned owl there on Tuesday. Was it in an old cottonwood?"

Stacy shrugged. "It buzzed my head and landed in a big tree. And made noises. And stared at me. It was kind of creepy."

He tried not to laugh. He managed to keep it to a tight grin. "Noted. Sounds like I need to mark that trail off limits. What's your schedule coming up? I'd like to see you again."

She bit her lip and looked down. "I can come up late next weekend. Same as this one, except I'll be able to stay until dinner time on Sunday. I won't be able to do the following weekend."

Luke nodded. This was how it went. Always. He was used to juggling two, sometimes three relationships every season. He knew this pattern. The mountain was an escape from the real world, and he was the bonus feature. Great for a weekend here and there, but not an all-the-time thing.

Usually, that was the way he liked it, but he wanted more with Stacy. That scared him a little. So, he nodded and steered their conversation on to safer topics. Then it was time for her to go. He tangled his hands in her hair and kissed her, determined for her to leave here wanting to return for more.

* * * *

Later that afternoon, Cat delivered the guest list for the week. She propped her butt on the table and folded her arms.

"I wasn't sure which one of you to ask first, but, since you're the one with a staff cabin, I'll start with you," she said. "Will Stacy need a room on her next visit, or will she be staying with you? Works either way, I need to know for reservations."

She pushed herself up from the table and crossed the mess hall, then turned by the door. "If she's staying with you, there's no charge." She winked and left.

Luke didn't know what to make of any of that. Everything in him said his employer knowing about an affair with a guest was a problem. Except, this didn't seem to be. Kind of the opposite actually.

He sighed and dropped a text to Stacy, then got back to work, checking the guest list and making sure they had the right staff to cover any likely needs. He kept himself busy to avoid having to process the way his thoughts had been going about her.

After dinner, unable to sit still and with not enough moon to justify a nighttime hike, he hit the lights on the slopes and took run after run until his legs shook with exhaustion.

His phone flashed with a new text message, but he forced himself to ignore it until he'd showered. He didn't pick up his phone until he was in bed. He thumbed open his messages and sucked in a breath.

Your call. If you're comfortable sharing space, I'm fine with that. It would make things easier.

She needed a response. She'd need to make the reservation if she was staying in her own room. Luke swallowed hard and typed.

I'm all for easy. And I like not worrying about the room next door hearing you call out my name. See you this weekend. Goodnight.

He hit send and stared at his phone like it was some strange thing. *What the hell are you doing, man?*

Chapter Twenty-Three

Stacy, Friday, January 15

"I think that's everything." Caylan ran his finger down the list Stacy had given him. "Yep. I just have one question." He leaned back in his chair and stuck his hands behind head as if he were relaxing at the beach. The move accentuated his baby-face and made him look even more like a teenager wearing his dad's suit.

Stacy shook those thoughts out of her head. "Let me guess. Why am I doing this and not turning it over to you interns?"

He gave a one shoulder shrug. He was right to question. She wasn't happy about it, but after she'd finished the audit, Mr. Smith had dropped this research project on her desk and made it clear he expected it would take up her entire week.

"No one has come right out and said it," she said, "but I feel like I've been demoted. Maybe not in title, but definitely in responsibility."

Caylan's entire body snapped forward. His hands slapped against his knees, and his normally pleasant features creased into a scowl. "You're serious? Wait, never mind. Of course you are. You come here to get the prestige on your resume, not for career progress."

Too bad no one told me that years ago. Stacy shrugged and saved the file they'd been working on. She still needed to put the whole thing together into a simple presentation and send it and the supporting documents off to Mr. Smith, but she could do that faster on her own. Since she wanted to get on the road to Bristol Park tonight, faster was ideal.

"Good work," she said to Caylan. "I appreciate the help. Now go home. There's no sense in both of us staying late." She glanced at the time. "Okay, well, later."

She knew the long hours interns put in. Often with no additional pay. You got a flat stipend for the semester. Most worked another part-time job to make ends meet. Safe bet Caylan was either in student housing, or in an outer borough, if not farther, with a long train ride home.

To his credit, he didn't question. He shut down his computer, gathered his things and wished her a good night. Once he'd gone, Stacy sighed and moved to her desk. Only a handful of people remained in the office, so at least it would be quiet, and she could do this kind of work in her sleep.

She had just hit send on the email to Mr. Smith when Lily Dixon stopped by her cubicle. Stacy suppressed a groan. Lily had been a senior associate for ten years. By all standards, she should have gotten a promotion years ago. She also worked in a different division, so there was no reason for her to be coming to Stacy's desk.

"Rumor is you're jumping ship." Lily leaned against the cube's entry as if this were a normal, everyday conversation.

"Rumors are often wrong," Stacy replied as she shut her system down and locked her drawers.

Lily gave a short laugh. "You came in here expecting to be a rock star, but you know it doesn't matter how good you are. It's all about connections."

Tell me something I don't know. Stacy wanted to scream at the woman. She wanted to demand she get to her point. Stacy couldn't tell whether Lily thought she was helping, or if she was being a bitch. Either way, she didn't want or need help from someone who'd been stuck for a decade, and she had no time for petty bitchiness. She'd left that shit behind in college.

"A word of advice," Lily said. She cupped her hand near her mouth like a teen about to share juicy gossip. "Don't rock the boat. Keep your head down and do your job. You'll survive, take home a nice paycheck and have an impressive sounding career."

She gave a self-satisfied nod and left. Stacy stood as Lily made her way to the door. Stacy braced her hands on the cube wall and waited, she'd give it a minute or two before she left. The last thing she wanted to do was get stuck in an elevator ride with Lily.

As soon as the office door swung shut, Stacy finished shutting down her office, grabbed her things and peeked her head into the hall. Empty. Her luck held, and she was the only one in the elevator for the whole ride down.

She hurried home as quickly as she could and rushed into her apartment, dropping work things onto her couch — she'd deal with those when she got back on Sunday night. She'd already packed her bags, but she still had to swing by her parents' and pick up a car, and it was already nearly nine.

If she were staying at the main house, she'd be texting Cat that she'd come in the morning. But she was staying with Luke. That thought sent a pleasant shiver through her. She usually enjoyed having her own space, but she reasoned it made sense to share since it was only for two nights, and they had so little time together anyway.

She thumbed open her phone.

Got out of work later than anticipated. Still have to get the car. It's gonna be past midnight by the time I get there. Come now or in the morning?

She grabbed her bag and headed right back out the door. If he said morning, she could stay in the guest room at her parents'.

Her phone pinged as she was getting off the subway.

If you're not too tired to drive, come tonight. Looking forward to seeing you.

She sent a thumbs-up and climbed the steps leading out of the station, feeling happy for the first time this week.

Chapter Twenty-Four

Luke, Friday, January 29

The whistle blew and half a dozen ten-year-olds pushed off from a T-position and glided down the ice. Acceleration drills had been the bane of Luke's existence when he'd been in sports. He wanted to go fast, not stop and start every time he turned around. Watching Brandon coach the kids not just in the how, but in the why, was eye opening.

Two kids wobbled and came to a stop. A third got lower and lower until he was almost skating in a squat before he finally landed on his butt. The other three made it to the marker where Luke stood ready to give high fives all around.

"Not bad," Brandon called out. "Today, we're working on balance — there's gonna be a lot of gliding. But we're also going to focus on explosive movement — getting speed from a stop and also when you're already in motion."

He turned to Luke. "Let's see you show off. That's what you're here for."

Luke barely restrained himself from flipping Brandon off. The truth was, Luke was there because Brandon had tired himself out earlier with the younger kids and wasn't sure he could manage a clean gliding start.

Luke got moving, keeping himself angled so the six boys watching could see his feet and legs. He set himself, dug his toes in and built-up speed until he whooshed around Brandon and the students. He didn't miss Brandon's eye roll.

"Luke's strong points on the ice are power and speed," Brandon said. "Who noticed what he did with his feet?"

Luke skated to the edge where Brandon's fiancée, Gina Tellis, sat with a laptop perched in front of her. She looked up as he sat at the other end of the bench.

"Thanks for covering this," she said. "I know you've got company coming in later."

It was Luke's turn to roll his eyes. Small-town life. Everyone knew your business.

"Erik sucks at acceleration drills. Besides, Andre got his walking cast today, and they've got concert tickets. I'm not such an asshole I'd get in the way of that."

Gina closed her laptop and arched an eyebrow at him. "No comments on the company, huh?"

"She's meeting me here," he replied.

Gina's grin went a mile wide. "Oh, so we get to meet her. Cat can't stop talking about how pretty she is."

He'd bummed a ride to the rink with Brandon and Gina after Stacy had said she could probably be in town by a little after eight. The hockey club program would be ending, and they could maybe do a little skating before going to his place.

It had been two weeks since he'd seen her, and his weekends had been busy. He felt like he'd missed a lot of her company. This weekend was supposed to be light, and she was making it up earlier than usual, so he hoped to have more time together. He glanced back to the ice where the kids were finishing their first drill.

"Duty calls," he said as he rose and skated toward Brandon. They worked on some balance exercises, then finished with a speed skate. It ended the session on a fun note rather than on the tedium and repetition of drills.

Parents started showing up as they were breaking the kids into free skating and allowing them to get a little silly. Gina started calling kids off the ice, and Luke got out of the way. He marveled at the teamwork between Gina and Brandon—though it shouldn't surprise him. He had years of working on a professional team, and she was a teacher.

Something in the room shifted, and Luke looked up to see Stacy standing at the edge of the ice. His heart beat a little faster, and he knew damn good and well he had a goofy grin on his face. Then his breath caught as Gina handed the last kid off to their parents and strolled over to Stacy.

Brandon skidded to a stop next to him and laughed. "You know you're in for it," he said. "You've been the topic of the coffee club gossip since you showed up. There are going to be some disappointed single women."

He was smiling and sounded like he was joking, but Luke wasn't entirely sure.

"What coffee club? And...wait...what?"

He'd been living in his own little bubble for a year. Sure, he'd come to town to buy groceries. He'd had more than a few chats with the old guys who hung out at the general store—after getting over being vaguely creeped out by them, or at least feeling like he was in some alternate universe where people still played checkers on the porch.

He shook himself and glared at Brandon, who gave him a subtle middle finger and not at all subtle smile, no different than Luke would do to Erik—big brother energy. *Except that's my role.* Fine, Brandon wanted to be the obnoxious older brother, well, Luke had an excellent example of the bratty kid brother thanks to Erik. He could channel that, no problem.

Guess we're being twelve-year-olds today. Okay then. Luke skated backward, gave Brandon two fingers and stuck his tongue out. That earned him an eye roll and a roar of laughter in return.

By the time Luke made it over to Stacy, he was laughing as well.

"Something amusing?" she said, then leaned in, wrapped her arms around his neck and kissed him. Something bumped his side, and he looked down to see a pair of beat-up tan ice skates, complete with toe pick.

Luke hooked a finger in the laces she had slung over her shoulder. Part of him wanted to get to his cabin as quickly as possible. Then there was a quiet part stirring as if waking from a deep sleep.

That part wanted to spend time with Stacy. He wanted to get to know her. What made her laugh? Why did she choose finance and how challenging was that as a woman? He wanted to know more than her pretty face, sexy-as-fuck body and how good she was in the sheets.

And that was something he hadn't felt in…well… maybe ever. He and Becca had been childhood friends and high school sweethearts. There wasn't anything to get to know. With Stacy, it was a whole world of discoveries.

"How does a snack stand hot dog and some skating sound?" It wasn't exactly a gourmet dinner, but it was the only way he could think to get the time he wanted.

"Add in a shake and maybe share a plate of nachos and you're on," she replied. She pointed her thumb over her shoulder. "So, I've met Gina. Who's the tall ginger?"

He didn't like the tiny stab of jealousy he felt and squashed it as best he could. He made introductions, and somewhere out of nowhere, suggested Brandon and Gina stay.

The two looked at each other, then back at him.

"My treat on hotdogs," Brandon said. "But then we've gotta go."

The four of them sat at one of the big plastic tables, laughing over chili cheese dogs and shared nachos. He'd known Brandon and Gina for a year, and Stacy for barely over a month, but this felt like…well…family.

Stacy put down her chocolate chip shake and laid a hand on his arm. "You okay?"

Luke tried to manage a cocky smile, but it felt awkward and wrong. He settled for what he hoped was a sheepish grin. "Yeah, realizing how long it's been since I've been home to see my folks. Weird, I know."

Brandon and Gina helped clean up and took off shortly after that, then the night manager shut everything down except the rink lights and reminded Luke to shut the main lights down when they left.

Stacy laced up her skates. "That was fun," she said. "Did the kids tire you out? Think you can handle skating and…" She raised her eyebrows at him, lust painted all over her face. Every shred of jealousy he'd felt earlier disintegrated.

"I'm an adrenaline junkie," he replied. "The harder I go, the more I want."

Now that they were alone and on the ice, he tried asking how her week had gone and got short, impersonal answers. It was like she didn't want to let him too close. The trouble was, close was exactly what he wanted.

"How's your grandmother?"

Stacy turned to face him, effortlessly switching to moving backward. Then she moved in close. Her body pressed to his and any other thoughts died. All he wanted was more of her. He brought his hands to her hips and held her there, then lowered his mouth to hers.

Her lips parted in an instant. They slowed, and he steered them to the edge of the ice. He brought a hand to her throat, and Stacy tipped her head back with a smile. He rested his fingers there, gently holding her against the wall as he explored her neck with his lips.

Stacy moaned as he grazed her skin with his teeth, then she wrapped both hands around his wrist and somehow maneuvered them around, so he was against the wall. She kissed him, slowly, as if they had all the time in the world. Then she sank to a squat and smiled up at him.

He didn't give it a second thought. He undid his belt, and Stacy had his jeans unbuttoned before he could take another breath. She slid cool fingers around his cock and gave a little hum.

He was a skilled lover, but he'd never had anyone treat his body as their own personal buffet of delights before. Usually, he was the one doing all the giving.

Her warm mouth closed over the head of his cock, and Luke's eyes rolled back as she took him into her throat. *Fuck, she is so good.* Her fingers stroked the base as her tongue swirled on the tip. She turned a blow job into an art form, and he was one hundred percent a fan of it.

Hell, he was one hundred percent a fan of her. He clenched his fingers into her hair, forcing himself to hold loosely. To let her be in control. He was dimly aware of her shifting her body somehow, but then she twirled her hand and squeezed, and he didn't care about anything else.

"Stop." He managed to croak the word out. Stacy paused and looked up at him. Her eyes were glazed with the same passion he felt. "You keep that up and I'm gonna explode. What about you?"

She slid her hand up his length, over the head and back down. Luke's entire body shook in response.

"We already know you can go more than once in a night," she replied. "And I know you'll take care of my needs."

A weak chuckle escaped him. Her last visit, they'd had so little time neither of them had slept and they were both sore at the end of the weekend. *Worth it.*

"I want to taste you," she said. She gripped his wrists and guided his hands to her hair. "Hold tight."

Then her mouth was on him again making everything she'd been doing before feel like a tease. She tipped her head and swallowed his entire length and fuck if that wasn't the hottest thing he'd ever experienced.

She pulled up, then slid down and repeated, keeping up a steady, long stroke that had him on the edge of losing control. Then she sped up and he did. He managed a warning before it happened, but Stacy didn't stop.

Her fingers clenched around him as he spasmed. She pulled back slowly, flicking her tongue over the tip of his cock as she went. Then she stood as if the last however long squatting on ice was nothing.

Luke wrapped an arm around her waist, hauled her against his body and fitted his mouth to hers. "My turn." He practically growled the words before he pulled them off the ice to one of the team benches. He tugged off his sweatshirt and laid it on the bench, then peeled Stacy's leggings down to her ankles and sat her on his shirt.

He'd never unlaced skates so quickly in his life. Hers were off in a flash and her leggings and panties followed. He straddled the bench between her legs and lowered his head.

Stacy cried out his name the moment his tongue traced her labia. Then again when he narrowed in on her clit and pulled it gently between his lips.

She was amazing and delicious, and he feasted on her, relishing her cries of pleasure as they echoed over the ice.

She grabbed his hair when she came and held him tight. His cock roared to life as she ground against him. He didn't stop until she was pushing him away. He straightened and looked down at this beautiful woman spread out in front of him.

Luke reached into his pocket and retrieved a foil packet. He held it up between his fingers.

"Here, or after we get to my cabin?"

He knew the answer. It was all over her face.

"One condition," he said as her fingers closed over the condom. "You ride me. Show me how you touch yourself. Use my cock, my fingers, your fingers, anything, to make yourself come for me."

Stacy's lips parted on a gasp. She sat up and kissed him—hot and fierce. Then she pushed him back on the bench. She didn't bother to take his pants down. In seconds, she had the condom on him.

His cock twitched as if in anticipation. How he could be so hard and so fucking horny right after that amazing blow job was beyond him, but he needed her. Now.

She stood and straddled him. She leaned down and whispered in his ear. "Do you want your dick in me?"

Fuck. Yes. That was the only thing he wanted. He grabbed her at the hips and pulled down. Stacy smiled and guided him. She hissed in a sharp breath as the head of his cock pressed into her, but she shifted her legs and slid farther down.

She settled onto him, leaned back and beckoned him to sit up. Her body tightened around him as he shifted on the bench. She braced her hands on his shoulders and started rocking against him.

Luke gripped her hips and lost himself in the feel of her warmth surrounding him and the sound of their breathing, punctuated by Stacy's cries of pleasure.

Then she lay back, still rolling her hips on his cock, and her fingers traced her clit. Luke watched, transfixed, as his cock slid against her slick skin. He watched the way her fingers circled, then pinched, then circled again.

"That's it, baby." Watching a woman masturbate was hot. Watching Stacy play with herself while grinding on him was off the charts. "You are so fucking beautiful."

Her fingers sped up and her back arched. "Yes!" Stacy's cry echoed over the ice as her entire body spasmed. She sat up, grabbed him by the nape of the neck and kissed him deeply. Her tongue thrust into his mouth, and her muscles clenched around his cock. Another stroke and it sent him careening over the edge into a second orgasm.

Chapter Twenty-Five

Stacy, Saturday, January 30

Stacy leaned back in the booth and surveyed the coffee shop. A small group of women sat at the front table, clearly people watching out of the big window. She took a sip of her latte — it wasn't too bad.

"Y'know, I've been in town only once to pick up from Dolly's and I don't think I noticed any of this," Stacy said. Luke gave a short laugh and smiled.

"It's not a big town," he replied. "I don't know how you missed it."

His hand covered hers and squeezed, somehow conjuring up images of the night before and sending warm tingles through her body.

"I've never been the small-town type, I guess?" The tingles spread, and she told herself it was left over excitement from their sex at the ice rink. "C'mon, every ski resort is surrounded by small touristy towns."

Except Abbeydon didn't seem touristy. Businesses lined Main Street for a few blocks, but it wasn't the usual collection of antique stores, bookstores, gift shops and tourist traps she was used to seeing. There were a few antique shops, but mostly it was businesses that clearly catered to folks who lived in the area. The general store and coffee shop were across the street from the bank and post office. Dolly's sat at the other end of the main town area.

The door opened and Gina came in. She waved at the women clustered at the front then strolled to where Luke and Stacy sat. Gina squatted by their table and smiled.

"I'm on a mission to find some volunteers," Gina said, and her smile got even wider. "The school's doing a Sweetheart Dance on the thirteenth, and I need a couple extra grownups to help oversee the decorating committee on Friday night."

Luke shook his head. "Sorry, high school life is my brother's gig, not mine."

The image of Luke clambering all over a high school gym to hang streamers and whatever else passed for decorations at a small-town dance sent Stacy into a fit of giggles. She coughed into her hand to cover it.

Gina arched an eyebrow and poked Luke's arm. "Haha. The Sweetheart Dance is at Bristol Park. Erik is already helping out, and he told me you'd say that. C'mon, I've got plenty of people doing the hard work. I need two more and you are the perfect candidates."

That made Stacy's laughter dry up. *Oh hell no.* "As exciting as that sounds, I'm afraid I'm not coming up that weekend."

It was Valentine's Day weekend, and she had a long-standing rule — that was self-care time. She already had her spa day booked.

A look of concern flashed on Luke's face so quickly she wondered if she'd imagined it. He shot Gina a lopsided, carefree smile and leaned back in the booth.

"I'm guessing you'd prefer a pair?" His grin shifted to a more serious expression. "If you can't find enough help, hit me up. I'll step in."

Gina's gaze flickered between Stacy and Luke, as if trying to read their faces. Stacy maintained a pleasant expression. She'd withstood scrutiny from far more intimidating people than Gina.

"Great," Gina said and stood with a smile. "I'll add you to the list." She turned and headed toward the front table.

A chuckle pulled Stacy's attention to the man next to her. Luke drained the rest of his coffee and cleared his throat.

"I'd forgotten what small-town life was like," he said. "We hadn't talked your upcoming schedule yet."

The words were soft, but there was an undercurrent of tension in them, and Stacy wasn't sure what to make of that. She focused on the first half of his statement.

"You've spent the last ten years in ski resorts," she said. "Don't those tend to be smaller towns?"

"Sort of, just not in the same way—especially when you're a seasonal employee." He leaned closer and caught her fingers in his. "I enjoy your company, and I know it's a long drive and you can't always get away for the weekend—but you kinda caught me off guard there."

He wasn't letting go of the schedule and something in his tone tugged at her. An unexpected pull of emotion. This was supposed to be a casual fling. It was a long-standing joke with her girlfriends—men were

Stacy's boy toys, and, like any toy, their purpose was strictly fun.

"I'm sorry," she said. "We hadn't gotten around to talking about it yet. I have plans for that weekend."

She could tell him those plans involved a full-body massage and a facial, but she shouldn't have to. They had no promises between them. She didn't owe him an explanation. His expression remained neutral.

"Well, we're on the subject, so, should we consult our calendars?" He gave her a questioning look that had her laughing. Here was the Luke she'd gotten used to — lighthearted, flirty and fun. She pulled out her phone and waited until he retrieved his from his pocket.

"The first few weeks of February are hell. I won't be able to make it up until the twenty-sixth, maybe the twenty-seventh. Depending on work."

Luke typed the dates into his phone and added a smiling devil emoji to the days. Everything about him was perfect. *Well, almost everything.*

For the first time in her life, Stacy understood why someone would settle for less than an exact match in a relationship. Here she was, making plans with this gorgeous man, who had a good sense of humor, was kind and generous, thoughtful and intelligent, a damn good lover and almost everything she could ever ask for in a partner.

Except he's content to be a seasonal employee and work as a ski bum. There was more to his job than that, and she knew it, but it still came down to the same thing. Luke lacked ambition and drive. He seemed happy in his little world.

Were she wanting a long-term relationship, Luke would be tempting. Very tempting. The trouble was, she knew how that story would end. Her parents provided living proof of that. As far as she could tell, her biological father was like Luke — a wanderer content to follow his passions with no concern for money or prestige.

She knew all too well that her stepfather was almost the exact opposite — a man who put money, power and prestige above all else and never seemed to show a shred of passion for anything.

On top of that, Luke's world kept him in remote places like Abbeydon, while her job required a major city.

"Locked in," Stacy said as she saved the dates. Luke smiled at her, and she wanted to get lost in the cool depths of his eyes, and that was dangerous territory.

That train of thought completely derailed as Luke leaned toward her and kissed her. His hand cupped the back of her neck as his lips caressed hers. She wanted to devour him on the spot. He broke the kiss and pressed his forehead to hers.

"What do you say we get out of here?" His voice held a note of gravel. She moved her hand up his thigh, but he caught her fingers and shook his head. "Naughty girl."

Stacy slid from the booth and leaned over, giving him a good view down the low neck of her top. "You like it when I'm naughty," she said, then straightened and walked toward the front.

He caught up with her at the door. He held it open and let her go through ahead of him. She stayed a couple of steps ahead of him as they walked to his car. She was used to being the one in control. Luke tended to turn the tables on her — in a good way. The second she rounded the corner, his arm whipped around her waist, and he hauled her against his chest.

"I do like it when you act the bad girl." He growled the words into her ear and tingles of pleasure went straight to her nipples and clit. *Oh, this man is dangerous fun.*

"So, who won our little game, do you think?" The low rumble of his voice tickled her neck. His arm was like a vice around her middle and his body felt like a brick wall. *If brick walls were warm and sexy.*

"I think it's a draw, don't you?" She tipped her head, trying to see his face, but he had his mouth against her ear. "I mean, I invited you in, but you talked sex first."

His fingers clenched on her ribs, and she felt the smile spread across his face.

"I propose round two," he said. "Right now. We go to my cabin, and I take my time finding every pleasurable spot on your amazing body. Sound like a good start?"

She couldn't have stopped herself from nodding if she'd tried. Her breath caught and her heart pounded at the idea.

"I won't fuck you until you beg for it," he continued. The throbbing of her pulse spread until her nipples ached with the need for his touch.

"Sounds good to me," she replied, managing to keep her words steadier than she felt.

"But there's a catch." His voice had dropped to a whisper, pitched so low it vibrated the tiny hairs on the back of her neck. "If you beg for it, I win."

Now her pulse vibrated down her body and settled in her pussy. She licked her lips and swallowed against a throat that was suddenly dry. "What do you get if you win?"

His low chuckle had her wet in an instant. "What are you offering?"

He walked them to his car, somehow managing to unlock the door and open it while still holding her around the waist. Luke maneuvered her into the open door and turned her to face him. A look of primal need darkened his eyes.

As intense as their sex had been so far, something told her there was more, oh so much more, possible. Luke was on the edge of abandoning whatever restraint he'd been exercising until now.

All too often, men treated her like some fragile thing. Luke had already proven that wasn't the case with him, and now, if she was right, she could nudge him a step farther down that path.

Her lips parted on an involuntary gasp as he leaned closer. "For starters, I want my cock in your beautiful mouth." He brought her hand to his crotch. His dick throbbed and pulsed under his fly. "We can talk about the rest on the ride. Now get in the car."

Chapter Twenty-Six

Stacy, Tuesday, February 2

A tray of tacos slid into Stacy's vision, followed by a pitcher of what had to be margaritas. Brit deposited both onto her coffee table. Kylie pulled an ottoman over and sat the tray of toppings on it while Brit retrieved glasses.

"I gotta admit," Brit said as she came in and poured three drinks. "I can't decide what I want to hear more about first—boy toy or shitty work. And I'm still not saying I told you so."

She handed out the drinks, and they all clinked glasses like they'd been doing ever since they were kids with glasses of lemonade.

"To Taco Tuesday," Stacy said, as if it were the most serious thing ever. They raised their glasses in a toast, and all took big gulps in unison. Then all three burst into laughter. The same as always. *Why can't all of life be this easy?*

"I work in a male-dominated industry and even I don't have to deal with the shit you do," Kylie said. She paused as she scooped guacamole onto her taco, before pointing the spoon at Stacy. "I'm all for fighting the good fight, but at a certain point, you have to consider throwing in the towel."

Brit snagged a taco of her own and doused it in hot sauce. "She's right. If you came into the office with this stuff, we'd be talking options — I mean you know this, and I understand why you don't want to go that route. But then why stay?"

Stacy took another drink and tried to figure out the answer to that question. After Lily's visit, she'd debated following the woman's advice. The trouble was that wouldn't get her what she really wanted. *No, what I really need.*

Independence. Sure, she could go Chad's route and find some glorified closet of a studio apartment or move to Brooklyn or Queens. Brit had moved in with her grandmother a few years ago and was set to take over the apartment when Grams moved to Florida. Kylie had taken money she'd inherited from her grandfather and invested in a one-bedroom condo in an up-and-coming neighborhood.

The help Stacy got from her family came with too many strings.

"Never mind the job," Stacy said. "And never mind the boy toy. I got this via certified mail today." She put the letter on the coffee table. Brit picked it up and her eyes flew over the page.

"Holy shit."

"Are you gonna tell me what it says?"

Brit handed the page off to Kylie. "TLDR — Grand-mère is kicking Stacy out of the apartment."

Kylie rattled off a few choice phrases from the letter as she read, but Stacy had the whole thing burned in her brain.

"My little 'case of histrionics' at Christmas was the last straw, I guess." Stacy took the letter and stuffed it in her pocket. "I kept waiting for her to say or do something. Turns out, she had decided to give me a month to change my mind. And here's the consequence to not doing so."

Her friends stared at her, open-mouthed. Stacy had known her grandmother was petty and controlling. She had known she might lose the apartment over her holiday outburst. Her friends didn't. Even after years of knowing Stacy and her family, they still thought families loved each other and protected each other.

"What are you going to do?" Kylie's eyes were wide in shock.

"You move in with me for starters," Brit said with an air of finality. "The letter said you have until March thirty-first. Grams bought a place in Florida, and it closes at the end of this month. She's planning to move the beginning of March."

Part of Stacy wanted to argue with her friend. She wanted to say it was too much. Another part knew that sharing an apartment with Brit was her best temporary solution. The place was small but nice, had two decent bedrooms, each with their own bathroom. Gramercy was a twenty-minute train from work.

"I want to do this myself."

Kylie threw up her hands and Brit just smiled.

"Fuck that," Brit said. "I'm not telling you to give in to your grandmother's bullshit control, but I am telling you that you need to take off the blinders and realize that accepting help from friends isn't the same thing."

"We don't come with quite so many expectations," Kylie chimed in.

Brit shrugged. "We've roomed together before in worse circumstances. You pay a reasonable rent. We'll do this all legally, paperwork and all. Whether it's a month, a year or forever, I don't care." She leaned forward and put a hand on Stacy's knee. "It's time. I know it's hard and I know you're scared and you're not where you want to be yet. But she's forcing you to make a choice. So, make it. Live life on your terms. We've got your back."

Kylie added her hand on top of Brit's, and Stacy covered them with her own. Tears pricked her eyelids, and she blinked them away.

"Now will you fucking eat something?" Brit said. "You're halfway through that drink, and I know you've not touched food since you opened that letter."

Stacy laughed, grabbed a paper plate and started building her taco.

"Housing crisis solved." Kylie sat back with her plate of food. "Work or boy toy?"

Stacy stuffed a bite of taco into her mouth and chewed. She made Kylie wait until she swallowed.

"Can't we talk about your lives for once?"

Both women roared in laughter.

"No thanks," Kylie replied. "I work from home, have minimal office drama since going freelance, I date low drama people and my family is chill. I'm boring."

Brit shook her head. "Don't look at me. I went through my drama phase. You two kept me sane through coming out and transition and all of that. Your turn to reap the benefits of friends."

"Fine," Stacy replied. "Work continues to be shit, and I think they're trying to quiet fire me. I can't get on any decent projects, they've pulled what few accounts I was managing and the only advice I get is keep up the good work." She sighed and scooped more cheese onto her taco. "I've been working long hours during the week so I can have weekends free, but nothing I do seems to be enough. There's a team building event this weekend that I'm going to."

She didn't have high hopes for that, but she wasn't ready to quit yet. Dwelling on work was not the way she wanted to spend downtime with her best friends. That left Luke. The boy toy. Last weekend hadn't felt like a fling, and she didn't know how to process that.

"Short version. Your grandmother is a petty shit, and your company treats women like shit as well," Kylie said.

Brit rolled her eyes. "She's not wrong. What's the story with the hot ski dude?"

"He's amazing in bed," Stacy replied. Not like she hadn't shared that before. Kylie looked bored but Brit leaned closer.

"What's going on?"

There was no escaping the penetrating look in Brit's eyes. They knew each other too well. Still, Stacy hadn't wrapped her head around anything with Luke, and her grandmother's latest attempt at exerting control over her life wasn't helping her focus.

"I think I've been too harsh on my mother for the choices she's made in her life." That was the best she could come up with right now. She picked up her plate and focused on making another taco. "I'm going to stuff my face with tacos and margaritas," Stacy said. "Maybe after I'm full and good and drunk, we can talk the boy toy. Because he confuses me and that's a new thing."

Chapter Twenty-Seven

Luke, Friday, February 12

The rec room glowed with soft light thanks to string upon string of tiny LEDs hung across the ceiling to seem like a night sky. Luke folded the ladder and stuck it in the hallway. Erik was across the room, hanging a sheer curtain over a shower of white lights.

"Luke, can you grab that box of glittery stuff?" Cat nodded toward the wall where a pile of open boxes sat. As far as he could see, everything was sparkly or glittery or shiny. Her hands overflowed with iridescent ribbons in shades of pink and red.

Brandon and Gina directed a flow of chaos in the form of teens running between the boxes and the walls as they hung sparkling streamers and layer upon layer of hearts and shiny starburst things.

He made his best guess on which box and followed Cat to where his brother perched on a ladder at the end of the curtain.

"Ribbons first," Erik said. He looked down at the box in Luke's hands. "Perfect. That one's gonna take two. We'll need the other ladder."

Luke rolled his eyes, put the box down and retrieved the ladder. It only took a few minutes to finish the wall thanks to Cat's help getting everything centered. When they were done, the three of them stood back and admired their handiwork.

"That's the photo backdrop," Cat said. "Tomorrow, the dance committee will do all the balloons. Do you know what a pain in the ass it is to find this many non-latex balloons? I'm really excited about the LED ones for the corners."

He helped clean up and by dinner time, the rec room had emptied out, leaving him and Erik.

"That went faster than I figured," Erik said. "Wanna grab dinner? And maybe uh, drop me off at home? I caught a ride with Brandon and Gina."

They closed up the room and headed for Luke's Subaru. Once in the car, Erik turned in his seat, crossed his arms over his chest and glared at his older brother.

"What the fuck has you in such a piss poor mood today?"

Luke ignored his kid brother until they were on the road to town. He needed a burger and maybe a couple of beers. Hell, he needed more than a couple, but considering tomorrow the entire place would be overrun with teenagers because they'd decided to close to regular guests and do a whole weekend special for the high school, being hungover did not sound like a good idea.

"Maybe I'm not cut out for hanging around one place too long," Luke said. It was bullshit, and he knew it. The trouble was exactly the opposite. He'd enjoyed the last year. He loved the small resort and the town. His bosses were amazing people.

"Not buying it," Erik replied. "You've seemed happier here than I've seen you in years. I mean, genuinely happy."

Luke shrugged. His brother was right. He'd wandered for years, never thinking about settling down, but Abbeydon felt right. He felt like he belonged.

"I think I fucked up with Stacy." The words came out of his mouth without thought. He didn't so much as glance at Erik, but he knew his brother was scrutinizing him.

"Like she got emotional and is going to cause a problem fucked up? Or you forgot a condom and she's pregnant fucked up?"

Leave it to Erik to jump to those two. Luke let the silence stretch. He wasn't even sure how to put his feelings into words. He'd spent the last ten years either mourning or keeping himself emotionally isolated. Numb was better than the anguish of grief.

"More like I got emotional," he said finally.

Erik coughed, but it wasn't enough to cover the fact he was laughing. He cleared his throat and apologized. "How is that fucking up?"

The kid was right. It shouldn't be a problem, but it was, at least to Luke.

"She's not the relationship type," he said. "Let's start with that. Even if she were, she's in New York and not about to move. I'm not about to go live in a city. I mean, what would I do for work? That's the start of the practical issues."

Like the fact she has multiple degrees and a professional agenda, and I'm a college dropout who has no desire to even visit a big city, let alone live in one.

"I've got till the end of next month to decide if I'm taking the operations role at Bristol Park," Luke continued. "Part of me knows it's the right thing, but it's scary. Another part feels like that puts a nail in the coffin with Stacy. Then I wonder why I should care so much about a woman I barely know."

No smart-ass remark greeted that statement. No jokes or teasing. Just quiet. Luke glanced at his passenger. Erik looked dumbfounded. His eyes were wide and his mouth slightly open. Then he blinked.

"Eyes on the road," Erik chided. "I know this may sound callous, but it's been ten years. It's not surprising that you're finally reaching a place where you can move on. And I mean that with work and women."

Erik wasn't saying anything Luke didn't know. Hell, he'd been through enough therapy, trying to process the guilt and the shame. He knew damn good and well why he liked people and jobs to be disposable.

None of that made it any easier to suddenly start feeling again. Especially when the person he was falling for was herself emotionally closed off and unavailable.

"I think the job answer is easy, if you think about it," Erik said. "As hard as it is to accept, not every person comes into our lives to stay. Sometimes they're there for a reason, and that reason has an expiration date."

It didn't surprise Luke that his kid brother was more relationship savvy than he was. Luke had had one serious relationship in his life, and she'd died at nineteen. Since then, he'd never allowed himself to get attached to anyone. He wasn't sure he'd ever truly understood love.

He'd had a number of years where he'd almost exclusively dated older women — usually ones who had just been left or done the leaving themselves and were looking for someone young and fun to make them feel good again. He'd been happy to oblige, knowing he was a temporary thing for them. That was how he liked it.

"Yeah, the job part is easy," Luke replied. "Still seems weird even thinking about it, but it feels right."

He turned down Main Street and Erik started laughing. "Did you forget that Dolly's closes at five?"

Fuck. He had forgotten.

"Guess we're going up the road a bit more."

He swung the car around and headed to the highway. There was a burger joint near the ice rink, and they'd be open late on a Friday night. Plus, be less likely to have a bunch of locals eavesdropping on what could be a very uncomfortable conversation about his love life.

Chapter Twenty-Eight

Stacy, Sunday, February 28

The image on the screen blurred then came into focus, and Stacy still squinted to see. "There's a bird in there?"

Luke chuckled and glided his thumb over the controls and the image zoomed in enough she could make out a large bird in the nest.

"Yep, that's the demon bird."

Luke tapped the screen, then moved the drone and tapped again. "Getting pictures," he said. "And that is a female great horned owl. As far as I can tell, she laid eggs about a week ago. So, we'll stay on this side of the meadow."

Stacy was fine with the idea of staying far away from the demon bird. Especially now that she knew there were two of them. One had been scary enough.

"Isn't there some like forest ranger or game person or something to keep track of these things?"

Luke brought the drone down in front of them and knelt to fold it up. "This is private property. If there's a problem, yeah, there's the Division of Environmental Conservation, but they're not actively involved in keeping tabs on every critter out there."

He stuck the drone into his pack and slung it on his shoulder. "We keep track of wildlife mostly because of guests—don't want skiers disturbing nesting birds or stumbling across some bears."

He picked up his ski poles and led the way out of the clearing. Stacy unzipped her jacket a bit. The day was cool, but she warmed up quickly when they were moving, despite the sun hiding behind low, gray clouds.

"When should the baby demon birds hatch?"

She knew they were great horned owls, but the yellow eyes and her first encounter with the thing would always label them demon birds in her mind.

"Usually it takes about a month," Luke replied. He turned at the end of the meadow and took them to higher ground. A week of unseasonably warm weather meant some of the trails had turned slushy. "Around the end of March, I'd guess."

"So that trail is off limits the rest of the season?"

He stopped and turned, then pointed his pole along the trail they'd come up.

"We'll keep all of this flagged into spring. At least until the owlets are flying well."

She'd missed three weekends in a row, and it was still winter, but the trails were already changing.

"I bet this is amazing in spring," she said. Luke snapped his head around and his eyes were wide with surprise. Then his mouth turned up into a big smile.

"It is," he replied. "Bright green in spring and the meadow is filled with wildflowers. Then in summer, the trees turn darker green."

His face registered wonder and delight. Nothing in Stacy's life gave her that much anticipation and pleasure. Watching the seasons march through the city was nice, sure, but there was nothing magical about it.

Stacy took in a deep breath and surveyed the meadow with fresh eyes. She'd been places where the scenery was more spectacular—Instagram worthy photo ops everywhere—but none of them had felt like Bristol Park. There was something special here.

Strong arms wrapped around her waist, and she tipped her head back against Luke's chest. This felt good. He felt good. Too good.

"I'm starving," she said and craned her neck around to catch his expression. He gave a lopsided smile and kissed her forehead.

"Then let's get back and get to dinner," he replied. "You okay eating here tonight?"

Stacy nodded and they set off down the trail. They made it in time to shower and change for early dinner, and Luke found a quiet table near the fire.

As they finished their meal, she tried to imagine Luke's life here. Weekends spent dealing with guests. The rest of the week catching up on trail and equipment maintenance. Driving half an hour or more to get to a movie theater or a date-night type restaurant.

"There she is." Cat's voice pulled Stacy from her thoughts. Cat squatted next to their table. "Nate's on baby duty so I can come socialize. Brody is being a little bit fussy of late. It's been a while since we've seen you up. Welcome back."

As always, Cat was the picture of elegance. She was one of those people who would look good in a paper bag and could make even the simplest outfits seem like a fashion statement.

"Yeah, work has been hectic," Stacy replied. "I'm curious, I know the history here—like how you inherited the place and it had been closed for years, but where were you before?"

A cloud passed briefly over Cat's face, and Stacy kicked herself for being rude. Then Cat smiled and gave a little laugh. "I forget there are folks who don't know the whole thing. I was in New York City, managing my then husband's shipping company. He passed and I didn't know what to do with myself. Then I found out about this place. Sort of a fairy tale, really."

Well, that explains a lot.

Cat stood and brushed her hands down her pants legs. "There is coffee and dessert in the sunroom if you'd like. Enjoy the weekend."

After she'd left, Stacy turned to Luke. "I hope I didn't step in something there. She seemed kind of... I don't know. Weird."

Luke reached across the table and squeezed her hand. "There's some ugly history there and everyone here already knows it all. You didn't step in anything and it's no big secret. Kinda hard to have secrets here."

Stacy clamped her mouth shut on the laugh that threatened to bubble up. She could walk down the street in Manhattan, and no one would pay any attention. The hot dog vendor near her work knew her. As did the doorman in her building. But those were passing things. Casual, surface relationships that held no depth or meaning. Here...

Stacy shook herself. *What the hell has gotten into me?* Luke squeezed her hand and arched an eyebrow as if he were waiting for her to respond to something he'd said.

"I'm sorry, I must've missed something?"

His smile quirked wider. "Did you want dessert?"

His expression made it clear what he wanted, and she was more than happy to go there. That was why she came here, after all. As beautiful as this place was, Manhattan was home, and Luke was a boy toy — maybe the best she'd ever had, but still just a diversion.

"I want stress relief," she replied. She needed to shut off her brain. She was sure the only reason she was suddenly so enamored of rural life was because work was such a shit show. Plus, she had a month to get out of her apartment. And she didn't care about any of that right now.

She leaned closer to Luke and caught his gaze. "I've got a long drive home tonight, and I need to forget my own name before I leave. Think you can help with that?"

Chapter Twenty-Nine

Luke, Sunday, February 28

Every brain cell and blood cell seemed to rush straight to Luke's cock at the look on Stacy's face. He crossed his fingers that his jeans were heavy enough to hide the raging hard-on, then stood and pulled Stacy up next to him.

He leaned into her and whispered into her ear. "I think we need to explore more of your naughty side. You seemed to enjoy that last time."

Her cheeks pinked quickly, and her tongue slid out along her lips. Luke had to restrain himself from kissing her right in the dining room. Instead, he led them to the entry to collect their coats, then straight down the hill to his cabin.

He'd made his peace with his growing feelings for Stacy. While he hoped they were reciprocated, the reality was it was unlikely. He wasn't thrilled with that, but he'd cope. She wanted to forget her name, well, he could help her there.

Their last time together, he'd discovered she liked being teased until she was begging for his cock. Then she'd wanted it fast and hard. Tonight, he'd see how much farther down that road she wanted to go.

Once inside his cabin, he slammed the door shut then turned to Stacy and let his gaze linger over her, top to toe. Her rich, dark hair was piled into a messy bun, and she had on only a little makeup. He helped her off with her coat then motioned at the couch. Stacy sat without question, but her eyes narrowed. He perched on the chair opposite.

"You said you want to forget your name," he started. "Would you like to continue what we started last time?"

Her narrowed eyes opened wide, and her cheeks flushed even brighter. "Yes, please." Her words were soft and quiet, but to Luke, she might as well have shouted.

"Do you know what a safe word is?" He mentally crossed his fingers he'd been reading her right. Her lips curled, making his cock twitch in anticipation.

"Yes," she replied. "Red is simple, isn't it?"

Luke nodded. *Holy shit.* "Since you seemed to like our little game, I want to play a slightly different variation." He swallowed hard. *Assuming I can keep it in my pants long enough.*

"I want to make you orgasm, repeatedly. But every step of the way, you have to ask for what you want," he said. One side of her lips quirked up a little more. He could imagine what she was thinking—this sounded like a repeat of last time. It was, but he was about to add a twist.

"I want you to beg for it and I want you to be explicit," he said. "No euphemisms. No hints. Let me hear exactly what you need."

Her lips parted on a gasp. Now he was getting in her head. Time to up the stakes. "We know you're a naughty girl. So, when you beg me to eat your pussy, or fuck you, before I do that, before I give you every single thing you want, I will spank your gorgeous ass."

Stacy's entire body twitched, and her nipples printed clearly on the lightweight turtleneck she wore.

"It won't be hard. Just a light smack on the ass. Unless you ask for more. Are you okay with that?"

She licked her lips and swallowed. Her eyes blinked rapidly, and her teeth sank into her lower lip. Her breasts rose and fell with each breath. Finally, she looked up and those caramel eyes bored into his.

"Yes, I'm more than okay with that."

His cock throbbed, but that would have to wait. "Anything I need to know? Anything you want to ask?"

She shook her head and Luke rose. He closed the few feet between them and stood over her. "No touching," he instructed, then stepped closer. He bent down and placed his lips near her ear.

"You are beautiful," he whispered. "I plan to taste every inch of you tonight. I want to hear you calling my name." He straightened then took her hands in his and pulled her to stand.

Luke grazed his fingers over her body, relishing each shiver she gave. Then he tugged her sweater over her head. He traced his thumb over the cups of her bra until her skin prickled in visible goosebumps.

"Did you want something?" He hooked a finger under her bra strap and gave a gentle tug. "Maybe something taken off?"

She rolled her eyes, and he stepped back. The lost look that crossed her face was almost his undoing, but she took in a slow breath and closed her eyes.

"Please take off my bra."

Luke stepped behind her, so close his body pressed against hers. "Why do you want your bra off, Stacy?" He trailed his thumb down her back and rested on the hook.

"I want..." She took a shaky breath. "I want your fingers and mouth on my nipples."

Luke wrapped one arm over her shoulders and across her chest and held her tight. He stroked her perfect ass, gently kneading one cheek, then he smacked it. One light tap, but enough to make her jump.

"Very good," he whispered in her ear as he unhooked and removed her bra. True to his promise, he turned her to face him and bent his head to take care of her request. Her hands cradled his head as his lips closed on her nipple and he stopped.

"No touching," he reminded. She dropped her hands, and he took her nipple between his lips again. He lavished first one then the other with attention, licking and sucking and biting until Stacy was gasping with pleasure and her body arched against him.

"Please," she gasped. "I want you to do that to my...um... Please eat me."

Luke chuckled against her skin. Not as explicit as he'd like, but good enough. He released her nipple and led her to the dining table.

"Hands on the table," he said. She complied, and he took a moment to admire her curves. Then he slid her pants down and off. A purple thong set off her ass cheeks beautifully. He laid his hand on the cheek he hadn't smacked yet.

"Are you ready?" He waited for her to nod, then raised his hand and brought it down a little harder than the first one. Stacy gasped and quivered as Luke slid her thong off.

"Lay your chest flat on the table and spread your legs." The moment she did as told, he kissed his way up from her ankles to the curve of her ass. He stopped before he got to the best part.

"I did say explicit, didn't I?" He planted a kiss on the top of each ass cheek. "What do you want me to do?"

Her legs trembled and a low moan escaped her. "Please put your mouth on my pussy."

Luke swatted her ass twice, once on each cheek, then knelt and buried his face between her spread legs. He had no trouble reaching her clit with his tongue and he teased lightly. He gripped her hips and stroked with his tongue until she was grinding against his face.

"More please!"

Luke retreated, and Stacy let out a soft whine of protest.

"Please, Luke, make me come with your mouth."

Oh, fuck, she's hot. He stood, curled one arm around her waist so he could continue stroking her clit, then he delivered four more swats on her ass cheeks. She barely even jumped. He turned her around and slid her onto the table and pulled up a chair.

"Put your feet on the arms and spread your legs wide." He waited until she was settled, then kissed her inner thighs before licking his way along her labia. She was sweet and spicy, and he never wanted this to end. He pulled her clit between his lips and let his tongue tease until the already swollen bud poked farther from its hood.

Another lash from his tongue, and Stacy's body tensed, then exploded as she cried out his name. She'd barely stopped shaking when she sat up, tangled her fingers in his hair and lifted his head. Her face was pure lust and passion.

"Fuck me, Luke." Her breasts rose and fell as she panted. "I want your dick in me."

Somehow, he stopped himself from standing up and doing exactly that. Instead, he gently pulled her hands from his hair and smiled.

"Go get on my bed. On your hands and knees. And wait for me."

She didn't bat an eye. Her feet dropped from the chair, and she headed straight for his room. Luke took his time following her, hoping to regain a shred of control for what he wanted to do.

The sight of her naked on his bed, ass in the air, almost made him lose it. He got undressed and stood at the foot of the bed.

"Bring your ass up here," he said. "You have one more spanking coming, then I want your mouth on my cock getting me all nice and wet before I fuck you like you asked."

Stacy backed right up to him, and Luke smacked her ass a little harder this time. His hand left a light-pink mark on her ass cheek, and she sucked in a sharp breath, but arched her hips up for the next one. "Turn around." He ground the words out and she was facing him almost before he'd finished.

Her lips wrapped around the head of his cock, and she took him down her throat. He let her continue for a few strokes then he pulled out and turned her around.

He rolled down a condom and knelt behind her, pressing the head of his cock against her entrance. "Back yourself up on me," he said.

She took him in one push, and Luke moaned in pleasure as her warmth wrapped around him. He stroked slow and shallow, forcing himself to wait until she asked for more.

"Harder, please."

He slapped one butt cheek and did as she asked. Every time she said harder, or faster or deeper, he'd slap his hand lightly against her ass just before he delivered what she wanted.

He rested his hand on her ass and let his thumb press against her entrance. She didn't flinch. Luke slowed his strokes and reached for the bottle of lube. A little on his thumb and he circled around. Stacy let out a moan, and he slid his thumb into her ass. Her muscles clenched around him.

"Luke, fuck me hard, please."

He slapped one cheek and pressed his thumb deeper into her ass as he ramped up his thrusts until the sound of their bodies slapping together echoed off the bare walls of his room. He reached around and found her clit, stroking in time to their rhythm.

She clenched again, and her moans turned to sharp gasps, then warm wetness cascaded down his hand. That sent Luke over his own edge, and he pulled her up to him as he came.

They collapsed onto the bed, and Stacy curled against him. Luke felt something shift inside him, as if a door with rusty hinges suddenly stopped resisting and cracked open.

Stacy rolled over and slid out of bed. "I've got to shower before I go."

He wanted to grab her hand and tell her to stay, and not just for the night. He wanted to talk and find a way to make this work. Some long-dead part of him stirred to life at the idea of not waking up next to her. He loved this woman, and he wanted her in his life.

Well, fuck.

Chapter Thirty

Stacy, Friday, March 5

The empty box sat on her table, seeming to mock her. Stacy plopped onto her sofa without taking off her coat or shoes. Another fourteen-hour workday done. She was exhausted, but she needed to start packing. Leaving things to the last minute was not an option as far as she was concerned.

She pushed herself up and kicked her shoes into the closet by the door. Her phone rang as she hung up her coat, and she answered before she noticed who was calling.

Big mistake. Her mother's profile pic filled her screen, and Stacy braced herself for yet another uncomfortable conversation.

"Hi, Mom." Stacy pushed the closet closed and headed to her bedroom. If she was going to pack, getting out of work clothes was a must. "More lectures on how I'm screwing up my life?"

Her mother's sigh echoed over the line. "I think we've covered that enough, don't you?"

Her tone of voice said otherwise, but Stacy wasn't in the mood to argue about it.

"I didn't call to go over the same ground we've covered multiple times already," her mother said. "I'm trying to make sure you have a plan."

Stacy sat her phone on her nightstand and stripped. "When do I not have a plan? I have been planning my entire world since middle school."

She tugged on leggings and a tank top. Packing called for comfort.

"Look, I know what finding a place is like in the city. I need to know that you've got everything covered."

Stacy rolled her eyes. Her mother and stepfather had been in the same place since they first got together. It had been at least twenty years since her mother had to consider housing.

"What's this really about, Mom?"

Another long sigh. "Are you going to come to Easter?"

That explained her mother's strange talk about plans. She rarely got straight to any point, preferring to come at you sideways, seemingly from out of the blue.

"I wasn't planning to," Stacy replied. "I mean, really? After the whole Christmas thing, and her refusal to even talk to me? And now the apartment?"

Her mother's 'tsk' sounded like a gunshot in Stacy's head. It was the sound of disapproval and disappointment and it echoed from childhood.

"It might have helped had you apologized for your behavior at Christmas."

Stacy laughed. She couldn't have held it in had she tried. "I tried," she said quietly. "Grand-mère wanted to know if I'd changed my mind about going back to school. When I said no, she hung up on me."

"She only wants what's best for you," her mother said. The same refrain Stacy had heard all her life. The only time her mother had fought back had been ice-skating—she hadn't been able to pursue that dream as a child, but she enabled Stacy to.

"No, Mom," Stacy replied. "She wants what she wants—it has nothing to do with what might be right for me."

Again with the 'tsk', only this time, it didn't sound so loud. "Well, you're wrong, but you've always been like this."

That was the final straw. Stacy rubbed a hand over her face and bit her tongue, but it didn't stop the tide. "What happened to 'you can be anything you want to be' and 'be true to yourself'? Huh? Look, I'm sorry I have somehow failed to mold myself into whatever it is Grand-mère thinks I should be, but..." She stopped.

There was no point. They'd beaten this topic into the ground time and time again. The only things Stacy could say that might get through to her mother would be hurtful, and she had no desire to be that person. There was enough of that in her family already.

"It doesn't matter," Stacy said. "Maybe this is for the best. I've been enjoying all the perks of this family while trying to get out from under Grand-mère's ridiculous expectations and conditions."

She straightened up as if someone had removed a weight from her shoulders. "That was my choice and maybe my mistake, but she took care of that for me. I'm done, and if going it entirely on my own is the cost of that, well, I'm more than happy to pay it. So, no, I won't be at Easter. Thanks for asking me, though."

Stacy barely heard her mother's goodbye. She tapped her phone off and stared at the empty box. She had to make sense of what she was taking and what she was storing, and she had a little over three weeks to do it.

All while trying to find a way out of whatever professional pit she had landed herself in and navigating the strange complex emotions she had over Luke. She sighed as memories from last weekend flooded her mind.

He was sweet and amazing and the best lover she'd ever had. Her body clenched in recollection of his hands on her and the way he laid claim to every part of her body. All those same parts wanted her to go to bed, pull out her vibrator and relive those memories. But that damn box wasn't going to pack itself.

Besides, Luke was just a boy toy. He wasn't long-term material. Not for her, at least. That thought didn't sit right. It chaffed and burned in her stomach.

She jumped as her phone buzzed with an incoming text. She was tempted to ignore it, but she glanced at her screen, then snatched up the phone when she saw Luke's name.

Dunno why, but something told me to reach out to you and say hi. So…hi. Maybe I'm missing your company this weekend. I know I've said it, but I really appreciate the way you gave yourself to me last week.

The burning changed to butterflies bouncing around. That and warmth spreading to points south, beckoning her to satisfy the thoughts she'd just been having. This is what she got for not masturbating all week or finding someone far more local and easy to get to. Not that any of that mattered — she'd been too busy and too tired to even feel horny. Until she thought about Luke.

Stacy sent a kissy face emoji then started typing.

I keep thinking about that. I really enjoyed it. More, please?

She hoped he'd get the hint. Maybe some naughty pictures or sexting would get her head in a better place.

So, my high-powered financial woman likes to be spanked. What did you want more of?

The heat that had spread turned into a muscle clench and suddenly Stacy couldn't care less about packing. She headed to her bedroom and found her vibrator. She suspected she was going to need it.

She laid on her bed and typed.

All of it.

She wriggled out of her clothes and arranged herself on the bed, then snapped a picture that perfectly highlighted her breasts and hit send.

Good to know. You really seemed to enjoy something in your ass.

She sucked in a breath. It hadn't been the first time a guy had done that. She'd done anal with former partners. She'd never been all that impressed. Luke was something different. It had just been his thumb, but it made her want all of him.

That thought brought another involuntary muscle clench as she tried to imagine handling the size of him. She didn't know how to respond to his last message. Was he hoping for confirmation?

I did.

A smiling devil emoji came back almost instantly, followed by the little dots that said he was typing. They stopped, then started, then stopped again. An agonizing minute ticked by before a new message appeared.

Nice pic. Looks like you want something. What are you craving, Stacy? Remember, I like it when you get explicit.

She should have known he'd go that route. She'd hoped he'd get the hint and it seemed like he had, but instead of running with it himself, he was going to make her spell it out. Stacy had never asked for that in her life. It had always been something a guy suggested when she was on her period or something like that.

I'm not sure I could handle you.

Her phone rang and she thumbed it open the second she saw Luke's name.

"You've been thinking about this, haven't you?"

His voice was low and rich, and it sent shivers down her spine.

"Yes," she replied, and it was far more breathy than she'd planned. She was rewarded by his throaty chuckle. She could almost see his eyes light up and his lips curl into that lopsided smile.

"Lots of lube, lots of warm-up and lots of patience," he said. "We don't have to rush it. But you do have to tell me." There was more than a hint of command in that statement. "Tell me what you want me to do to you."

Am I really going to say it? Can I?

Her phone buzzed and an image popped up. Luke's hand wrapped around the base of his shaft. Straight-up dick pics weren't normally her thing, but his made her want to lick the screen.

"Tell me where you want this cock," Luke commanded. His words triggered a rush of wetness as her body told her mind to quit fighting it.

"In my ass," she replied, whispering the words.

He let out a low groan. "Good girl. I want you to touch yourself while I tell you everything I plan to do to your beautiful body. I want to hear you call my name tonight."

Stacy thumbed her vibrator on. This man was magic, that was all there was to it.

Luke's voice became silk in her ears — smooth and soft and seductive as he told her how he'd kiss her all over and what he'd do with his lips and tongue and teeth. She was on the verge of an orgasm by the time he got around to talking about sliding inside her and the idea of taking his dick in her ass pushed her over the edge.

"Good girl," he said. "We should have done video for that."

They talked for a few minutes, but it was getting late, and Luke had an early morning, so Stacy reluctantly said goodnight. Tempting as it was to simply curl up under her blankets and sleep, there was an empty box on her dining table, and she needed to do something about moving forward with the rest of her life.

Chapter Thirty-One

Luke, Saturday, March 20

Two weeks of warm weather and sunshine meant even with snow machines going full blast, the snowpack was on the anemic side. Luke slushed his way down the easiest run. He came to a stop at the end a few feet from where Cat stood and wiped mixed snow and mud from his pants.

"You were right to call it," he said. "I think last week was the end of good skiing. This is…"

"Yuck," Cat finished for him. "Well, it is the first day of spring. The melt is a little earlier than we'd hoped, but not a big deal. Let's go ahead and figure on taking down the machines next week."

She pulled out her phone and tapped the screen. Luke knew from experience she was making herself a note. The woman's organizational skills were a little intimidating.

"I don't want to push, but have you had a chance to consider the offer?" Cat arched an eyebrow at him. He had until the thirty-first to decide, but he couldn't blame her for being curious.

"I'm uh… Yeah, I have." He pulled in a long, slow breath and surveyed the slopes. There was a lot of work to be done here if they were going to expand. A year ago, if someone had told him he'd be signing on for a second year here, he'd have laughed. He never would have imagined he'd be agreeing to take on a larger role.

"You planning on telling me something here, or do I have to wait for the deadline?" Cat crossed her arms and tapped her foot in the slush.

"I'd like to talk a bit more about what that operations role entails."

He'd been rolling the idea around, never letting his brain really settle into it, but saying it out loud felt good. Maybe Erik was right. It was time to let go of the past.

Cat whipped out her phone again and tapped in another note. "Added to the agenda for next week. Meanwhile, take it easy this weekend. Stacy's visiting, isn't she?"

If she ever gets here. It was nine and Stacy hadn't sent a text saying she was on her way.

"Yeah," he replied. "Work ran late last night, so she'll be up sometime today."

Cat tipped her head to the side and gave him a penetrating look that made him squirm a little. Then she flashed a bright smile. "Well, if you two don't make it out of your cabin, say hello to her for me." She waved and headed toward the house. He shut the lift down and hung the sign indicating the runs were closed.

Cat had said they'd keep the seasonal employees on till the end of the month. It was time to shift everyone from dealing with guests to dealing with shutting the operation down. Equipment needed to be cleaned and stored. They'd have to inspect and catalog everything and make lists of what needed to be repaired or replaced.

Things he'd given little thought to at other places but here were part of the job. Now that he'd said a sort of yes to the operations job, that was even more true. He made his way to the mess hall and stowed his gear.

Top on the to do list – get a proper base set up.

If they were going to expand, it would mean a full office, adequate storage, and so much more. His phone buzzed, and he snatched it from his pocket to find a text from Stacy.

Finally on the road. Sorry for the delay. Long story. Can't wait to see you.

He sent a thumbs-up then joined the crew dismantling the tubing hill. Normally, he'd expect that to be the last thing to close, but with as slushy as things had gotten, he wouldn't be comfortable sending anyone down the thing.

He stayed busy till lunchtime when everyone gathered in the mess hall for the soup and sandwiches Cat had sent down. He had to stop himself from constantly checking his phone, even though he knew it would buzz if a message came in.

He hated feeling antsy and anxious like this. His phone buzzed just after one. She'd turned off the highway and would arrive by half past.

You gonna be hungry?

The kitchen was still open. He could get a sandwich and have it ready for her.

Had a late breakfast and grabbed snacks. I'm good thanks.

He hurried to his cabin and jumped in the shower. He'd already changed the sheets on the bed and tidied the place up. Tires scrunched on the gravel outside as he was pulling a flannel over his undershirt.

Then she was inside and in his arms. Her lips warm and giving under his, and her hands roaming his body. Luke inhaled her scent, filling himself with her.

Part of him knew this was temporary, but how could he ever go back to casual flings after her? No one else in his life had made him feel the way Stacy did. Maybe they could find a way to make it work.

"I missed you," he said, breathing the words against the soft skin of her neck. "You're later than usual today."

Her body tensed in his arms, then she pulled back, her lips turned down and her forehead furrowed.

"It's a long story," she said. "Short version—I normally borrow a car from my folks. Today, they said no. So I had to get a rental."

Her tone said there was more to the story, and also that she didn't want to discuss it. She kissed him again and his world narrowed to the feel of her lips and the touch of her hands.

Sliding into her was pure bliss. Seeing her lost in pleasure was better than any high. They had a little over twenty-four hours together. He'd make sure the memories would be enough to sustain them both.

Hours later, Luke brushed a lock of hair from Stacy's face as she slept. Golden light filtered through the window, and he leaned against the headboard. Her hair splayed across a pillow now smudged with traces of her pink lipstick.

Thinking about how that smudge got there brought a big smile to his face.

He should wake her up so they could shower and grab dinner, but he lingered. It wasn't just that he didn't want to disturb her sleep. He didn't want this moment to end. Ever.

Realistically, they had no future. For years, he'd been content with strictly physical relationships. Emotional entanglements were not his thing. Now, he wanted more — with Stacy, but she'd made it clear she wasn't interested in anything beyond a fling. Even if she did want more, the idea of driving in the city made him cringe. Living in one, even temporarily, was unthinkable. Her career meant living near a major financial center — and that meant a large city.

I had to go and fall for the impossible.

Stacy stretched, the sheets slid down, exposing soft skin and her perfect breasts, then her eyes popped open and fixed on him.

"I'm hungry," she said. Before he could respond, she slid down and took him in her mouth. All thoughts came to a screeching halt as every brain cell he had focused on the feel of her lips and tongue gliding over his cock.

The golden light had faded to sunset by the time they finished and stepped into the shower. He wrapped his arms around Stacy's waist and held her close. This was heaven.

Chapter Thirty-Two

Stacy, Sunday, March 21

"We have to be careful with the drone now that the owlets are here." Luke tipped the screen so Stacy could see the image of the nest. One large bird sat along the edge, but she couldn't make out any baby owls in the mess of feathers and twigs.

Luke zoomed in and pointed at what could have been a ball of fluff. "There's one," he said. "The other might be hiding."

Stacy squinted at the screen. It was hard to believe that lump was a baby owl. "Last time you were able to get in closer. What changed?"

Luke pulled the drone back and set it on a return path to them before turning to her. "The male attacked a drone when I got too close one day. That was right about the time the owlets hatched, so he probably saw the drone as a potential threat."

The image of one of the giant demon birds taking down a drone sent unpleasant shivers through her. Those things had beaks and claws. They hunted small animals.

"We got some great footage of the attack," Luke continued.

Stacy waved her hands at him. "Don't show me. That bird creeped me out enough just sitting there, staring at me and hooting."

Luke chuckled. "We're in their territory."

That was exactly why she liked her nature in small, controllable doses. She could admire the beauty and respect the ebb and flow of the world without being that up close and personal, thanks.

Spring had definitely started—bright flowers bloomed along the edges of the meadow and the trees had the pale green cast of emerging buds. While there was snow on the ground, none clung to the branches.

Luke squatted to pack up the drone. His golden hair shone in the warm sun. She was used to seeing him outside with a hat on, but today, his hair was tied in a loose knot. He'd stripped off his jacket and his broad shoulders strained the seams of the gray flannel he wore. Luke glanced at her, and his lips parted in a grin that lit his face.

He is one truly beautiful man.

He seemed more like a Viking than ever. Maybe once the weather warmed up, she could convince him to do a little dress up and role play. The idea of Luke standing over her bare chested, with the sun glinting off his muscled arms, had her considering whether or not the rock she sat on would work for sex.

"What put that expression on your face?" Luke slid a finger under her chin and tipped her face to him. His hair created a halo in the sunlight, and Stacy bit her lip to keep from asking him to fuck her.

How can I want sex again? We just did that this morning. And countless times yesterday.

Her body ached from the activity. He'd left fingerprint bruises on her hips, and she knew she'd left a few scratches and bite marks on his shoulders. Still, she wanted him again. Right now. Never mind that they were outside.

So much for restraint.

She grabbed the collar of his shirt and pulled him closer. "What's the likelihood of getting caught out here?"

His eyebrows furrowed and for a split second, she worried he didn't get her meaning. Then his lopsided grin peeked out. "Virtually zero," he replied. "Did you have something in mind?"

She wanted him, but she didn't want to be the aggressor. *Well, that's new.* Maybe it was the whole Viking thing, but she wanted Luke to demand what he wanted. *How do I tell him that?*

She pulled in a shaky breath and looked up at him, trying to find the words to convey her desires. If she could give voice to what she wanted, Luke would meet her needs. She knew that just like she knew the sun would come up every morning.

"Ah," he said, drawing the word out in a long sigh. "My naughty girl wants to be taken."

His words burned through her like some erotic fire. She clenched her fingers against the rock and swallowed. "Maybe?"

Luke leaned in close and tipped his head. "I need more than a maybe if that's what you want."

Her nipples hardened at the tone in his voice. "Yes," she whispered.

Luke's grin spread, and he stepped to where his pack sat on another rock. He pulled out a small blanket and stood back, his eyes roving over her and the rocky outcrop where they had propped their skis and stowed packs. He nodded and laid the blanket down on a shelf of rock about his hip height.

Things had been heating up and now he was all calm and methodical. Luke turned to her and any confusion she had disappeared at the look in his eyes. Here was the conquering Viking she'd sensed lurking behind his sweet, Minnesota-nice exterior.

His was the face of a man about to claim a hard-won prize that might bite him if he wasn't careful. Luke stepped close, and in an instant, his hand caught in the hair at the base of her neck and held tight.

"Use your safe word if you want me to stop," he growled. "Fight me if you'd like. In fact, please do."

He flashed a wicked grin before lowering his head to claim her mouth in a bruising kiss. Stacy breathed into it for a moment, then his words registered — 'fight me'. She pulled her head away and shoved her hands against his chest, but the fingers in her hair clenched tighter.

His other hand captured one of her wrists and, despite her struggling against him, he hauled her to her feet and held her against his body. His next kiss was no more gentle than the first, but he stopped before she managed to get her free hand between them to push him off.

Luke spun her so her back was to him, and she twisted, trying to get out of his grasp, but he held her fast. She was not a petite girl, and she was physically strong, but Luke had no trouble restraining her. The whole being taken thing had never been her fantasy before, but Luke was quickly changing her mind.

Luke wrestled her to the rock where he'd spread the blanket and pressed her down. He held both of her hands over her head then bent over to whisper in her ear.

"Is this what you wanted?" His free hand slid over her hip to her belt and quickly loosened it. Stacy struggled, but he slapped her ass and told her to stay still. He got her pants unbuttoned and unzipped. "I expect an answer. Is this what you wanted?"

Fuck yes! Everything in her cried out as if this were the thing she'd been needing all her life but never gotten before now.

"Give me an answer, or I stop," he said. "We can play this game harder, but we need to have a much deeper conversation first."

Stacy bit her lip. This was what she'd been fantasizing.

"Yes," she answered, her voice raspy with lust.

His answering growl sent pleasant shivers through her. "To be clear, my naughty girl, I plan on getting your pants down, fingering your beautiful pussy until you come on my hand, then fucking you so hard we'll both be feeling it for days."

She nearly came at his words. She managed to strangle out a "yes, please" before Luke got her pants shoved to her knees. He let go of her wrists but tangled that hand in her hair to hold her down. His other hand slid between her legs.

"Baby, you're wet," he crooned into her ear. "You like this." His fingers slid into her, and his thumb grazed her clit. "Oh, you like this a lot. Such a naughty girl."

True to his word, Luke stroked his fingers inside her, finger-fucking her in slow, hard thrusts until she was panting and pressing her ass back against him. His thumb stroked harder, and she trembled with the first spasms of an orgasm.

"That's it," he said. "Come for me."

Another stroke and she tipped over the edge. He kept going until her entire body shook. The sound of his belt buckle had her trying to lift her head, but he pinned her to the blanket.

"Stay down," he instructed. Crinkling sounds told her he'd put on a condom. His hand coiled in her hair again, and he pulled up until she arched and lifted herself off the rock.

"Tell me what you want."

She wanted him. In any and every way possible. She wanted the passion and caring Luke brought to everything.

"Fuck me," she cried out. "I want you inside me."

Luke pressed the head of his dick into her wetness and pushed. Stacy gasped at the pressure, but he kept pushing until he was buried in her. Even tired and sore, her body welcomed him, and she arched her back to give him deeper access.

Luke chuckled and tightened his grip in her hair. His next stroke was hard and sharp, driving her hips into the blanket-covered rock. He slid his free hand between her legs and teased her clit as he pounded into her in a punishing rhythm.

Stacy called out his name as she came again and again.

"You wanted to be taken," he growled into her ear. "You like getting fucked hard and rough."

There was only one thing that would make this better. "Please..."

She couldn't bring herself to say it. Luke stopped and pressed her down into the blanket. "Don't move."

He slid out of her and rummaged in his pack, then dropped a small bag on the rock next to her. His hands caressed her exposed ass, and Stacy hissed in a breath.

"Tell me where you want this cock," he said. Memories of their phone sex sent a new rush of wetness and Stacy moaned. Something clicked, then the feel of lube hit her ass.

Luke slid one finger into her pussy and his thumb pressed against the entrance to her ass.

"You said you wanted to be taken," he repeated. "Well, I want all of you. Every. Single. Bit." His thumb pressed in as he spoke. He took his time, stroking her clit as he slowly worked another finger into her ass.

She was rocking against him, panting and speaking gibberish she was so close to another orgasm, then he stopped, and she felt the head of his dick where his fingers had just been.

"Tell me," he commanded.

Stacy swallowed hard. "Please fuck my ass." It came out as a plea, barely a whisper. Luke growled and sank one hand into her hair and clenched. Then he pushed forward, and Stacy gasped.

"Relax and breathe," he said. "I'll go slow."

True to his word, Luke moved inch by inch, easing himself into her until she was ready to scream and demand he fuck her already. He added more lube, then he was in and sliding in and out. His other hand stroked her clit until Stacy's hips rocked in rhythm.

She'd never had anal like this. It had always been about the guy getting off. Luke made it all about her as his fingers worked magic on her pussy.

"That's it, baby," he said. "Fuck yourself with my cock. When you're ready, I'll take over."

The pleasure built until her fingers clenched into the blanket. She wanted, no, she needed it harder. Luke chuckled behind her.

"There it is," he said. "Hold on tight, baby."

He let go of her hair and braced himself against the rock. His other hand cupped her pussy, trapping her clit between his fingers. His next thrust gave her everything she wanted, and she arched to meet him.

"Yes!" The word came out loud and clear and Luke responded with another deep thrust. The next orgasm ripped through her like a tornado. She barely registered Luke calling out her name as he came.

His touch was gentle as he helped her roll over on the blanket. She jumped at the sensation of a warm, wet cloth on her.

"How…? What…?" She craned her head and caught his wink as he dropped the washcloth into a plastic bag and recapped a small thermos bottle. "You planned this."

He feigned a look of innocence. "We'd talked about it, so I was prepared for the possibility."

He'd somehow read her like a book, giving her exactly what she wanted and needed, even when she couldn't find the right words to ask for it. There was no settling when it came to Luke.

Except there is.

That was like a dash of ice in her face. Their relationship might be perfect, the sex out of the world, but Luke would never fit in the city, and she had no desire to fit outside of it.

They weren't anything more than a fun fling. He was meant to be just a boy toy, and she had to find a way to break it off before she got herself hurt. She suspected it was already too late for that precaution.

Chapter Thirty-Three

Luke, Sunday, March 21

Luke tossed Stacy's bag into the trunk of her rental car. The past twenty-four hours had been magic, and he didn't want to wait weeks for a repeat. He knew her schedule was heavy, but he had to ask.

"When will we have time again?"

Stacy dropped her purse in the passenger seat and turned to face him but didn't meet his eyes. "I've got to finish packing and get moved. And storage. And unpacking. And..." She shook her head and looked up at him. "Probably not before the middle of the month."

Three weeks. Maybe four. *Fuck. Wait, moving?*

Something must have registered on his face because Stacy's expression morphed from sad to mad in a split second.

"Unless you plan on helping me move, that's the way it is."

He wasn't prepared for her harsh tone. He was even less prepared for her suggestion. "I'm not much of a city guy," he said. "I'd be more likely to hire someone to help you move. And this is the first you've mentioned moving."

The second the words came out he knew they were wrong. Her mad face set even tighter, and she rolled her eyes.

"You don't owe me anything," she said. "Like I haven't already paid for movers. I think I'm in a better position to do that than you are."

What? Fuck. This was not how this conversation was supposed to go.

Luke put his tongue between his teeth so he wouldn't say something he'd further regret, but Stacy didn't back down.

"I'm busting my ass to save my job," she said, her voice rising enough that Luke cast a glance around to make sure no one would overhear. Unfortunately, Stacy noticed.

"Don't worry," she continued. "I won't make a scene or cause problems at your job. Not that it should matter. You've worked at plenty of places over the years. What's one more, right?"

He stuffed his hands in his pockets. Whatever had triggered this had very little to do with him and everything to do with all the rest of her life that she refused to talk to him about. Like the fact that she was moving, or that her vague complaints about her job were more than just complaints. That alone should have told him about his non-existent place in her world, but he'd gone and fallen in love.

"I'm sorry," he said, hoping to smooth things over a bit. "I don't mean to be pushy. I enjoy our time together and I look forward to the next. Whenever that happens to be."

Stacy threw up her hands. "I don't know when I'll have time again."

Luke knew that line. It was code for 'this is getting deeper than I expected and I need distance'. Maybe, like him, she wanted more. Maybe it was that she sensed the shift in his feelings. Either way, it didn't matter. He could give her that space and hope the good between them was enough to bring her back.

"It's all good," he said. "We both knew what we were getting into here."

He held an arm out and Stacy stepped into his embrace. Her kiss was bittersweet, and Luke savored the way she felt in his arms.

"Lemme know when you make it home, yeah?" He dropped his forehead to hers and waited for her nod. "When you've got time, we'll figure something out."

She nodded again, but when she stepped away, she didn't look him in the eye. She kissed him lightly, then slid into the driver's seat. Luke waited until her car was out of sight down the drive before he turned to his cabin.

The last thing he wanted to do was go inside where Stacy's soap and shampoo and perfume still hung in the air. Where the rumpled sheets reminded him of how they'd spent the last few hours together. He sure as shit didn't want to unpack the bag he'd taken with them this morning—the one with a blanket and lube, and all the things they'd want if things went...well, the way they went.

Fuck it.

He pushed through the door and left it wide open, then opened all the windows. Hard stuff first—the bed—sheets in the laundry. He didn't stop. He gathered towels, the blanket and his clothes from their morning skiing and stuffed those in the basket to be washed next.

"You planning on turning into a polar bear?" Erik called from the doorway. "I know it's spring but it's not that warm."

Luke's brother stopped in his tracks, his head turning side to side as he surveyed the cabin. Erik closed the door, then went around closing windows.

"Light a candle or burn some incense. It works better," he said with a wink. "I take it you and Stacy ended?"

Luke sank into a chair and shrugged. "There was never anything to end."

Erik rolled his eyes. "Yeah, that's a load of bullshit. Try again."

"Fine. I'd call it more of a soft break up than an ending. I've done it often enough myself I know the tricks. Not that I mind the company right now, but what the fuck are you doing here?"

Luke stopped and took in the six pack now sitting in the middle of his table. "So, I wasn't the only one who had a shitty day?"

He pulled out two beers and handed one to his brother. Erik twisted the cap off and took a long pull.

"Andre and his ex got back together."

Luke sucked in a breath. Erik had seemed happy, and everything appeared to be stable.

"Ouch," he replied, then cracked open his own beer. His issues could wait. He'd known what he was getting into with Stacy—he just hadn't planned on falling for her. Erik, on the other hand, had gone into this relationship thinking long term.

"Shoulda seen it coming," Erik continued. "But... whatever. Tell me what the fuck happened with Stacy."

Luke laughed. "Nothing to tell. I caught feelings when it was supposed to be casual. First time for everything. But you didn't come out here with a six pack to talk about my shit. So, spill."

His kid brother needed to talk, and Luke would damn well listen. Besides, it took his mind off his own shit show for a bit.

Chapter Thirty-Four

Stacy, Friday, April 2

The lights flickered as Stacy climbed the steps up to Union Square. She rushed the last few treads, thankful to get into the relatively fresh air outside the subway station. Normally, none of the usual subway smells bothered her, but tonight had been an exception. She chalked it up to being exhausted from a near eighty-hour work week, and she still had a six-block walk to her new place with Brit.

The move had been easy, despite her grandmother demanding she return the keys in person. Stacy had feared another lecture, but her grandmother had met her at the door, held out her hand, then slammed the door in Stacy's face as soon as she turned over the keys.

Just another opportunity to demonstrate her opinion.

Brit's apartment still smelled like her grand-mother — the sweet floral of Anaïs Anaïs and the sandalwood and patchouli incense she favored. It was an odd mix. They had cleaned the carpets and drapes, but the scents lingered. Considering the woman had lived in the apartment since the seventies, it was probably in the walls themselves.

Stacy tossed her raincoat and shoes in the hall closet and went straight to her room to change. Then she'd figure out food. Brit was out for the weekend and ordering takeout was tempting.

She had just pulled on a pair of yoga pants and an oversize shirt when her phone buzzed. She grabbed it to see who was calling and hit the answer button by mistake.

Shit. Luke's name flashed on the screen. *Double shit.*

"Hey." She should have hung up, but she'd ignored his last text, and she didn't do ghosting.

"Hey yourself." That deep voice sent her mind whirling into places she didn't want to go right now. "I figured I'd get voicemail, but I wanted to see how the move went and I dunno…talk."

A pang of something ripped through her stomach. *Guilt? Regret? Whatever.* No matter how much she liked Luke and no matter how amazing he was, she couldn't date him. She wouldn't. She had a career to get back on track, and after busting her ass all week, things seemed to be improving.

"Move was okay," she replied. No sense in being rude or mean. He hadn't done anything wrong. He wasn't the right guy for her, that was all. "Work is brutal and it's going to stay that way for a while. I just got home."

He let out a soft, low whistle. "Sounds like you need a bath and a glass of wine."

Both of those sounded magical. Then again, so did his particular brand of magic that involved his tongue and… *Stop it!* Stacy shook herself.

"Yeah, I might do that." Too late she realized the possible invite in her words. Just two weeks ago, that would have prompted a sexy exchange and maybe some pics.

"You wanna tell me about it?"

Stacy closed her eyes and fought the rising tide of arousal.

"Work, I mean," he said. His clarification did nothing to tame the fire hearing his voice had started.

"Nothing to tell," she lied. There was a lot to tell, but if she confided in Luke like a friend, it would be harder to walk away from him. And she needed to walk away. All she had to do was look at her family for the proof of why — everyone tied to Grand-mère's support.

The disastrous relationship between her mother and now absent father. She was certain her mother had married her stepfather more as a matter of convenience than out of love or passion. In the Astor family, everyone made the Grand-mère-approved choices and settled for less than they wanted.

"Yeah. I forgot. We don't talk about your work."

The note of sadness in his tone tugged at her, and she stuffed those feelings down. Love hadn't done anything good for her parents.

"I'm kinda tired," she said. She needed to do this. Needed to tell him it was over. That she couldn't come up anymore.

She'd fallen for the guy. Completely and utterly, and it was clear he felt the same. She couldn't let herself give in to that. The more she saw him, the harder it would be to let him go. Better to deal with the hurt now than later.

"Long work week, I guess," he replied. "Okay, I'll get right to it. I know this month is busy, and I am not trying to pressure you, but…" He trailed off and his sigh carried through the phone.

Stacy could see him, leaned forward, shoving a hand through his hair, then looking up at her with a ghost of a smile. *Stop it, right now!*

"Bristol Park hosts a big May Day thing," he said. "It's on a Saturday this year, so it's gonna be pretty special. I thought maybe you'd like to come spend it with me."

There it was—a yes or no situation. She could hedge and say maybe, but that was delaying the inevitable.

"I can't," she said. She didn't offer any excuse or reason.

"It's fine." His tone said it was anything but fine, not that she planned on calling him on it. She needed to pretend she didn't care about hurting him. "I'll uh… You get some rest…" Another long sigh.

"Yeah, no, I'm not fine." His voice was still soft and low, but the Minnesota accent was a little more pronounced. "I'm… Aw, fuck it, I'm gonna give it a shot here. I feel like we're…well, coulda been, something special. And I feel like you've been pulling away."

Stacy sank her teeth into her lip to keep from responding. Her heart wanted to ease the pain in his voice. Her head told her to suck it up and deal. She should have known better. She let this go too far and she needed to end it.

"Maybe I'm wrong, but I don't think so," he continued. "If there's something we need to fix, talk to me. If there's nothing to fix, and you're done, we're done, at least let me know."

There it was. All she had to do was tell him there was nothing to fix. That she was done. Luke was genuinely nice. He'd listen and he'd back off.

"You and I have different needs." It was a nice enough start. It was honest, but kind. "I'm in the city and you're way out there. I've got a career I need to focus on, and you're content to...to..." She stopped. That had gotten away from her.

"I'm not sure we're all that different," he replied, and his voice had gone cold. "Not underneath where it really matters. I've been running from myself for years, but I've found something amazing at Bristol Park. And with you."

Shit. Stacy's heart cried out, and she clenched her fists against her mouth to keep from saying "me too." That wouldn't help her achieve her goal of independence. It wouldn't help further her career.

"We never had any promises or expectations," Luke said. "We were supposed to be a fun fling. This is entirely my doing. I have one question for you, then I'll wish you the best and let you go."

Stacy braced herself. She'd heard some nasty shit from men when they were rejected. Not that Luke seemed the type.

"You said it yourself. I'm content." Silence stretched for what felt like an eternity before he continued. "I'm happy where I am. At the end of the day, I'm fulfilled."

His voice had dropped to a soft whisper.

"Are you happy?"

The question hit like a punch to the gut. Stacy ground her teeth together trying to hold back a rising tide of indignation. *How dare he? What the fuck? This is my dream.*

"I don't think it's your place to question that," she snapped. The words flew from her mouth before her brain could reel them in. "You're right, we never had any promises. I'll let you in on a little secret — among my friends, you're called the boy toy. It was fun while it lasted, but this was never meant to be long term."

Oh, why the fuck did I go there? No need to be mean. But she hadn't been able to stop the flow of words. Once she'd opened her mouth, they spewed out like vomit.

"Nice. Well, happy to have been of service," he said. His tone was crisp and professional. It was the sound of a salesclerk or server who was ready to get you out of their hair but didn't want to be rude. "Guess the rest was not what I thought it was," he continued, sounding much more like the Luke she knew and adored. "I made a promise—one question, then I'd wish you the best, so... I hope your dreams come true. You are a remarkable woman, Stacy Barclay, and I'm happy to have shared some time with you."

The phone went silent. Stacy stared at it, trying to figure out what the fuck she'd done. She'd made an art of safe breakups. A few times of guys losing their shit when they were rejected meant she'd developed some pretty strong armor and an arsenal of tools to let men down gently so as not to bruise their egos.

She'd failed utterly with Luke, and yet he'd still been nice in the end.

I need ice cream.

She texted Kylie. Like a true friend, forty minutes later, Kylie came in bearing bags of Chinese takeout and another bag filled with quarts of ice cream and bags of cookies.

"Gods bless the bodega near my place," Kylie said as she dumped a dripping bag of ice into the sink. "I don't think this stuff would've survived the subway otherwise."

She ushered Stacy to the dining table and stuck an opened box of *lo mein* in her hands. Stacy pulled apart her chopsticks, then looked up at her friend.

"Did you get...?"

Kylie slid a small plastic tub of chili crisp across the table. "You are so weird. Ever since you dated that one dude, you've gotta have the spicy shit."

Stacy dumped the spicy oil and chili mixture into her noodles and stirred. "Don't knock it."

Everything came out between bites of noodles and the crispy perfection of the crab rangoons. By the time Stacy crumbled a couple of speculoos into her salted caramel ice cream, she'd unloaded the whole story, including her own confused feelings for Luke.

"You're not gonna like me," Kylie said. "I just want to remind you that I showed up with noodles and ice cream. Okay? Remember that."

Stacy laughed and rolled her eyes but internally braced for something hard to hear.

"He's right." Kylie stabbed her spoon into her tub of rainbow sherbet and took another bite before she continued. "You're so focused on a career you chose years ago, and on getting out from under your grandmother's thumb, that you've lost sight of what actually makes you happy."

Stacy opened her mouth to protest, then closed it. She wasn't sure she agreed with Kylie, but there was some truth there, and that meant it was time for some introspection.

After more ice cream.

Chapter Thirty-Five

Luke, Monday, April 19

Spring had sprung at Bristol Park. Flowers bloomed everywhere and the trees were dusted with bright green, new leaves. The transformation from snow-covered and stark to teeming with life never ceased to bring a smile to Luke's face.

A team of surveyors and engineers scaled the slopes, determining where to install a second lift. Cat was around somewhere, probably talking to the experts in resort architecture. The property was amazing, and had a lot in place already, but to expand and modernize, Cat had wisely called in help.

Luke checked the last item off his list and closed the storage pod. The past few weeks had been a flurry of activity as he and the ski staff packed all the equipment into portable storage sheds. The end of the mess hall seemed empty without the clutter of desks, equipment racks and everything else that had made up his day-to-day for two seasons now.

"Looks weird, doesn't it?" Nate shifted the wriggling eight-month-old baby in his arms.

"End of season is always a little strange," Luke replied. "I just swept in here. I won't say it's clean, but I don't think there's anything that'll hurt him."

Brody had started crawling at five months, and since then, there was no stopping the kid. He wanted to be moving. All the time. Nate shrugged and sat the baby on the floor. Within seconds, the kid started exploring this new environment.

"Last year we shut everything down and packed up the computers. This..." Luke waved his hand at the wide-open space. "I'll be honest, it also feels a little weird to be closing out a second winter and hanging around."

Nate cocked his head to the side. "Good weird?"

"Yeah." Luke had been tempted to leave after the thing with Stacy, but that hadn't lasted long. Instead, he'd found even more reasons to stay and had accepted the contract for the operations role. "Very good."

Brody squealed and moved with a purpose toward something along the wall. Luke swooped in and snagged a battery he'd somehow missed in his sweeping. Nate tossed him a plastic key ring, and Luke handed it over to the baby, who immediately stuffed it in his mouth.

"Teething, huh?" Luke pocketed the battery and smiled at the chubby baby. The kid had Nate's black curls, but Cat's bright green eyes. Cute, if you were into babies. Luke wasn't sure on that front. He and Becca had talked about kids in the vague way two nineteen-year-olds could. It was always an 'eventually' — after college, once their careers were settled, that sort of thing. Since then, a baby was the last thing he wanted, to the point he'd considered getting snipped.

"You're good with kids," Nate commented. "I don't mean just Brody."

Luke shrugged. "I was the big brother. Erik's the closest. I was twelve when my youngest sister was born. So I spent my teens babysitting. Plus, this gig? I started off manning the kiddie slopes."

The baby let out a sudden cry that echoed in the empty space. Nate scooped the kid up and smiled. "Guess it's his lunchtime. Come on up to the house in about an hour. We can start talking May Day."

Luke nodded and went to figure out lunch. He could go to the kitchen, but he'd already discovered his fellow staff asked where Stacy was this week. He cleaned up then scrambled some eggs with a little ham and toast. He may not like eating first thing in the morning, but he did love breakfast foods.

Up at the house, he found Cat and Nate in the kitchen with the baby monitor on the counter between them.

"Nap time," Cat explained. "You want a soda? Water? Coffee?"

Luke shook his head and hooked out a stool. Cat had her ever present tablet and a stack of papers spread out around her.

"Most of the organizational stuff is done," Nate said. "We got all that in place months ago. We've already got staff and volunteers."

Luke braced himself for whatever was coming next. He'd signed on for a job that included a whole lot of 'other duties as assigned' and he was fine with that. He suspected this was one of those moments.

Cat handed over the tablet. As expected, a detailed spreadsheet outlined everything in the week leading up to May Day and continued for a few days after — until all cleanup was done, and all rented or borrowed equipment returned.

"We figured we'd let you have first choice of what you wanted to help with," Cat said.

Luke scanned the list again with renewed interest. He skipped over the maypole activities, then saw something interesting.

"I can do the kite building station," he said. "Need a couple extras to help with the flying. And I'll bring hotdish for the potluck."

Cat's eyebrows went up, and Nate gave him a curious look.

"Sounds great." Cat regained her normal composure and tapped the screen. "Just put in what you're bringing."

Luke was confused for a moment, then remembered not everyone understood hotdish. "It's a Minnesota thing," he said. "It's a casserole — usually ground or chopped meat, cream of something soup, some veggies and tater tots or mashed potatoes on top. Just… hotdish."

He filled in two slots on the list and handed the tablet to Cat.

"Wonderful, thanks. Maybe a sensitive subject, and feel free to not answer — what's up with Stacy?"

Luke coughed at the unexpected turn in the conversation. *Here's where the shit hits the fan.* Except that didn't make sense, and Cat didn't seem like an angry employer, but a concerned friend.

"Uh… Well…" He cleared his throat. How to summarize what had gone down between him and Stacy? "We were a casual, temporary thing."

That seemed like the easiest and nicest way to say it. That is, until Nate barked out a laugh, and Cat fixed him with an 'oh really' expression that rivaled anything his mother had ever leveled at him.

"We both knew it going in," Luke said, not sure why he was being so straight forward with his damn bosses.

Cat's expression softened. "You caught feelings."

Luke nodded. Hearing it from someone else made it feel even more miserable. Ten years of no emotional entanglements. He'd never been tempted to get involved, not once.

"You know, the city isn't that far," Cat continued. "You could visit."

The idea of driving into the city turned Luke's veins to ice. Nate slid a cup of coffee in front of him, then handed one to Cat before he sat down. Luke sipped the scalding brew and tried to wrap his head around the idea of being in a city.

"I kinda actively avoid cities whenever possible," he said. "Even traveling to different resorts, I'll choose smaller airports when I can. It's uh…"

He pulled in a slow shuddering breath. "In college, my girlfriend was killed in a carjacking in the Twin Cities—Minneapolis Saint Paul." He added the last when he remembered not everyone spoke Minnesotan. "I've spent the last ten years numb and avoiding anything that makes me not numb."

He stared at the dark liquid in his cup. His hands were steady, at least there was that. Usually when he thought about this shit, he had to fight the shakes.

"But even if I managed to convince myself to go, Stacy would have to want me there," he said. "And she doesn't seem so inclined."

She'd made her lack of continued interest clear. He suspected she had feelings and was running from them, but that didn't change the fact that she'd spelled it out—he was a toy and meant to be discarded when she was done playing. Whether she meant it or not didn't matter. She had ended things between them. Continuing to pursue her now would go against everything he was.

"You the type to need to stay busy, or are you more the 'disappear for a few days to get your head on straight' type?"

Leave it to Nate to boil it down that simply. The hell of it was, Luke didn't know. He did know what he was inclined to do.

"Planning on marking a lot of trails this week," he said. "I've gotta go over the email from the guys about the mess hall renovations—make sure it's got everything we need for a ski shack."

He stopped when he caught their amused faces. "Guess I'm the stay busy type."

"I'll share the master project list with you," Cat said. "If you see something on there you're comfortable handling, put your initials on it. No pressure. Take on as much, or as little, as you feel like."

She cast a glance at Nate and a soft smile played on her lips. "We've all been there."

A soft cry erupted from the baby monitor, and Nate pushed back from the counter. "I'll get the little tyrant. Safe bet he needs a diaper change." He dropped a kiss on Cat's head and turned for the door, then stopped with his hand on the jamb.

"Abbeydon tends to attract folks who are at a crossroads. Sometimes it's one they can't even see. Everybody who comes here needs something—but it can take digging to find it, and it isn't always comfortable."

Cat gathered the empty cups and deposited them in the sink. "He's right," she said. Her eyes turned to the window and the view down the hill to the first row of cabins. "This place can show you who you really are. I know I changed for the better after coming here."

She wiped her hands on a towel and tossed a baggie at him. Luke caught it easily then looked down. *Brownies?*

"I was up late with the baby and baked. Enjoy."

He held the bag up in mock salute. "I will. Thank you. For everything."

He was almost out the door when Cat spoke again.

"Luke, I'm glad you're here," she said. "This is also a place of healing."

He had no response to that. Until recently, he'd have said he didn't need to heal. He was perfectly fine going along just the way he was.

Now he realized how wrong he'd been.

Chapter Thirty-Six

Stacy, Friday, April 30

If digital clocks could tick, this one's hands would be going backward. Stacy had finalized the big audits, then she'd been given a portfolio and told to create a five-year plan for the client. She'd sucked in a happy breath when she saw the client's name — Abbot.

Maybe they were giving her back the account.

Mr. Smith had her final proposal and was supposed to review it with her this afternoon. If all went well, this would get her on track and working with high-profile clients again. She could make associate by the end of the year if she played her cards right.

She practically leapt to her feet when the call came in to report to Mr. Smith's office. Stacy forced her expression to remain neutral, even though she felt like walking on air. She wanted to text Kylie and Brit and make plans to celebrate. She wanted to text Luke and share the news with him.

Stop it. She'd managed to go all week without thinking about him — much. Mostly because she worked over eighty hours and was exhausted by the time she got home.

Sam Smith's secretary waved Stacy into the office and her budding smile froze. Chad sat opposite Mr. Smith and the two were laughing. They looked up as if she'd interrupted some private moment, then her mentor cleared his throat and gestured Stacy to the other seat.

He held up the portfolio and smiled. Some of her nerves quieted. "This is good work."

The band that had clamped over her chest loosened a notch.

"I've assigned the Abbot's account to Higgins," Mr. Smith said, and the band suddenly constricted so hard that Stacy forgot how to breathe for a moment.

"I'm also reassigning you and redefining your duties," he continued. "You have a good eye for detail and do excellent work at matching clients with an ideal long-term plan that meets their needs and comfort zone."

Wait, what? He's praising my work? She was able to take a full breath. *Then why did the account go to Chad?*

"Starting Monday, you'll report to Chad Higgins and Peter Murray as their assistant."

All the air exited Stacy's lungs in a whoosh. *Chad Higgins is to be my boss? Oh hell no. No. This is not happening.*

Their mouths were moving, but Stacy had no clue what either of the men was saying. She hadn't agreed to this. It was completely the opposite of her goals.

"Come in an hour early on Monday, and we'll get it all straightened out with HR."

Mr. Smith spoke as if this were a done deal, but he hadn't given her anything to sign. This was a major change in job duties, and in supervisor. She could still fight this. There had to be a way.

"I look forward to working with you," Chad stood and offered his hand. Stacy shook on reflex. He leaned closer. "No more early Fridays." His voice was so low it wouldn't carry, not that she believed Mr. Smith would care.

It was official. She was well and truly fucked here career-wise. She forced a bright smile and pulled her hand out of Chad's grip.

"I look forward to discussing this opportunity with HR on Monday."

She didn't ask permission to leave. She didn't excuse herself. She turned and walked out. She would have slammed the door, but the office had a highly unsatisfying pneumatic thing that closed softly.

What the fuck was that? She hurried to the ladies' room, checked there was no one else there and locked the door. Then she texted Kylie and Brit. Replies came back almost instantly.

Jump ship. That was Kylie.

This has reached complaint territory. Call HR right now and request a meeting on Monday morning and do not sign anything. That was Brit.

Hands shaking, she pulled up the contact info for the firm's human resources department. Naturally, it went to voicemail. She left a message that she hoped was coherent and hung up.

"*Are you happy?*"

Luke's question echoed in her mind, or maybe it was whispering through the room like some strange ghost-like thing. Tomorrow was May Day and a whole festival at Bristol Park. She shoved that thought aside and texted her friends.

Message left for HR. I dunno what I'm gonna do on Monday. I do know tonight I'm drinking. You in?

She splashed water on her face and looked in the mirror. Relatively normal. So long as you didn't pay attention to her eyes. Even to her, they seemed haunted and empty.

She propped herself on the sink counter and pulled up the company directory. She scrolled through to find every woman listed — there weren't that many. She knew there were other women on staff, but they were secretaries and — fuck Mr. Smith and Chad Higgins and, why not, Peter Murray — assistants. The ones with their names in the company directory were the ones who interested her. Those were women who had, or should have, power.

She pocketed her phone and exited the bathroom with a purpose. She was going to take a tour to see the workspace of every woman who held a major role in the company. She found the one female vice president in a small, open office that was not much better than a cubicle. The four women who worked as associates shared an office, while their male counterparts were two to an office.

The one female attorney didn't maintain office space in the building — she worked at a firm down the street. Within the company, everywhere she looked, women were stuck at a less senior level than the men.

The few successful women lived their entire lives in the office. She knew those stories — she'd been here long enough to hear them. Most had been divorced more than once. So had most of the men, but the difference was, no one judged the men for it. At least not out loud.

This was her future here.

Could she fight it? Sure. It wouldn't do much good.

"Are you happy?"

Stacy stopped in the middle of the empty hallway, convinced she'd heard the words as if they'd been spoken aloud. *I bet he's the type who would put flowers in his hair and dance around a maypole. And be totally hot doing it.*

Her phone buzzed with an email — an invite to a meeting with HR on Monday morning. She hit accept then blindly stared down the hall.

Nearly six years wasted.

Well, not wasted. She'd learned a lot and this job would look excellent on her resume. Assuming she got a good reference and could keep herself from saying nasty, bitter things about her time here. She'd have to practice that shit in the mirror.

She had enough in savings she could make it a few months if she quit on Monday. That might damage her hopes of getting a good recommendation. Or she could suck it up and start searching elsewhere. Not that she'd have time or freedom to interview. She'd figure it out. She had to.

Fuck it.

Stacy headed to her desk, set her email to an out of office message and shut it all down. She gathered her things and left. She'd get no more work done today. If Chad had a problem with that, he could pound sand.

He wasn't her boss until Monday, and if she had anything to say about it, he never would be.

She made it to the elevator without running into anyone and stabbed the down button. The door opened in no time, and she hurried in, punched the door close button, then the ground floor.

"Are you happy?"

"No," Stacy said to the empty elevator car and the ghost-voice of Luke echoing in her head. "I'm not."

Chapter Thirty-Seven

Stacy, Friday, May 7

Stacy flopped into the hard wooden chair next to Brit's desk. She cradled her coffee rather than risk toppling one of the towering piles of folders cluttering the desk surface.

"Gimme a second." Brit grabbed the closest stack and stuck it on the floor, then moved more stacks until a corner of her desk was clear. "Class action lawsuit. The research is tedious. So, you said you needed your lawyer friend. I'm guessing you got an offer. Lemme see."

She settled into her chair and pulled up the email Stacy had sent. "Pretty much a boilerplate, which isn't necessarily a bad thing. Quick offer, too. You just interviewed on Wednesday, right?"

Stacy nodded and sipped her coffee. She'd gotten the call within hours of submitting her resume. That alone was unusual. Getting an interview the next day and an offer two days after was unheard of.

"They're a small company," Stacy said. "The owner left Godmann and opened his own business. Only a year ago."

Brit cringed. A start up in the investment world was dicey at best. "Company doing well and expanding? Or did someone leave?"

Not surprising, Brit echoed the same things Stacy had wondered. The trouble was, she hadn't gotten clear answers during the interview, and the offer email hadn't addressed her concerns either. Combined with a generic offer, it didn't give her warm fuzzies.

"On the plus side, at a small company, gaining experience and climbing the ladder are kind of a given," Stacy said. "Negative side, it means doing a lot of extra work, long hours, and not the greatest pay. And it's a gamble. A huge gamble."

A short man with a wispy beard popped his head into Brit's office. "Sorry to interrupt, but the building super says they're shutting down water for some sort of emergency repairs. We're closing the office for the day. No water is just barbaric."

Brit threw up her hands and let out a string of expletives. "Gotta love pre-war buildings in desperate need of renovation. Thanks Alex." She shut her computer down and waved Stacy out of her seat. "I'll finish this stuff tomorrow. Toss that." She pointed at the paper cup in Stacy's hand. "Let's grab a drink."

They took the stairs rather than deal with the crowd of people in the elevator lobby. Outside, late afternoon sun cast a pale glow across Tompkins Square. The day tempted Stacy to suggest a rooftop bar, or someplace with outdoor seating. Both would be crowded on a sunny Friday, and neither would be all that conducive to conversation.

Brit turned along a side street, then down a short flight of stairs to a plain, gloss-black door. Kylie might be the queen of finding great travel options, but Brit was the undisputed ruler of the best out of the way places in Manhattan. The Spot was her favored choice for times that called for serious talks.

The door opened onto a short, brick-lined hall and finally, a long, dark room with low ceilings and an ambiance that always made Stacy feel like they'd stepped back in time. The place had once been a speakeasy, and it still had that vibe. A short bar, a few scarred tables and a wall lined with high-sided booths that guaranteed privacy.

The menu was simple — food truck type fare, and the drinks uncomplicated. The bartender was likely to throw you out if you tried ordering something too fancy or that took too many steps. Stacy grabbed a booth while Brit put in an order for chicken strips and fries, then came back from the bar with a pitcher of beer and three glasses.

"He's gonna bring waters with the food, and Kylie's on her way," she said as she slid into the booth. "Aside from the obvious yellow caution tape surrounding this whole thing, what's on your mind?"

She pressed a cold glass into Stacy's hands then leaned back and tapped her fingers on the table. Stacy took a slow sip then sighed.

"I don't even know where to begin," she said. "I thought I knew what I wanted. I had a plan. Everything went great through college. Hell, I made great progress from intern to junior analyst, then analyst."

This was old territory. It was the same thing she'd been saying for a year. Stacy sucked in a breath at another reminder of how much time she'd poured into the company, trying to make her dream a reality.

"What do you think changed?" Leave it to Brit to ask the hard questions.

"Maybe I'm not as good as I think," Stacy replied. She didn't believe it. Not in her strong moments, anyway. She knew she was good. Her work was solid, and she had never failed to deliver.

"I don't know," she said. "Most of the women in the company have similar trajectories—a rapid rise and boom! Glass ceiling. Dead stop."

The smirk on Brit's face said more than words ever could. "I think the 'I don't know' is bullshit."

"What's bullshit?" Kylie slid in next to Brit and poured herself a beer. "Somebody catch me up."

The bartender came by with their food and waters. Brit summarized, and editorialized, everything while they ate. When the last fry was gone, Stacy braced her elbows on the table and propped her chin in her hands.

"What the fuck is your secret?" She waved one hand at her friends. "You two are both doing what you love, making ends meet and not dealing with the shit I've got."

Kylie and Brit exchanged wide-eyed looks then both laughed.

"Well, for starters, we both have much more supportive families than you do," Kylie said. "Maybe not as well-off, but the help doesn't come with ridiculous expectations. But, ummm…" She bit her lip and shot a pleading glance at Brit, who closed her eyes, drew in a slow breath and nodded.

"You asked, so here is the unvarnished truth," Brit began. "You have been chasing money over your own peace of mind. What do we do different? We've both compromised in some things in order to pursue work that brings us joy."

Coming from anyone else, those words would have pissed Stacy off. Coming from her best friend, they stung, but the truth of them resonated somewhere deep in her soul.

"I could be making a hell of a lot more working for some government whatever," Kylie said. "But I hate the idea of going to work in some secure location, or having to give up my colorful hair, or being surrounded by a bunch of folks whose politics do not align with mine." She refilled their glasses and waved at the bartender for a fresh pitcher of beer. "I want free time. I want to be able to grab lunch with friends. So, I live in a tiny condo in a neighborhood where housing is not as expensive, and I work. A lot. But at least I work on my schedule."

Brit reached across the table and grabbed both of Stacy's hands in hers. Her gaze was steady and filled with love, but her mouth was set in a hard line.

"I've lived with my Grams," she said. "Partly because she needed someone and partly because it was cheaper. You've seen the shithole office I'm in. None of these are better choices than yours. They're just different. There's no one-size-fits-all solution."

None of this was new to Stacy, but it felt like she was really hearing it for the first time. She'd always seen compromise through the lens of her family. She'd never considered seeing it from her friends' perspectives.

"I'm sorry," she said. "I think I've been a bit selfish and shitty to you both."

Kylie blew a piece of hair off her forehead and looked away, but Brit leaned in closer.

"We're your friends, and you've been fine," she said. "The question is, what are you going to do moving forward? Does this work make you happy, or is it just the money?"

There it was again. *"Are you happy?"*

"I like the challenge," Stacy replied. "I like parts of the job. I love working with clients."

She stopped. She'd never thought about work in terms of her satisfaction beyond a job well done and a fat paycheck. She'd never questioned whether it was fulfilling. She'd made no secret she was doing it for the money, even though she'd had moments of feeling heartless as Brit worked in a field that focused on people.

"Got your tablet?" Kylie piped up from across the table. "Do your spreadsheet thing. Lay out all the job options. Just like you did in college."

"You're a genius!" Stacy pulled out her iPad and opened a spreadsheet. The three of them huddled over the screen as Stacy put her entire set of life choices into a series of columns and rows. Every now and then, one or the other of the women would poke at the screen and make a suggestion.

Another pitcher of beer, some onion rings and an order of chips and cheese dip later, Stacy was no closer to getting her answers.

"I don't get it," Stacy said, scowling at the screen. "Normally, I do this, and I can see a path. Something makes more sense than everything else. But this… It's just… Well, I don't know."

She flopped against the hard booth and let her head thump into the wood.

"Last call." The bartender's voice rang through the room and Stacy opened her eyes to survey the mess on their table. Brit settled up with the bartender while Stacy and Kylie stacked dishes and tidied the table a bit.

"My place," Kylie said. "I'll pull out the futon, make some magic juice, and we'll get to the bottom of this. Tonight."

"Haven't thought about that stuff in a while," Brit said with a laugh. "You never did tell us what's in it."

Kylie batted her eyes and tried to appear innocent. "My family's secret anti-hangover concoction. And c'mon, it works. Have you ever been hungover after I've made it? Answer—no."

Stacy had to give her that. Kylie used coconut water and hibiscus tea as a base, and that's all Stacy knew for sure. She suspected there was pineapple in it as well, and definitely something full of B vitamins, and maybe something caffeinated, but Kylie was tight-lipped. It wasn't half bad, had a vaguely tropical flavor and did the trick of keeping you hydrated. Which was probably the secret to avoiding a hangover.

"There's one more thing you need to add to that spreadsheet," Brit said.

Stacy got to the top of the steps and turned to scowl at her friend. "I covered all the job possibilities, and even listed going back to school. What am I forgetting?"

Brit laid an arm over Stacy's shoulder. "There is someone you owe an apology. That boy toy of yours. And it had better be a very, very good one."

Chapter Thirty-Eight

Luke, Friday, June 4

A team of teens and parents descended on the pavilion with what had to be yards of lights and acres of streamers and who knew what else. Luke gave the group a wide berth lest he be roped in for some decorating.

He found Nate, Erik and Brandon in chairs on the back patio. Baby Brody stood next to Nate's chair, looking like he wasn't sure how he got into that position, but it was pretty cool. Luke dropped into the seat next to his brother.

"Prom committee?" Luke pointed down the hill toward the pavilion.

"Yeah, they're all over in the house, too," Erik replied. "Kinda why we're out here."

Erik pulled out his tablet and tapped the screen. "The hockey club is gonna have to run September through June. There's too much uncertainty over summer, and the rink has a whole Summer Saturdays thing they do. This year, the figure skating team from Margaretville are using the space while their home rink is refurbished. All that would limit when we could use the place."

"That's helpful," Luke replied. "We're booked solid all summer, and it's not like winter where it's mostly weekends. I won't have much time."

Nate cleared his throat and pointed a finger at Erik's screen. His kid brother switched to another tab, and Luke recognized Cat's organizational system.

"You've got plenty of local staff," Erik said. "But you're gonna have to train up some supervisor types. That still won't give you much time off. So..."

He highlighted the staff tab.

"Are all middle children like this?" Brandon reached over and tapped the screen, so the tab opened. "Short version—Erik and I can help this summer. That way you're not busting ass seven days a week, and he and I get some income during the off months. You might even talk Gina into helping out here and there. Win all around."

Erik rolled his eyes at the man. *Poor kid has two big brothers now.* "Not to mention, if Brandon isn't busy, he gets a little testy."

"This is where I come in," Nate said. "We've been operating with a very light managerial staff and relying on having great workers. But if any of us want a vacation, it's time to expand. These two are stepping up for part of that. We've got the kitchen covered. It may be a juggle this year, but by next, we'll all be taking a vacation together."

If someone had told Luke before he came to Bristol Park, that he'd think the idea of taking a vacation with his kid brother and his bosses was a great plan, he'd have wondered what they were smoking.

Now? It did sound like a great plan.

"It all sounds great," Luke said. "And I know that a lot of that was Cat's organizational superpowers, so where is she? I'm kinda missing her sneaky intro to things."

Nate threw his head back and laughed. Brody startled and sat down abruptly. For a moment, he looked like he was considering crying. Instead, he grunted and pulled himself up the chair leg.

"We have a new tenant at my old place," Nate said. "We've been using it as a vacation rental since Brandon moved out last year, but they're moving in today and Cat's getting them all squared away."

The baby lost his grip and tumbled backward, but Nate was quick and caught him. Still, the kid's face scrunched up and fat tears started. "I think someone is hungry and tired. Back in a bit."

Luke waited until Nate was inside, then turned to the other men. "Am I missing something?"

Brandon chuckled. "Nah." But Luke caught the look Brandon threw at Erik.

I'm missing something.

They went over the plans for the hockey league and worked out a tentative schedule for summer coverage on tubing, which opened this weekend.

They were finishing up when Nate stuck his head out of the sunroom door and beckoned them inside.

"There's a buffet set up in the dining room for all the volunteers," Nate said. "We can join them, then chip in with cleaning up."

The dining room buzzed with conversation as parents and students filled their plates and found places to sit. Brandon and Erik got pulled in more directions than Luke cared to think about. Gina came in with a group of giggling girls, all of them covered in splotches of bright paint.

Erik sat down with his phone out and a grin on his face. Luke leaned in, trying to catch a glimpse of the screen, but Erik stuffed the phone in his pocket.

"New love interest?" Luke asked.

A pink flush crept up Erik's cheeks, but his grin got broader. "Maybe. It's early, but yeah. Cat introduced us near the end of last year, but timing didn't work out. But now...he's just moved back to Abbeydon."

It was good to see Erik smiling. "Is that who's renting Nate's old place?"

"No, he's got one of those cute little houses in downtown."

Someone from the committee stood up and gave a bunch of thanks, triggering hooting and hollering all around. Brandon pulled a pair of earplugs out of his pocket and stuffed them in his ears while Gina shifted her chair, creating a path for him in case he needed to leave.

At some point, Cat slipped in, whispered something in Nate's ear, then got herself a plate and joined them.

This was like no place he'd ever worked. Lots of companies paid lip service to being 'like a family', but Bristol Park was the only time he'd ever seen it be true and not an excuse for toxic behavior.

"We should have Mom and Dad visit," Erik said. "And the girls. End of summer would be nice. After the busy season."

Over the years, Luke had managed to have his family visit occasionally — since most places he worked were booked up months in advance, it often meant last-minute plans when cancellations happened. He'd never had the whole bunch out at once. He hadn't seen everyone together since the week after Becca's funeral, when he'd packed a bag and put Minnesota behind him.

"I'd like that," he replied.

"That's a great idea," Cat chimed in. "Family and community are what this place is all about. That sense of belonging is what keeps people coming back."

Luke had to agree with that.

Bristol Park felt like home—he belonged. He'd settled into the rhythm of the place. He'd thought Stacy had been a part of that. For the first time since Becca, he'd found someone he wanted to share his life with. Too bad she didn't feel the same.

"Is this seat taken?"

Luke snapped his head up, unsure he hadn't conjured her out of his imagination. Stacy balanced a plate in one hand as she slid out the empty chair. Her dark hair was piled up in a messy bun and she was in battered jeans and a baggy T-shirt. She still looked amazing.

"Thanks for inviting me," she said. "I've still got a ton to unpack, so there's no way I could manage dinner on my own tonight."

Unpack? She'd been moving at the end of March. Why was she still unpacking? His brain jumbled, trying to put it all together. There was no way that city-girl Stacy had rented Nate's out of the way cottage.

"You're welcome to a room here if you haven't had a chance to get enough done to stay the night," Cat said.

Holy shit. He had to be in some alternate universe. An elbow jabbed into his side and Luke scowled at his kid brother.

"Close your mouth," Erik whispered. "People will think you're in shock."

"You knew?" Something dug at him. The look Brandon and Erik had exchanged earlier when Luke thought he'd missed something.

The conversation at the table continued around him as if there were nothing unusual going on. Stacy laughed with Gina over something someone had said, then she pointed her fork at Erik and shook her head.

Luke watched, transfixed, as she slipped back into his world like she'd never left. Like she belonged. There had been an empty chair at the table, as if she'd been expected. No one else seemed surprised that she was here. *What the fuck is going on?*

He leaned toward Erik and tried to keep his voice low enough no one else could hear. "Why didn't you say something? When?"

Luke pushed his fingers through his hair. She'd rented Nate's place—maybe it was temporary. A vacation rental. But Nate had said they had a new tenant, not a short-term renter.

"About two weeks ago," Stacy said, pulling his attention to her and the soft expression in her caramel eyes. "I start my new job on Monday."

Okay, not temporary.

Erik got up and left and within a minute, the rest of the table followed, leaving him alone with Stacy. Or as alone as they could be in a room full of chattering people.

"That was planned, wasn't it?" He tipped his head toward Cat and Nate who were near the door, talking with one of the parents and the woman who managed the dining and catering side of Bristol Park.

"Maybe a little bit," Stacy replied. She took in a slow breath. "I was nervous, and I called Cat for help."

That made so much sense. Once she'd talked to Cat, the wheels were in motion.

"Can we maybe find a place to talk?" She arched an eyebrow at him. She looked uncertain, as if she didn't know how he might respond.

For him, there was only one possible response. He stood and offered his hand. The moment Stacy's fingers touched his, all was right with his world. He stuffed that feeling aside. No matter how good it felt, they had some talking to do.

Starting with what in the hell she meant about her new job.

Without planning or talking about it, they both turned down the glassed-in hall and headed straight for the bench they'd sat on the night they'd first met.

She sat next to him, and her spicy floral scent called up memories of exploring and tasting every inch of her skin. Not where he needed his brain right now.

"We didn't exactly part on the best terms," he said. "You maybe want to explain why you're here?"

Stacy flinched, then a small smile curled her lips. "I deserved that." She shifted on the bench, turning to face him. "The last time we talked, you asked me a question. Do you remember it?"

For days after, Luke had thought of nothing else. He'd chastised himself for pushing her. He'd asked himself the same question. His own personal hell was that, aside from whatever had gone sideways with Stacy, he was able to answer 'yes'.

"Are you happy?"

Stacy nodded and her eyes tightened as if she had a flash of pain. She pressed her mouth into a thin line and let out a short, harsh laugh. "I thought I was," she said. "I was busting my ass to fulfill a dream."

She tipped her head back until it thumped into the wall. "The last Friday in April, work went to shit." She stopped and scowled. "No, that's not right. Work was already shit, and I was too stubborn to see it. The blinders were yanked off, and all I could hear was your voice, asking if I was happy."

She reached out as if to take his hand but stopped. Luke met her halfway and curled his fingers around hers.

"It's not a fun moment to realize your dream has become a nightmare. I didn't like who I'd become, and I liked the path ahead of me even less. I spent that weekend pouring my heart out to the girl squad. Then on Monday…"

She trailed off in a series of bitter sounding chuckles. "Well, that's a long story. The short version is by the end of Monday, I was unemployed. My severance package was executed, so I had a buffer."

She squeezed his hand and gave a shaky smile.

"All my life, I've avoided settling — no compromises allowed. I wanted to live life on my terms. It's why I was working so hard to get out from under my grandmother's control. Relationships were no different — I refused to get emotionally involved because I knew perfect for me didn't exist."

She pulled her hands from his, hung her head and let out a sigh. "Until I met you. Except, you didn't fit my goals, or my image of what my life should be like, so how could you be perfect for me? I'm sorry. I was a shit to you. I hated myself the moment I said those words, and I'm sorry."

Luke grabbed her hands. She was vibrating with tension, and he acted without thought. He slipped a finger under her chin and gently nudged until she lifted her head, and he locked his gaze on hers. Tears hung in the corners of her eyes.

"Pretty sure I understand where it was coming from," he said. He didn't know what had changed her mind and brought her here, and he didn't care. There had been something amazing between them, and maybe they could get back to that. He hoped they could.

Her lips trembled, then curled up. Then she let out a laugh that sounded like relief.

"Can you forgive me?"

Luke cupped her cheek in one hand. "Ask something hard next time. Of course I can."

Chapter Thirty-Nine

Stacy, Friday, June 4

The urge to grab his hands and drag him to his cabin was nearly overwhelming. That wouldn't fix what she'd broken. Stacy pulled in a slow breath and looked into his gorgeous blue eyes. She'd done a lot of soul searching in the last month, and only one thing was a constant. She tipped her face into his hand, relishing his touch.

She didn't have the words to erase what had gone wrong between them, but she had the time now, and if they were to have a chance, she couldn't live in fear or shut off her feelings.

"Luke, I..." Stacy stumbled over the words she wanted to say. She'd never said them to someone she was dating. She'd said them to her family and her girlfriends, but never in romantic love.

His eyes locked with hers and he smiled. That lopsided grin she knew so well. His fingers clenched on her neck, then slid into her hair and his chest shook as he took a sharp breath.

"Say it when you're ready," he whispered. "And same."

Something broke in Stacy — like a dam cracking under the stress of too much water. A half-sob, half-laugh escaped her lips. Luke stood in a rush and took her hand. They went down the hallway, past the stairs to the guest rooms, to the alcove where he'd first suggested their little game.

Instead of pinning her to the wall like he'd done before, Luke leaned against it, wrapped his hands at her waist and pulled her to stand between his legs.

His eyes flicked over her face, and she couldn't read his expression.

"I think I just realized how very alike we are," he said. "Maybe different reasons, but similar outcome. I don't...didn't...have relationships for the same reason I don't go to the city. And I think we both need to air some past demons before we can move ahead together. I wanted someplace more private than a bench in the hall, but I don't think we'd get much talking done at my cabin, so..."

He pushed open a small door and led her into a narrow galley space. He flicked a switch and soft light illuminated glass shelves in front of a mirror opposite a wooden bar.

"What's on the other side of that window?" She pointed at the bar, framed by what should have been a big opening, but a roll-up door closed in the space.

"Rec room," Luke said. "It's already set for prom. They'll do dinner in the dining room and the dance in there, but I think they're opening the sunroom, too.

This is supposed to be a bar, but they haven't gotten around to renovating yet, and it needs it. But…"

He hooked a couple of stools out from the corner and dusted them off. He sat and looked up at her, his eyes haunted and his mouth set in a hard line. Stacy wanted to reach out and smooth the furrows in his brow. Instead, she sat, knees touching his.

"When I was nineteen, I saved up and bought an emerald ring for my girlfriend," he said. "I was all set to propose at my family's on Christmas. Except she never made it there."

He closed his eyes, and his fingers clenched on her waist. "Someone shot her during a carjacking." Stacy gasped, then covered her mouth with her hand as he told the rest of the story. She couldn't imagine facing that decision, but especially not at such a young age.

When he was done, something in his face had changed. He seemed more relaxed, as if sharing his past with her had removed a barrier of some sort.

In light of his story, her own seemed petty and childish, but she shared it all the same. The pain of watching her parents' divorce, and seeing her father grow more and more distant. Or her beautiful, vibrant, passionate mother slowly fading into a colorless, soulless shell of herself. And, of course, her grandmother and how she ruled the family with her purse strings.

"I guess I learned that love is conditional and means losing yourself," Stacy said. "Or, at the very least, compromising yourself."

Luke took her hands in his and squeezed. "That's why you didn't want to settle for less than perfect in every way. I can understand that. So, what brought you back here?"

Stacy chuckled. This was the part that was hard to explain. "I went home, and I asked myself that question."

"Are you happy?" Luke whispered.

Stacy nodded. "I knew the answer was no. So, the next question was — what would make me happy. And I had to think about that a lot. For most of my life, I thought independence would make me happy, and I had a picture of what that meant."

Stacy looked up and found him focused on her, a rapt expression on his face. "Then I met you," she said. "The day you took us all on that cross-country trail and had us close our eyes in that meadow — I felt peace like I'd never known before."

His smile was gentle and warm and made her want to see more of that every day. He was right. She needed to open herself up like this. She needed to trust him with all of her if she was going to give him her heart and deserve his in return.

"I had already interviewed at other financial firms. I had an offer on the table from one, but it didn't feel right. Nothing felt right."

She closed her eyes and took a deep breath before going on. "I talked to my friends," she continued. "We sat at a bar talking until last call, then went to Kylie's and talked till sunrise. Both Kylie and Brit are successful, they're not as successful as they could be — but they're happy."

That realization had been a hard one. They were both amazing women, but they had both turned down opportunities that would have been financially better for them. All because they would have had to give up things that mattered more.

"It was..." She paused and shook her head. There was no easy way to summarize the whirling thoughts in her head. "It was confusing. So, typical of me, I made a spreadsheet of my options. Pros. Cons. Long-term outcomes. Everything I could think of. And none of it helped."

She didn't know how to tell him — she'd been thinking with her head, not her heart. She'd been trying to analyze everything as if there were a formula for happiness.

"Then I did something on a whim — I googled Abbeydon and saw the bank had an opening in investments and loan counseling. It's sort of temporary as the regular person is about to go on maternity leave, but she may only come back part-time, or not at all."

Here it was, the point that she had to risk herself.

"I have never been with anyone who makes me as happy as you do," she said. "And I'm not talking about the sex. It wasn't just the distance getting in our way. It was me. I thought, well, maybe I can fix the distance, and we can see if we can work it out. So, I applied. And...here I am."

She licked her lips. "Think we can try this thing again? Only this time, for real? No games. No restrictions. We give it a go. All in."

He leaned in to press his forehead against hers. "All in."

His kiss started out gentle and Stacy melted against him. Oh, how she'd missed his touch and the feel of his hard body against hers. She tugged at his shirt, but Luke grabbed her hands.

"You know I'm all for unusual places but uh, no condoms. Plus," he tipped his head toward the rec room on the other side of the closed window. "Even if

I wasn't worried about parents, or worse, kids, coming through for a last-minute check... I wasn't the type to get freaky in the bleachers when I was in high school. These days, I'll take comfort."

Stacy crossed her arms and stared at him. "Worrying about being interrupted I'll give you, but comfort? This from the man who had me bent over a rock in the snow."

He laughed as he took her hand and led her through the small door then out into the parking lot.

"To be fair, it was sunny and unseasonably warm," he said as he headed down the hill to the staff cabins. "And the snow was melting."

The smell of dew on the grass and the whisper of trees in the night were very different than honking horns and the constantly varied smells of the city. Stacy breathed it in. This was the world she was signing up for with Luke.

He opened the door to his cabin and gestured for her to go ahead of him. Once inside, he had her in his arms, and Stacy thrilled at his touch. Luke lowered his head and pressed his lips against her ear.

"So it's clear, I want to make love to you tonight," he said. Stacy trembled against him, surprised at the rush of emotion those words brought up.

He took his time undressing her, stopping every so often to kiss or caress her body. Then he stood back and the look of admiration on his face was plain. It was her turn to get his clothes off. Following his lead, she went slowly, letting her hands linger on his exposed skin.

Once they were both naked, Luke pulled her into his arms and lifted. Stacy wrapped her legs around his waist as he carried her to his room and laid her on bed. He kissed his way up her legs and parted her thighs with gentle pressure from his hands. Then he lowered his head and used his lips and tongue to tease her to a languorous orgasm.

She was dimly aware of him reaching into his nightstand, then the sound of a foil package opening. Then Luke held himself over her, his eyes never leaving hers. She gasped as his dick pressed into her, but Luke moved in smooth, short strokes, slowly getting deeper.

Passionate, wildly abandoned Luke was amazing. Tender and loving Luke was mind-blowing. He rocked against her, setting up delicious friction until she came again, shaking and crying out his name.

"That's my girl," he said as she clutched at his shoulders. "My god, you feel so amazing."

Stacy brought her legs up higher until her feet rested on his butt. He smiled and shifted his weight, pushing deeper into her for a few strokes before he gripped her hips and rolled until she was on top.

"You are beautiful," he whispered. Stacy sat up and shifted so she could ride him. He ran his hand up her thigh until his thumb rested on her clit. Stacy moaned as he stroked gently. His touch had her climbing right back up the hill toward another orgasm.

"Take what you need, baby."

Stacy sped up, and Luke matched her rhythm perfectly, his touch getting a little harder as she ground down onto him. She braced her hands on his chest and rocked her hips against him. The feel of him buried inside her combined with the friction and his thumb still stroking her clit with unerring precision sent her over the edge.

She dug her fingers into his chest, then collapsed against him. He rolled them once more and his cock hit her g-spot, keeping the wave of orgasm rolling. Then Luke ground out her name and his body stiffened.

Later, after they'd showered, they sat curled on the couch and wrapped in blankets as Luke talked to her about accepting the operations role at Bristol Park. Stacy rested her head against his shoulder and in that moment, knew contentment. She let out a soft sigh.

Luke chuckled. "So, the last time you were here, we got a little wild."

Stacy laughed. "Yeah, are you hinting you want something?"

"I think you liked it," he said. "In fact, I think you more than liked it."

"I did," she said. "Probably about as much as you liked doing it."

His low chuckle turned into a full laugh. "You said no games, or I'd propose a deal."

Stacy lifted her head and looked at him. That lopsided smile was back. "I'm listening."

He tipped his head and nuzzled her neck. "Those words you aren't ready to say out loud? When you're ready, you'll say them. And that is the next time we'll do that."

She sat up, not caring that the blanket fell off her shoulders. "Not until then?"

He shook his head. "I mean, only if you agree. What do you think?"

"I want to be sure I understand the parameters here," Stacy replied. "So, you won't do that until I say those words. Once I do, is it like…a right-away kind of thing, or a that's-back-on-the-table kind of thing, or what?"

He rolled his eyes. "Right away, or as right away as possible. Circumstances permitting and all. Sound fair?"

Stacy pretended to give it some thought. Then she stuck her hand out to shake on it. "Deal."

Luke shook her hand. Stacy shifted and laid on his chest, snuggling in close.

"I love you," she whispered.

Chapter Forty

Luke, Sunday, July 4

Luke padded down the stairs in the quiet, early morning light. He brewed coffee on autopilot then stared at the pot until he could pour a cup.

"There better be enough for two," Stacy said, then wrapped her arms around his waist. "Why are we up so early on a Sunday?"

Luke handed her the first cup of coffee. She bent over to get milk from the fridge and the oversize shirt she wore rode up, exposing polka dot panties. Luke tore his eyes away. He didn't have time for that distraction.

"Because it's July fourth, and there's a lot going on at Bristol Park, and some of that is my job." He dropped a kiss on her forehead. "And because in case you haven't noticed, it's a bit of a drive between your place and mine."

Stacy made a face. "It's a bit of a drive into work every day, too, but at least there's no traffic."

"You could go back to bed and come later," he said.

She wouldn't, and he knew it. A month ago, he wasn't sure how Stacy would fit in around Abbeydon. She was a born and bred city girl. Then she'd surprised him by jumping in with both feet—she volunteered at Bristol Park and, thanks to Brandon and Gina, was set to present a financial literacy workshop for high school seniors in the fall.

She'd gone to the city for a couple of days to visit the girl squad, and they had come up for the holiday weekend. Stacy stayed with Luke half the time, and the other half, he came to her place.

Stacy bent into the fridge again and this time, Luke didn't resist. He slid behind her and ran his hand over the firm globes of her ass. She wriggled and laughed, then straightened and turned to him.

"How much time do we have?"

Luke hoisted her to the kitchen counter. "Enough for a quickie."

It took no time to remove her panties and tease her to readiness. The quickie turned out to be a little longer than he'd planned, and they rushed through their shower and getting dressed.

At Bristol Park, Stacy helped him set up for tubing, then headed to the main house to spend time with her friends. Luke had a few minutes of calm before the first guests hit.

The early folks were mostly families with young kids who stayed in the area just below a series of tiny rapids upstream. The water cascaded down a final set of rocks and created a wide, shallow pool with minimal current. It was a favorite swim spot.

The narrow choke point after that was where they had set up the launch. The first extraction point was a few hundred yards downriver — a short, peaceful trip they suggested for the younger kids. After that, the river hit another series of small rapids and crossed into state forest land and three more extraction points manned by Bristol Park staff.

"Damn, he's even better without all the cold-weather gear." Brit gave him a fist bump and surveyed the tubing set up. "This really is a sweet spot."

Kylie poked one of the brightly colored tubes. "How far down can we go, and do we need a ride back or what? I read about it online, but I've never tubed before. How does this work?"

Luke caught Stacy's gaze, she was laughing and shaking her head at her friends. He directed them to the big sign with all the rules.

"We're in a perfect location to give you the type of tubing experience you want." He launched into the standard spiel, describing the escalating adventure levels that went from lazy river to bouncing along a few shallow rapids that slowly increased to full white-water tubing by the final extraction point.

"Don't miss that exit," he said. "We don't have staff beyond that point, and it gets really rough a couple hundred yards later. The full trip takes about two hours, give or take."

He explained the shuttle and their options for staying and hanging out at an extraction point, then sent Kylie and Brit to choose their tubes.

"You could have given that whole speech," he said. "You've heard me do it enough times by now."

Stacy leaned in and kissed him. "Yeah, but you're fun to watch when you do it."

She hooked a purple tube from the selection, and Luke got their cooler tube set up then sent them off down the river. He was near the end of his shift when the girl squad returned. Stacy flashed him a smile before heading up to the house. A few minutes later, his phone buzzed.

We're gonna shower then join Cat and Nate on the back patio for drinks. You coming?

Luke sent a thumbs-up and stuffed his phone into his pocket. He handed the signup sheets over to his replacement and hurried to his cabin for a quick shower. He found the girls already settled in Adirondack chairs, drinks in hand. Cat squatted with Brody as he held her hands and took shaky steps.

"Alcoholic or non?" Nate asked.

"Depends on who did the mixing," Luke replied. He'd learned to avoid anything Nate mixed. The man didn't drink, and his cocktails were on the potent side. Cat, on the other hand, was sneaky and could make a drink that didn't taste of alcohol at all, but it packed a punch.

"Cat made sangria."

Luke took a glass and sat next to Stacy. She took his hand and squeezed.

Later in the afternoon, they played corn hole. Erik showed up with his new partner just before the real crowds started rolling in. By sunset, people were sprawled on blankets and in folding chairs on the grassy hill leading down to the river.

This is good. I could get used to life like this.

Kylie sat on an adjacent blanket, playing games on an iPad with a boy that might have been about six. Brit and Charlie Neeman, whose dad owned the general store, sat nearby, engrossed in conversation.

Finally, Luke looked at Stacy. The woman he loved beyond anything he could ever have imagined. He still worried that this was enough for her. Would she get bored? Would she tire of small-town life?

"I've got next weekend off," Luke said. "What do you say to a couple days away?"

Stacy's lips curled into a smile. "We kind of live in vacation land, but yeah, sounds great. What did you have in mind?"

Luke bit his lip. He'd given this a lot of thought. There had been many conversations with Brandon and Gina as he decided he needed to get over his fears.

"I thought you might show me around New York."

Her eyes went wide. "Really? You'd do that?"

Luke squeezed her hand. "Not saying it'll be easy, but it's past time. And with you? I feel like I can tackle anything."

She flung her arms around his neck and kissed him. "You're amazing."

He nuzzled her neck, enjoying the sweet scent of her. "I love you."

Epilogue

Stacy, Saturday, December 19

Sheer curtains billowed in the ocean breeze as Stacy twirled in the room and flopped onto the bed.

"I suppose that's one way of making sure the bed is comfortable," Luke said with a laugh. Their bags already sat at the foot of the bed.

"I was going to ask if you'd even looked at the view, but you're probably jaded by Jamaica."

Stacy sat up and glared at him. "One can never be jaded by the Caribbean."

She reached for his hand and tugged him to the bed with her.

"You doing okay?"

It was a week before Christmas. He'd said he was ready to lay the past to rest, but that didn't mean it would be easy.

"Bittersweet," he replied. "I don't have to erase the old to build something new."

She kissed his cheek, then hopped up and stalked to the wide-open doors and the tiny, covered porch with steps that led straight to pristine white sand.

"I've got to hand it to Gina and Brandon," she said. "They chose one hell of a destination wedding spot."

Cat's former brother-in-law, Tommy, had come through with a great deal on a cluster of beach cottages at an all-inclusive resort. It was a small group. Aside from Luke and Stacy, there was Brandon's mom, Erik and his boyfriend, and Cat and Nate, who had left Brody with his parents and entrusted Bristol Park to their remaining staff for a few days. A few other friends were staying in the main hotel on the other side of the narrow road.

"Well, what do we do first?" Stacy held up the little card that listed the wedding itinerary. "We don't have anything official until six tonight with the rehearsal dinner. I thought they were going to elope."

Luke plucked the card from her hands and tossed it into the room. "They were. Then Cat got wind of it, and, well..."

Stacy chuckled. Cat was a force of nature on two feet. She could only imagine.

"This is the compromise," he continued. "The vacation they wanted and a small group of family — chosen and related. I mean, c'mon, they're getting married in the sand."

Somehow, that didn't surprise her. Gina wasn't the big wedding type and Brandon hated crowds. Stacy had never pictured herself getting married — maybe as a very young girl, but certainly not once her teenage years hit. She had no idea what she'd want if she ever decided to walk down the aisle. Until Luke, she'd never met a man who made her even consider it.

Luke pulled her into his arms as they stood on the porch, gazing out at clear-blue water that sparkled like a gemstone.

"You know it's been a year since we met?" He whispered the words against her neck, sending shivers down her spine.

"Mmm, yes, you mentioned that last week," she replied.

He kissed his way up her neck, then nibbled on her ear. Stacy nearly turned into a puddle at his touch. They didn't have anywhere to be for hours yet. They had time.

Luke seemed to have the same idea as he slid the strap of her sundress down, exposing her breast. His thumb stroked her nipple, teasing lightly.

"Something I wanted to ask you," he said as his hand cupped and his fingers lightly pinched.

"Whatever it is, I'm sure the answer is yes." So long as he didn't stop what he was doing.

His low chuckle sent waves of excitement through her. That usually meant he was planning something delightful.

"You sure about that?"

She gave it some thought, or tried to with him distracting her the way he was. "Yeah. Pretty sure."

"Okay," Luke nodded, as if they'd just concluded some serious negotiation. Now Stacy worried what she'd agreed to.

"I debated being all romantic, but that didn't seem like your kind of thing," he said. "And I really wasn't sure about having this talk here, now. I mean, this is Gina and Brandon's day, or weekend, or whatever. Anyway, I don't want to take away from that."

What in the hell is he talking about?

"I suppose we should wait until we get home to announce anything. What do you think?"

The whole time he'd been talking, he'd kept playing with her nipples, and her mind was so fogged and confused she wasn't sure if she'd missed something or if he was being intentionally vague.

She looked up and he was smiling ear to ear. He knew what he was doing.

"You planning to tell me what, exactly, I'm agreeing to?"

She slid her hand down his side then in and cupped him through the thin linen pants he wore. Luke hissed in a sharp breath as her fingers tightened.

He lowered his head and touched his forehead to hers.

"You. Me. Making this thing between us official." He lifted his head and his gaze settled on hers. "I'm asking if you'll have me as your husband. Marry me?"

It took a few long breaths before his question fully penetrated her passion-fogged brain, but when it did, her heart skipped a beat. Then promptly went cartwheeling around her chest. She managed to rein herself in, just a little, and smiled up at him.

"Like I told you, whatever it is, I'm sure the answer is yes."

Luke's grin somehow got even wider, then he crushed her to him and claimed her lips in a kiss that left her breathless and wanting more.

When he finally raised his head, he spoke softly. "So, uh...the last thing I wanted to do was be a presumptuous ass, all ready to get down on one knee and pop open a box. On top of that, I really didn't want to rain on Gina and Brandon's parade, so I haven't bought a ring yet."

Stacy rolled her eyes. "You know me better than that."

"We can go shopping together when we get back," he said. "I love you and I want us to share life together. Always."

Stacy tipped her head back and kissed him. "I like this plan. I'm all in."

Want to see more from this author? Here's a taster for you to enjoy!

Logan County Love: Rekindled
Roxanne Blackhall

Coming April 2024

Excerpt

Flames leaped and crackled, tearing up the side of the makeshift building inside the Fire Research Lab, casting shifting orange and yellow light on the walls of the warehouse. Drea swallowed against the lump in her throat. Even through her respirator, the ashy air was sickly sweet from starter fuel mixed with the scent of burning pine. She clenched her fists and forced herself to watch as the ATF fire crew hauled out hoses. When the first hiss of water produced a cloud of steam, a tendril of panic coiled in her chest. She sucked in a sharp breath, refusing to give in to the rising tide of fear.

"Hey, Hidalgo!" The shout came from her side, and she tore her eyes away from the flames to Gabe Mattix who had her mask pushed back, eyebrows knit together. "I called your name three times. You okay, kid?"

Drea flipped her off—she'd known Mattix for years, their communication ranging from high fives to the bird—and shoved her mask back.

"I'm good." She steeled herself and turned to the group of trainees. "The purpose of this little exercise, aside from giving those hose jockeys an excuse to impress us all, is to encourage observation. You'll see things during the active phase of a fire that are clues."

She ignored the scoffing laugh of one trainee. Peter Adams was an incurable smart ass in class, but Drea thought he had the makings of a good investigator if his ego would stop getting in the way. She cleared her throat and addressed the group.

"What color were the flames? How about the smoke? These things can tell you a lot about the fire. What suppression methods were used? How long did it take?"

"I know all this shit. When are we gonna get in there and do something?"

Drea turned to face the trainee, and he had the sense to shut up.

"Well, Mr. Adams. Since you know it all, perhaps you would be so kind as to turn your back."

He blew out an exaggerated sigh, but she waved her hand at him and waited until he turned around.

"Good. Think about the perimeter. Anything combustible?"

She didn't have to see his face to know he had no clue. The uncomfortable shifting of his shoulders told the story.

"No, ma'am." His response came out sounding confident.

"Turn around and look again," Drea replied.

Adams turned and glared at her, then at the building. Drea pulled out her stopwatch, punched the button and waited for the ah-ha moment. It came nearly a minute and a half later when his eyebrows rose, and a muttered "shit" escaped his lips.

"There's a gas grill on the northeast side." He mumbled the words, barely audible in the noisy warehouse.

"Thank you." She turned the stopwatch, showing him the numbers, and Adams cringed.

"I'll repeat myself," Drea addressed the class again. "The purpose of this little exercise is to encourage observation. If you rely on what you know, or think you know, you will fail to truly observe, and you will miss things. That's true whether you're fighting a fire or investigating it. We're going to break for lunch and let this thing cool down, then we're going to get messy. Adams, c'mere."

She expected attitude. Instead, he looked down at his shoes as he shuffled over to her. She waited until all the other trainees were well out of earshot before she turned to him.

"I'm sorry, ma'am," he said before she could say anything. "I mouthed off."

Drea blinked in surprise. She'd been ready to give him a piece of her mind, but here he was apologizing.

"Did you learn something?" She waited for his nod. "Good. That's the point of all this. I'll be blunt. Questions are fine, attitude is not. You got a problem, you come to me one-on-one, like I'm doing with you now."

When he didn't smart back at that statement, or give her any other grief, she cracked a wide smile. "Instead of telling me how much you know, show me how smart you are. You wouldn't be here if you weren't, and I believe you've got the potential to go somewhere with this. See you back here in an hour."

Adams ambled off. Steam billowed off the burn, and the shouts of the fire crew faded, replaced with the roar of uncontrolled flames. Drea forced herself to look at the fire crew — hoses spewing water, the flames nearly out. The concrete floors of the warehouse were so wet they looked like glass. She breathed, in for five, out for five, then shoved her gear into her bag and hustled to the door, desperate for fresh air.

"I hear you're headed back to the field soon." Mattix leaned her nearly six-foot tall frame against the big roll-up door, arms crossed over her chest. Her dark eyes drilled into Drea.

"Yep. Final eval with the psych is next week." Drea did a little happy dance. "You gonna miss me when I'm gone?"

Mattix chuckled. "Shit no, Hidalgo. You've been a pain in my ass since your first day as a student in my fire science class. Seriously, you should switch to teaching. You're good with these guys."

"Oh, hell no," Drea said. She adored Mattix. The older woman had quickly gone from teacher, to mentor, and finally, friend. But after months of being in the classroom, Drea was itching to get back in the field. "I'm not staying. I got into this job to chase bad guys, not teach the good guys how to do it. As soon as I get my walking papers, I'm outta here. Love ya, but not that much."

"No bullshit." Mattix fixed her with a pointed stare. "How are you holding up?"

Drea waggled her hand so-so. Class time was easy. She could stand in front of a group of students and talk fire theory and investigative techniques all day. Being here, next to a burn, with soot and ash and smoke billowing was a different story. She swallowed hard and forced a smile. She'd be fine. She had to be if she was going back to the field.

"The occasional nightmare still," Drea said, and blew out a breath. The flashbacks still happened sometimes, too, but they were getting easier to control at least. "Even I'll admit I wasn't ready to get back in the field so soon the first time."

Mattix shook her head, sending her short braids bouncing. "I don't know why the doc cleared you."

Drea shrugged. "I seemed good. Everything seemed good. Then the ceiling caved in and landed on me, and yeah, I had a flashback, on a cold scene, with only my partner around. Not a huge deal. I got lucky. It could have been worse."

Mattix gave a sharp laugh and leaned back against the wall again. "And you're good now?"

Drea flashed a bright smile. "Hey, I held it together today, didn't I? At a live burn. I'm coping."

"Tell that to someone who doesn't know you so well." Mattix grinned. "Promise me you'll be honest with the psych, okay? If you're not ready, then you're not ready. There's no shame in that."

Drea wanted to be ready. Needed to be ready. Fire investigation was her career. Not teaching.

Her cell buzzed. Unknown number. West Virginia area code. All thoughts of fires and investigations and her upcoming psychiatric evaluation disappeared. Drea had only one thought... *Gramps.* She drew in a trembling breath and tapped the screen to take the call.

"Hello." Her voice far steadier than she felt.

"Ms. Hidalgo?" The unmistakable lilt of Appalachia came through in that short greeting. The caller waited until Drea identified herself, then continued. "Your grandfather requested we call. He was hurt while helping clean up after a fire..."

Drea sagged against the wall, her fingers clenched around her phone. Mattix shifted, her tall frame shielding Drea from any curious looks. The rest of the conversation passed in a haze of half-heard information as Drea's mind whirled on what she had to do next. She hung up the phone and stuffed it in her pocket.

"You're gonna eat before you go tearing off to West Virginia," Mattix said. "No arguing. Gimme your keys, I'm driving."

Mindless, Drea dug her keys out and tossed them to her friend. She didn't care about food. She wanted to get on the road.

Mattix drove, ordered burgers, and pulled into an isolated parking space at the back of the lot. Drea's hands shook as she unwrapped the burger. She tried to hide it, but Mattix didn't miss things.

"It's a six-and-a-half-hour drive to West Virginia, kid," Mattix said. "You could fly." Her eyes narrowed as she peered at Drea. Always assessing.

Drea swallowed and shook her head. "Still an hour from the airport. If I hurry, I can get to the Regional Medical Center before visiting hours end."

"What did the doctor say?"

Drea took in a shaky breath. "Gramps had a heart attack. The doctor wouldn't say much, only that he's stable, but they're keeping him for more tests."

They finished their burgers in silence. Mattix had never been one for filling every moment with idle chatter. When she spoke, it meant something.

"I need to pack," Drea blurted as she tossed her wrapper into the bag. "It's the end of this session, I've got a couple days. The Deputy Director will understand."

Mattix's hand closed over Drea's. "Don't worry about Wilkes."

At her apartment, Mattix helped her pack, then pulled Drea into a tight hug before she headed out the door. "Call me if you need anything." Mattix glared at her. "I mean that."

"Yeah, yeah." Drea waved her off and shouldered her bag. She didn't allow herself to think until she was past the sprawl of Manassas, on her way back to Orchard Creek and the home she hadn't seen in years.

* * * *

Whispered conversations and the chirp of medical equipment blurred into the background as Drea's footsteps echoed in the wide hospital corridor. She wiped her palms down her jeans, steeling herself for what was about to come.

"Andrea? Andrea Hidalgo?" A young woman in pale green scrubs came around the nurse's station. "We've been keeping an eye out for you. I recognized you from your picture."

"What? Sorry, I was woolgathering." Where did that word come from? Jesus, she'd just rolled into town and she was already sounding like a local.

"I'm Missy, the charge nurse. Paul told us you'd be coming. We didn't expect you this quickly. He's in four-nineteen, down the hall." She pointed before turning to the nurse's station. "Visiting hours end at nine. You've got about an hour."

Drea's feet felt like lead as she walked the rest of the hall to Gramps' room. She stepped through the door and into a world that felt at once foreign and familiar.

The beeping of his heart monitor and the hiss of the oxygen made an unpleasant symphony, calling up memories of her own time in the burn ICU after her accident. Noisy and hushed at the same time. And the smell. Hospitals all smelled the same — over-bleached linens and heavy antiseptics mixed with the cloying scent of flowers. In the bed, a gray, old man sat staring at the television. Lush white hair swept back from a forehead that was more lined and creased than she remembered. He seemed so small and frail.

Paul DeJarnet had been a big man when he was young and healthy. Strong and agile. He'd taken Drea hiking and fishing, and taught her to climb trees and rocks, despite Abuela's protests that girls shouldn't be getting their knees dirty and scraped up. Drea chuckled at the memory of the two of them standing on the back stoop, washing the mud off after a particularly messy excursion while Abuela stood in the kitchen doorway, hands on hips, trying to look angry.

His head turned at the sound of her soft laugh, and his face lit in a broad smile that dimpled his cheeks. Still handsome at eighty-eight. He patted the bed next to him, muted the TV, and beckoned her over.

"Little one." His pet name for her. His voice was whispery, like dry leaves rustling in the breeze. Drea sat on the edge of the bed, drawing in a shaky breath. She squeezed his hand and forced a trembling smile before looking away, unable to face the man her grandfather had become.

"What happened?" Drea asked.

"I've been around a long time and I'm worn out." He patted her hand. "I got out of breath."

"The doctor said you were helping clean up after a fire. Why were you out there? Never mind. Don't answer that." She knew the reasons. Orchard Creek was his home, and people took care of each other. "I'm glad you're okay. How long will you be in here?"

He lifted a shoulder. That noncommittal gesture said mountains. "A few days, at least. They have tests to run. And some procedure—an angioplasty. I'm sorry you had to come all this way, but I wanted to see you. Just in case."

Angioplasty. This is no minor heart attack.

"What did the doctor say, exactly?" Drea demanded.

"That I'm old." There was no laughter in that statement. "He said I have arteriosclerosis. They'll do this procedure, and that should be it."

He didn't look at her when he answered. His gaze roamed the room, settling on anything but her face. She knew that trick. She'd tried it herself, on him. It never worked.

"Uh-huh. What else?"

He let out a slow sigh. "The doctor said he didn't believe a bypass would be necessary, but he'd know more..." His eyes brimmed with tears, and Drea choked back tears of her own. A bypass meant surgery. She gripped his hand, her fingers curling around his.

"I should have come sooner," she whispered, "but I'm here now, and I'm staying until you're back on your feet."

His eyebrows knit together in a frown as he turned his gaze back to her. "What about your job?"

"I've got time off," she replied. "I took a few days leave to come see you and can take extended family leave. It's not a problem. The last class session finished, and I haven't started my new assignment yet."

He didn't need to hear she was uncertain what that assignment would be. She was eager to get back into the field, but also terrified. The psychiatrist said she was ready; she had one last review before being cleared. Mattix believed in her. But none of that mattered when she woke up at two in the morning, covered in sweat, a cry of pain and fear on her lips. Still, she was ready. Maybe.

A soft knock sounded and a nurse came in. Gramps joked with her as she took his vitals and made notes on the chart. Same old Gramps. Always a charmer.

Drea sat with him while he talked, slowly, of everything and nothing. His breathing labored and painful to hear. All too soon, his eyelids drooped and his head nodded.

"I think you need rest," she said. "I know I do."

"Your room is still set up." His voice was a soft whisper. "You'll stay there?"

"Of course, Gramps." She kissed his cheek, then rose to leave.

* * * *

The door swung open to her childhood home and Drea swallowed hard. Nine years, and she'd bet she could still find her way through the place in the dark. She'd last been here for Abuela's funeral, and the little house had been overflowing with people and food. Speaking of food...She sniffed the air. Vanilla and coconut. Cookies.

She dropped her bags at the steps and made her way to the kitchen that took up the entire back of the house and clicked on the lights. Boxes of buttery, jam-filled shortbread mantecaditos and chewy-crispy coconut besitos covered the kitchen table.

Every week, Gramps baked dozens of the traditional cookies, as his wife had done for years. And every Friday, he made the rounds, leaving boxes of cookies at nursing stations, the bank, the mechanic. Anyone who deserved a thank-you or needed something to brighten their day.

Drea groaned and searched for Gramps' delivery list. She found it stuck to the 'fridge, his once neat handwriting grown shaky with age. He'd never missed a week of cookie deliveries. Not even when his wife was sick. Abuela hadn't let him. Drea fingered the list.

The boxes of cookies sat neatly stacked on the table. Drea groaned again. She couldn't, didn't want to see all those people. Talk to all those people.

The sugary scent of vanilla and coconut filled the kitchen. Her stomach knotted and roiled. She should have insisted Gramps move to DC after Abuela died. Maybe then things would be different. Drea shook herself, dropped into a chair and skimmed the list again. *Suck it up, Drea. It's the right thing to do and you know it.*

Tonight, she needed rest. She'd deal with the cookies in the morning.

About the Author

Roxanne Blackhall is a former magazine and newspaper editor from San Diego, California, now living in the heart of Baltimore, Maryland. When not at her desk coming up with new ways to torment her characters, she can often be found in the kitchen, glass of wine in hand, cooking a meal for friends.

Roxanne loves to hear from readers. You can find her contact information, website details and author profile page at https://www.totallybound.com

Home of Erotic Romance

Sign up for our newsletter and find out about all our romance book releases, eBook sales and promotions, sneak peeks and FREE romance books!